Rebekah

Books by Jill Eileen Smith

THE WIVES OF KING DAVID

Michal

Abigail

Bathsheba

WIVES OF THE PATRIARCHS

Sarai

Rebekah

Wives *of the* Patriarchs • Book 2

Rebekah

A Novel

Jill Eileen Smith

Revell

a division of Baker Publishing Group

Grand Rapids, Michigan

Published by Revell
a division of Baker Publishing Group
P.O. Box 6287, Grand Rapids, MI 49516-6287
www.revellbooks.com

Printed in the United States of America

Library of Congress Cataloging-in-Publication Data
Smith, Jill Eileen, 1958–
Rebekah : a novel / Jill Eileen Smith.
p. cm. — (Wives of the patriarchs ; bk. 2)
Includes bibliographical references.
ISBN 978-0-8007-3430-5 (pbk. : alk. paper)
1. Rebekah (Biblical matriarch)—Fiction. 2. Bible. O.T.—History of Biblical events—Fiction. 3. Women in the Bible—Fiction. 4. Christian fiction. I. Title.
PS3619.M58838R43 2013
813′.6—dc23 2012034582

Published in association with the Books & Such Literary Agency, Wendy Lawton, Central Valley Office, P.O. Box 1227, Hilmar, CA 95324, wendy@booksandsuch.biz

13 14 15 16 17 18 19 7 6 5 4 3 2 1

To Jill Stengl, whose encouragement in this project kept me sane, whose faith gave me hope when I was certain there was no story to tell, and who believed in me despite my doubts that I could complete the work.

Thank you, dear friend, for the many hours you listened to my worries over Skype and for your many prayers on my behalf. This book would not be what it is without you.

Part 1

Some time later Abraham was told, "Milcah is also a mother; she has borne sons to your brother Nahor: Uz his firstborn, Buz his brother, Kemuel (the father of Aram), Kesed, Hazo, Pildash, Jidlaph and Bethuel." Bethuel became the father of Rebekah.

Genesis 22:20–23

Now Rebekah had a brother named Laban.

Genesis 24:29

1

HARRAN, 1969 B.C.

Light flickered from clay oil lamps in every corner of Bethuel's bedchamber, the effort valiant but feeble, useless to dispel the gloom. Attendants hurried in and out, the hum of their whispers mixing with the sounds of their movements as they refilled a water jar here, wrung out a cool cloth there, and adjusted blankets, fussing, fearing . . .

Rebekah stood to the side, unable to take her eyes from the form of her father lying prone on the raised wooden bed, his head engulfed in soft cushions and layered with cloths meant to bring his fever down. But his clear moments had been few, his words strained as though he were speaking through stretched and cracking parchment.

Tears filled her eyes, and she pulled the cloak tighter about her, desperate to subdue the shaking. *Not now, Abba. Please, do not leave me.*

She heard voices in the hall outside the room and swiped at the unwanted tears. Though the time for mourning was almost upon them, she did not want her grief put on public display. Not yet. Not while there was still a chance her father might recover.

Shadows danced over the tiled floor, and servants moved quickly to leave the chamber as her brother Laban and her mother, Nuriah, moved in. Laban carried a scroll and seal and walked with assurance to kneel at his father's side.

"You called for me, Father?" Laban spoke softly, but his words carried to Rebekah. She leaned closer to better hear him, catching Laban's glance and look of silent censure.

"Bethuel? Is that you?" Her father's eyes fluttered as he spoke. "Let me behold my namesake, my firstborn, that I might bless him."

Laban touched his father's arm even as a determined glint filled his dark eyes. "I am here, Father."

Rebekah's heart skipped a beat, and a certain dread filled her. What was he doing? She opened her mouth to speak, then changed her mind and turned to rush out and find Bethuel, but before she could move or utter a sound, her mother hurried to her side and clutched her arm with clawlike strength.

"Keep silent," her mother hissed into her ear, and though she leaned away from Rebekah, her grip did not slacken, her intent strikingly clear.

"I have brought the scrolls, Father. You need only to dip your seal in the wax and all will be well." Laban unrolled the parchment, took the small clay bowl, and poured the already heated wax onto the bottom of the scroll.

A rustling of robes filled her ear, and Rebekah turned, seeing two of her father's servants enter—two who had always favored Laban.

"Bring me Bethuel. I must bless my son." Her father's voice stumbled over the words, each one coming out painfully slow.

Nuriah stepped forward and touched her husband's chest. "You must do as Laban requests, my husband. He is the one whom you must bless."

Her father's breath grew labored, and Rebekah's own breath hitched as she watched him wince, as though her mother's words caused pain. Everyone knew her brother Bethuel was not quick-witted as Laban was, that his words and actions were slow, lumbering, and that he did not have the skill to run the estate the way her mother or Laban would want. But her father had always preferred him, and Rebekah knew that if nothing else, her brother would look out for her, would be fair and kind, unlike Laban.

"Mother, please." Rebekah's whispered words were met with a look like hardened stone. She clamped her mouth shut.

Laban took the seal and curled his father's fingers around it, pressing it into the wax.

Rebekah's stomach tightened as she recognized the scroll as the one her father kept secure in an urn buried in the dirt beneath the floor, the deed to all that he owned. The deed that should have been passed to his firstborn, to Bethuel. She glanced toward the door. Where was he? Why did he not stop this? Had Laban done something to her brother? But no, Bethuel was big and far stronger than Laban. He could break Laban's neck in his two hands, though he would not do so. Not for any reason.

She turned at the sound of rustling sheets. Her nurse, Deborah, was helping her father to sit straighter. Laban blew on the wax, waiting for the seal to dry, while her mother took her husband's hand in hers.

"Please, my husband, say the words you know you must say."

Rebekah's stomach twisted into knots at the pained expression on her father's dear face. *No, Abba. Do not listen to her.* But it would be useless to fight her mother and brother when they had obviously conspired together in this. Somehow they would have convinced Bethuel to stay away, to let them work things out as they had planned. And he was too kind and gentle to demand anything against them.

"Please, my husband." Nuriah's insistent tone made heat

rise to Rebekah's cheeks. Her arm still felt the nails her mother had dug into the skin moments before. There was no reasoning with the woman when she was siding with her favorite son, no matter what the cost to anyone else. Sometimes Rebekah wondered if her mother loved Laban more than she did her own husband. Surely she favored him above her other children or grandchildren. The thought brought a bitter taste to her mouth.

"May Adonai bless you, my son."

Rebekah leaned forward, listening, her father's words no more than a breath.

"May your mother's sons serve you, and may you prosper all the days of your life." He fell back among the cushions, his body spent.

Deborah lifted the thin sheet closer to his neck, and he closed his eyes. Rebekah watched closely, begging the God of Shem to let her see his chest rise and fall.

"Thank you, Father." Laban leaned close and kissed their father's sunken cheek, then gathered the scroll and seal and moved quickly from the room.

Her mother gripped Rebekah's arm once more. "See to it you say nothing of this to anyone. Your brother has done what he must. It is all for the best." She lifted a veined hand toward her husband's frail form. "He has always favored you and our weak-willed firstborn. But he was wrong." She wrapped her robe more tightly about her thin frame and hurried after Laban.

Rebekah stared after her, her heart thudding hard against her chest, a sense of betrayal and fury filling her. "He is not weak-willed." She spoke the words out of earshot of her mother. She knew better than anyone that her brother Bethuel was a gentle man—anyone watching could see the way he tended the lambs in his care, treating them with greater kindness than her mother had treated anyone in her life. Better than Laban did his own wife and children.

But it was Laban who had the sense for business and the wherewithal to command a household. Laban could charm the feistiest merchant and work his way into the most uncompromising heart. She was weary of his deceit and the way he controlled those around him. In the past, she could run to her father for aid. But now . . . what would she do without her abba? She looked again at his frail form, watching Deborah replace the cool cloths across his forehead and about his chest.

"Is he suffering?"

Deborah lifted a shoulder in a shrug, but a hint of worry filled her eyes. "I do not know, mistress. I do not think so. Not very much."

A sigh escaped her, and Rebekah stepped closer, kneeling at his side. She took his hand, clasped it between both of her own, and lowered her head to kiss it.

He rallied and cradled her cheek in his palm. "My dear Rebekah."

She strained to hear the words, leaning close so as not to tax his strength any further. "Abba, you must rest so that you can get well. We need you." Tears made her voice waver, and she could not stop them from freely flowing over her cheeks. "I need you."

A faint smile formed at the edges of his beard. "My Rebekah. My strong one." He paused, and she counted his breaths, silently begging him to continue, yet not wanting to press him.

O God of Shem, please do not take him now!

He opened his eyes once more, his look infinitely loving and sad. "Your mother knows best, dear one. She will find you a husband and all will be well. Do not fear."

"But I don't want to lose you."

She waited, but he did not respond.

Deborah came near and placed a hand on her arm. "He is sleeping, mistress. He will not likely speak again. He has spent his last words."

Rebekah gently squeezed her father's limp hand and laid it beneath the covers, watching the slow beat of his heart barely lift the sheet that was meant to warm him. She faced her nurse and fell weeping into her outstretched arms.

"My mother does not know best." The words came out broken and soft, though she knew Deborah could hear her.

"There, there, now. Obviously, your father does not agree. Perhaps he has already passed on his wishes to your mother. Soon you will live in the home of your husband and all will be well." She lifted Rebekah's chin in her sturdy hand. "Trust Adonai and wait and see."

Rebekah wiped the tears from beneath her eyes and willed her emotions under control. She glanced once more at her father, her regret and anger and hurt mingling with every labored beat of his heart. "All will not be well," she whispered, hoping he could not hear. She turned and held Deborah's sympathetic gaze. "I will have no say in the matter, and my father will not be there to defend me."

She was no match for her mother, but she would not cow to Laban's rule without a fight. She was not her father's daughter for nothing.

Hours passed, and the sun sank low on the horizon outside her father's bedroom window when the telltale sound of rattling in her father's throat jolted Rebekah. Deborah sprang to his side, but Rebekah stared, unable to move, watching as he strained to take first one breath, then another, until at last no more breaths would come. The sheet stopped moving, and his pinched expression softened in the unmistakable mask of death.

"Your father rests in Sheol now," Deborah said, her words barely registering at the fringes of Rebekah's heart. "He does not suffer any longer, dear one."

Rebekah nodded numbly as servants rushed into the room, and loud keening sounds burst from the waiting mourners' lips.

She staggered from the room into the hall where her brother Bethuel stood looking lost and forlorn. Their father had called for him, but the message had not been conveyed soon enough to bring him in from the fields, not soon enough to thwart Laban's plans. Anger flared once more at her mother and Laban and their callous indifference to this brother who had never hurt a soul in all of his life.

She touched his arm and looked up into his sober eyes. "He loved you. He wanted to bless you and would have. You must believe that."

He nodded but did not speak.

"I don't care what Ima and Laban have done. I need you, Bethuel."

He placed his large hand on her shoulder and patted it awkwardly. "I will take care of you, Bekah."

She reached both arms around his waist, relieved to feel his arms come around her. But as her mother's voice sounded in the distance, giving orders to the servants to prepare her father for burial, she felt little comfort from his reassuring hold.

Laban's and her mother's actions had changed her future. Nothing would be the same again.

The city gates loomed in the distance early the next morning. Laban cinched his cloak closer against the dawn's first chill, his nerves on edge with every step. There would be no problem convincing the elders the documents were real. His father's seal on the parchments would act as proof enough, and as long as Bethuel kept his tongue . . . He cinched his cloak again, glancing behind him at his father's steward—his steward now. The man would support him. All of the servants favored his leadership over that of his brother. There could be no doubt that his father's namesake was slow. Not exactly witless, but a clumsy oaf whose only skills lay in caring for the sheep.

Still, Laban tucked the pouch of parchments tighter beneath his arm as though holding them close would protect his assets. They would believe what he told them. Of course they would.

He shivered as a line of young maidens glided past him carrying jars on their shoulders, headed to the well outside of the city. He spotted Rebekah among them with her maid Selima, relieved when she did not stop or attempt to engage him in another confrontation. She alone had insisted that the firstborn Bethuel should carry the birthright of their father's blessing and had tried to convince both Bethuel and him that she was right. Thankfully, she'd stopped short of threatening to expose him to the elders. Her fate rested in his hands, and she knew it.

Lifting his shoulders in a shrug, he tried to brush the conversation aside, but the tension would not abate. The weight of guilt pressed in on him. It was ridiculous, of course. He had done nothing wrong. In fact, he had done the most prudent thing to protect his family.

He watched Rebekah's graceful form move beneath the gates toward the well as he approached the gate himself. Her beauty surpassed that of every maiden in Harran, and already he had received requests from several men willing to pay for the privilege of marrying her. He smiled, glad their father had not given in to the potter's request for his son Naveed. Rebekah's beauty belonged in kings' palaces.

But plans for his sister must wait for another day. He sighed, glanced at his steward, and entered the gate to meet the elders.

"Greetings, Laban, son of Bethuel. Have you come prepared to take your father's seat among us?" The chief governor of the palace motioned to the seat his father used to occupy as head of the merchants' guild.

"I am ready, Kenan." He handed the documents to the leader of the elders and took the seat offered him. "You will find everything in order there." He leaned back, confident that the documents his brother had signed along with his father's seal looked authentic even to the discerning eye.

The governor studied the parchments, running his fingers over the seal at the bottom. Laban waited, forcing himself to remain calm, to breathe normally, lest he show his anxiety. If he was caught deceiving these people, he could end up losing his place of honor and, even worse, be imprisoned for fraud. But they need not know the full truth. Any one of them would have done the same.

"Everything seems to be in order," the man said at last. He rolled the parchments up again and placed them back into the pouch.

Laban handed the pouch to his steward, relieved. He settled back, listening as the day's order of business commenced.

As the morning waned and the sun rose higher in the sky, the meeting at last came to an end, and the men left, most to attend business elsewhere. Laban moved toward the stairs leading to the streets below the city gate. At a touch on his arm, he turned.

"Laban, son of Bethuel." One of the elders approached.

"Yes, my lord."

"I would have a word with you."

Laban's heart kicked over in a silent surge of uncertainty, but at the look on the man's face, he relaxed and walked with the elder through the city gate toward the main thoroughfare of Harran's market streets.

"I am sorry for the loss of your father, may he rest in peace." The man lowered his head in a proper gesture of sorrow.

"Thank you, my lord. His presence is greatly missed." Laban touched a hand to his forehead, dutifully agreeing with the man's sentiment.

They walked in silence several moments, passing a baker carrying a tray of pastries on a wooden platter, headed toward his market stall, while street urchins raced in and around the patrons, nearly toppling the man's tray. Laban glanced at the sky, fighting the urgency to hurry the man along.

"Your father and I had discussed the possibility of a match between your sister and my son Dedan." The man cleared his throat, and though Laban looked him in the eye, he would not meet Laban's gaze.

"What did my father say about the matter?" By the man's

shifty expression, Laban knew the answer. His father probably thought the man a liar and a cheat and would never give Rebekah to such a man's son.

"Only that he was weighing several offers." At last the man stopped and faced Laban. "I am prepared to offer whatever you request. I think it will benefit both your house and mine to make such an alliance." His earlier disquiet seemed to disappear, replaced by sudden confidence. "My son is anxious to meet your sister."

Laban stroked a hand over his beard. He would find opposition from Rebekah and probably Bethuel if he acted too quickly in this. He lifted a brow, feigning uncertainty. "I am afraid this is a subject I am not as familiar with as I should be. If you will forgive me, my lord, my father's affairs are not yet fully set in order. I must consult with my older brother on this matter before I can give you an answer."

"I thought the papers indicated these decisions rest with you." Skepticism filled his expression, setting Laban's heart to a quicker beat.

"It does—they do. But like you said, my father had many offers, and I have not yet had the chance to look into them." Sweat pricked a line along his turbaned brow.

The man nodded, seemingly satisfied. "Of course. I understand." He turned to head in the opposite direction, and Laban breathed a sigh. "But do not keep me waiting long." He gave Laban a pointed look. "I am not a patient man."

"We will be moving at the end of the week." Laban leaned against the threshold between the cooking rooms and the area where they entertained guests during meals. The place where Rebekah's father had presided over family meetings and conducted urgent council business. But only days after her father's body rested in the family burial cave, Laban was already turning her world inside out. "Take whatever you will need to move to the house in Nahor in Paddan-Aram."

Their grandfather's home in Paddan-Aram, the city of Nahor, was larger by far than their house in Harran, where more people wanted to live in less space, where the king's palace and the seat of their government resided.

Rebekah turned from the table where she kneaded the dough for the next morning's baking to look from Laban to her mother, who was seated at the table chopping figs.

"Why should we move? Harran is our home." Rebekah shoved the heel of her hand into the soft, doughy mound, but it did nothing to release the sudden tension in her heart.

"If your brother thinks we should move, he has good reason."

Her mother's rebuke stung. Rebekah had argued with Laban all of her life. She would not follow his lead without question. She shoved the dough harder, turning it as she went, forcing back the ache that came every time she thought of her father.

"We won't all go. Not all at once," Laban said to Nuriah as though Rebekah were not in the room. "But I want you to take Rebekah and her maids and leave the city. Farah will stay with me for a time. People will understand during this period of mourning." Laban took a few steps into the cooking room, then seemed to think better of it and returned to prop one arm against the threshold.

Rebekah whirled to face him, flour-coated hands on her hips. "You cannot push me out of your life and send me away. Not until you have secured a proper betrothal for me." If she left, he might forget his responsibility to her.

"You're not coming with us?" Nuriah's thick brows furrowed, her mouth a tight line.

"I will visit often, and soon. Once things are settled here, Farah and I will join you."

Rebekah turned the dough over into a clay bowl and covered it with a cloth, refusing to look at him. "You still have not answered my question." She closed the distance to the table where her mother sat and braced herself, facing him. "Why should I leave?" She would find Bethuel and enlist his help to keep her here if she must. She had lived in Harran most of her life. Her friends were here.

"It is a safer place for you. Until I can sort out the many suitors who have come calling, it is better if you are not in the city."

A knock sounded on the outer door, silencing her protest. Laban moved into the sitting room while a servant went to see who had come to call. Rebekah glanced at her mother but ignored the shake of her head that told Rebekah to stay where she was. She walked quietly to stand along the wall and peeked around the corner to watch and listen.

"Baruch, welcome, my friend. Come in. Have some refreshment." Laban embraced the potter and kissed each cheek, motioning him to sit among the cushions.

"No, no. I would not think to impose on your hospitality so late in the evening." The potter rubbed a shaky hand over his beard, his gaze fixed solely on his feet. "I only wondered . . . that is . . . my Naveed is anxious for your answer." The man looked up, and Rebekah caught the hopeful glint in his eyes. Naveed's father had asked for her hand before her father died, and it was up to Laban now to give the man an answer. She waited, her breath held tight within her.

Laban nodded and placed a hand on the man's shoulder. "I am sorry to have kept you wondering, my friend. Your son is surely a worthy man that would make any woman proud."

But not your sister. She knew with the release of a sigh that Laban had no intention of giving her to the potter's son, the third born, who would inherit little and likely make only a modest, perhaps even a poor living the rest of his life.

"I am afraid, however, that the amount you offered for Rebekah's hand has already been exceeded by several other hopeful fathers just this past week. Unless you can offer much more than you already have . . ."

Disappointment filled the potter's expression as he slowly shook his head. "I have offered you all that I could spare. I am afraid I will have to withdraw the request." He bowed then and turned toward the door, looking back for a brief moment. "Thank you for your *hospitality*." He swept out of the house before Laban could respond.

Rebekah did not miss the man's sarcasm, nor the hint of anger directed at her brother. How many men of Harran would he offend by setting too high a bride-price for her? Was this why he wanted her to leave the city, so he could conduct his business without her knowing, so that she would not have to face the good people he had offended once she finally wed?

"It is just as well." Her mother's voice came from beside her. When had she moved close enough to hear? "Naveed was a poor potter's son. He would have never been able to provide for you as you deserve."

Rebekah stilled, her cheeks flushed with anger, a familiar feeling she had known too often of late. "Naveed was a good man. Better a poor man who is good than a rich, evil one."

"It doesn't matter now," Laban said, joining them in the cooking room again. "Pack your things. You leave in three days."

Rebekah's arms ached from lifting and carting heavy baskets laden with clothing, cooking utensils, and the washed wool for her weaving to the donkeys' carts, only to do the task in reverse once the small caravan reached her mother's new home. The city of Nahor in Paddan-Aram was situated in a lush valley surrounded by higher hills. Her grandparents' former home occupied one of the wealthier, more spacious sections of the town yet smelled musty from long disuse.

Some of the furnishings used by her grandfather Nahor, his wife and concubine, and their children still took up many of the rooms.

Rebekah explored the large estate as servants bustled about her, sweeping and arranging things the way her mother told them to. The air was cleaner here than in Harran, the noise decidedly lessened with the house situated far from the markets and some of the more pungent trades. She breathed deeply. Her weaving room was larger and more airy, and the view from her bedchamber's window was beautiful. She should thank Laban for sending them here, but she could not forgive him long enough to even consider such a thing.

She moved into the courtyard, where Deborah and Selima had begun preparations for the evening meal. The donkeys' carts sat outside the courtyard, empty now, the animals rubbed down and munching hay in the large stables near the house. She joined Selima near the millstone and poured the ground grain into a clay bowl.

"I think I could get used to living here," Rebekah said, adding oil to the flour and mixing them together. "There is so much room. Smells better too." She moved her hand in an arc. "But don't tell Laban I said so." She wrinkled her nose and Selima laughed.

"Your secret is safe with us, mistress." Selima's hands gripped the millstone, her body swaying with the motion of the turns. "It helps to have the animals in a stable away from the house, rather than below us."

"I do miss the sound of the camels when they belch." Deborah laughed and Selima joined her.

"I think the animals smell better than some of the people," Rebekah said. Her own brother among them, though in truth, Laban wore plenty of perfumes to mask his body's odor. It was the smell of his deceit she had grown to despise.

"I thought you liked the scents of myrrh and sweat."

Deborah bent over the clay oven, poking the fire beneath it with a long stick.

"I like the scents of the river and how a body smells when it is clean." Rebekah smiled, enjoying the company of these women. Even Naveed could have improved his habits of cleanliness, though he was better than some.

Naveed. Surprise filled her that she did not miss him or his offer of marriage. In truth, she could think of no one in Harran she pined after. She drew in a slow breath as she glanced through the courtyard's gates in the direction of Harran. Even the cone-shaped homes of the town were not visible from this distance, only a road that trailed into a thin line outside the city wall the farther it went.

"I wonder who your brother will pick for you."

Selima's comments brought her thoughts up short. Selima was obsessed with weddings and thoughts of marriage.

"I am like a prized camel in his eyes. He will sell me to the man with the biggest purse."

"And for such a purse you should be grateful. It is proof your brother cares for your welfare."

Her mother's caustic tongue set Rebekah's head to aching. She hadn't heard her approach.

"My brother cares only for the wealth I can bring him." Though she couldn't prove it, she suspected Laban kept back part of the gold she earned from her weaving, despite his assurances that he was giving her the full amount.

"Your brother thinks you are fit for a prince." Her mother stepped closer, carrying a basket of wool on her way into the house. She looked Rebekah up and down. "Though with that disobedient spirit, you should be glad Laban sent you away from Harran. That tongue of yours will get you into trouble, Daughter. Don't think I didn't warn you." She stalked out of the courtyard and into the cool interior of the house.

Rebekah stared after her, stunned. How was it possible

that her mother's words hurt more now than they ever did? She had endured the woman's scorn all of her life. But Abba had protected her then.

She swallowed hard at the touch of Deborah's hand on her arm. "She did not mean it as it sounds, mistress," Deborah whispered into her ear.

But Rebekah knew better. "I care nothing for spoiled princes. I want a man who treats me well. A man I can trust." She flung the words toward the house, certain her mother could hear.

"One day you will thank me," her mother called from inside, so self-assured, so matter-of-fact.

Rebekah turned her back to the house and looked at Deborah, refusing to continue her mother's argument. What could she say to such words? Deborah placed an arm around her shoulders and drew her toward the women's circle, where Selima glanced up from her grinding, her normally smiling face suddenly somber. Even her maids were weary of Nuriah's outbursts. With Laban away and her father gone, her mother had grown increasingly bitter.

Deborah, her nurse from the day of her birth, was more of a mother to her than Nuriah had ever been. And Selima, Deborah's daughter, was more of a sister than a maid, though social dictates did not allow her to be treated as one.

Rebekah scooped the ground grain from Selima's pile and sifted it through the sieve. She worked in silence for several heartbeats, and when she glanced into the distance, she saw a man walking the thin path toward their estate.

"Someone is coming." She set the bowl aside and walked to the edge of the courtyard to get a better view. The man drew closer, and she would have recognized his lumbering gait among any crowd of men. "It's Bethuel!" She snatched a linen cloth from the bench and wiped her hands on it as she ran toward him.

She reached him moments later, breathing hard, and threw

herself into his brotherly embrace. "How I have missed you, Bethuel! And now you are here!"

He twirled her in his big arms like he used to do when she was a child. "Laban needed me to watch over you." He set her down and moved a piece of hair from her face. "A house needs a man nearby, you know."

She clutched his arm. "And I could ask for no better man to protect me."

With Bethuel nearby, her mother would mind her tongue. Both her father and this brother had quietly commanded a respect Rebekah could not seem to gain on her own. One look from him would silence her mother's misguided words.

She smiled into his thoughtful eyes, pleased when he winked back at her.

"We will find you a good husband, Bekah. I will make sure of it."

"If you help Laban decide, I know all will be well." Bethuel could judge a man's character in one glance. If only he had remained the one in control of her fate. "But come, there is time enough to worry about protecting me. You must be hungry, and the evening meal is almost ready." She smiled at him again, relieved that he had chosen to come rather than go off to his beloved hills and be alone with the sheep.

He rubbed his middle with one hand. "I could eat a whole goat right now."

She laughed. "Well, unfortunately, red lentil stew will have to do."

"Spiced the way I like it?" He looked like a small boy the way he asked, and she suddenly was a young girl again learning to prepare her father's favorite dishes, pleased and proud when she succeeded in making him smile.

She patted his arm, her thoughts wistful, and wished her father were with them too. "Spiced just the way you like it."

They took their time walking back to the house.

A large clay urn rested atop Rebekah's shoulder, and she steadied it with one hand as she took the steps downward leading into the well's yawning mouth. Months had passed since she had been allowed to travel to the well outside of Harran, one she had used daily when they lived in the city. She was weary of begging Laban to give her the freedom to return to this task, and even now she was only allowed to come in the company of three of her maids, as if she were a prized flower Laban feared would be picked if he did not keep her surrounded and protected.

Irritation made her tighten her grasp on the urn as the voices of the village women drew closer, their varying tones echoing against the cavernous stone walls. She recognized her friend Iltani's high-pitched squeal among them.

"Rebekah!" Iltani sidled alongside Rebekah as she reached the last step and waited while she lowered the jar to the ground, then accepted Iltani's kiss of greeting. "I thought we would never see you here again! Where has that brother of yours been hiding you?"

"At my grandfather's house in Paddan-Aram." Though Iltani surely had already heard this news.

"But why? He has taken you away from your friends. The treks up and down these steps are not the same without you." Iltani laughed freely, and her eyes danced with too-obvious delight.

"You are happy about something. Tell me."

Iltani smiled wide, but when she met Rebekah's gaze, she sobered. "You may not think my news to be good."

"Of course I will! If it makes you happy, it will bring me joy as well." Though she could not deny a foreboding feeling in her heart.

Iltani took in a long breath and released it in a rush. "Naveed and I are betrothed! We will marry before the year is out. His father is already planning to build onto their house to make room for us."

"I thought Naveed would be moving away when he married." The words came out before she thought to stop them. She had no claims to Naveed. They had been childhood friends, and despite his attempts to marry her, those plans had long since changed.

"It is true that Naveed does not receive the inheritance of the firstborn, but Naveed is good at his father's trade, and his father wants to keep him on." Iltani dipped her jar into the spring, lifted the full water jug, and placed it gracefully on her head. "I hope you will attend me."

"Of course. I will be honored." She smiled at Iltani, but grew silent as Iltani chattered on about the wedding. She was happy for Iltani, truly she was. But the prick of jealousy in her heart mocked her. In the months since her father's death and their move to Paddan-Aram, Laban had turned away too many suitors, always hoping for one who would offer more.

"Are you coming?" Iltani moved up the steps and glanced back over her shoulder to where Rebekah stood at the water's edge.

"You go ahead. I'll be up shortly." She lowered her jar to the spring and waited as the water bubbled up into it.

"Will you go to the wedding?" Selima asked as the group surrounding Iltani grew distant.

Rebekah filled her jar, lifted it onto her head, and waited as Selima did the same. "If Laban allows it, of course." The thought of Iltani marrying ahead of her did not matter. She would not let it. Though at nearly twenty years on earth, she had already waited long enough.

"But," she added as they began the long trek to the surface, "if he does not allow it, I will not be disappointed."

The sun blazed a path toward the western ridge when Rebekah finally found Laban alone in the family courtyard. Servants had cleared away the last of the meal, and her brother sat near the fire, a clay pipe in his hand. She smoothed the wool of her skirt as she sat on a stone bench opposite him. "I trust you had a prosperous day with the merchants."

Laban put the pipe to his lips and drew in the smoke of the poppy leaves, then released a breath. "The woven garments you made brought a fair price." He jingled the pouch at his belt. "Your skills have given your family a tidy sum." He looked at her, and she caught the glint of affection in his dark eyes, a sentiment she had not detected from him since before their father passed.

He set the pipe on the bench beside him and lifted the purse, untied the strings, and poured several nuggets of gold into his hand, holding them out to her. She accepted them and dropped them into a pouch in her robe. "Thank you." She was surprised at the strength of the emotion his actions evoked. Perhaps he truly did seek what was best for her.

"You earned it fair enough." He picked up his pipe again and puffed. "Put it away for your future. When you go from this house to the house of your husband, you shall not go empty-handed."

Rebekah looked beyond Laban to the dying warmth of the setting sun, her heart stirred with the thought. Yet how often had he made such comments and done nothing to make them come true? Every time she handed over a newly woven garment or length of multicolored cloth to trade with foreign merchants, he handed her the same amount, giving the same comment. Yet no husband had come to claim her in the five years since she was nubile, and she feared Laban intended to hold her until her beauty faded and it was too late.

"About that husband," she said, forcing down her frustration. "When do you plan to find such a man for me, my brother? You have turned away every suitor who has come to call. Men will fear something is wrong with me if you do not act soon. Why do you hesitate?"

He avoided eye contact, dragging too quickly on the pipe. He choked and coughed for a long moment. She poured water into a gourd and he drank. At last he looked at her, but his gaze flitted quickly beyond her, as though he could not face her.

"Tell me the truth, Laban. I am tired of waiting for you to act." She was angry now, recognizing the sheepish grin poking from beneath the thick curls of his beard.

His head bobbed as he nodded. "You are right as always, my sister. I have only considered your best interests. What kind of man would I be if I sold you to a life of poverty?" He leaned forward and touched her knee.

She looked into his charming gaze, the one she had grown weary of him using to appease her. "Not every man that has come is poor. But I fear my brother expects too much. I want you to act now."

Laban leaned away from her and twisted the pipe in his hands, looking at the smoldering leaves as though wisdom could be found there. Silence grew, broken only by the sounds of voices coming from inside the house and the crackle of the fire in the stone hearth in the courtyard.

At last he looked up. "I will send servants to Ur, to some of our distant kinsmen, to see if a match can be made."

"I don't want to marry a distant relative or go back to a land we were forced to leave. Why can't you choose from someone nearby? Why would you send me away?"

"Would you choose a man like Naveed, who will inherit nothing from his father and has no means to get ahead in life? The men who have approached me could offer no better."

"Naveed is betrothed to Iltani." Sudden emotion at the thought surprised her. She was happy for Iltani. Truly she was.

Laban's brow lifted in a quizzical expression, a sure sign he had yet to hear the news. "Well, yes, then all the better for him." He smiled, plopping the pipe back into his mouth, then drew in the smoke and released it. "You will thank me someday that I turned him away. But do not worry, dear sister. You will marry soon."

She scrunched the fabric of her robe, kneading it between her fingers. Voices drifted closer, and before she could answer, her mother and Laban's wife Farah carried in baskets of wool and settled on benches nearby.

"Are we interrupting something?" Her mother smiled at Laban as she pulled the wool from the baskets and worked with Farah to separate the strands.

The moon ducked in and out of the clouds, an unsteady light over the courtyard. Night air brought a chill with it, but heat infused Rebekah's cheeks at Laban's audacious attitude. She rose, trembling, unable to share the same fire with her mother and her favorite son.

"Excuse me." She hurried from the courtyard into the house, past busy servants, and down the hall toward her sleeping chambers. She turned at the sound of footsteps and saw Selima coming toward her.

She entered the room and sank onto her couch. Leaning against the pillows, she let out an angry breath. "I am weary of his tricks. Laban is using me for his own gain. I am a prisoner in this house!" Defeat settled over her like a sodden cloak.

She looked out the window toward the starless heavens. The scent of rain hung heavy in the air, and her clothes felt damp from the weight of it. "Am I unworthy of marriage, Selima?"

"Any man worth anything would be honored to marry you, mistress." Selima plucked a pillow and fluffed it between her fingers. She was a pretty girl in her own right, but not well-to-do enough to marry at will unless Rebekah released her and had Laban find a man for her.

The thought depressed her further. She couldn't get Laban to do her own bidding, let alone help a servant. She walked to the window, wishing the rain would come and release its hold on the sticky air. Her gaze slanted upward, and she let go of her anger with a long, slow sigh.

God of our ancestor Shem, let me marry an honorable man, not one taken to the greed of my brother and mother.

She let the prayer leave her heart, wondering if it took wing and moved beyond her to the One she had learned of at her father's knee. Did He really exist? Laban would placate Him, if He did. But Laban placated every god in Harran.

Doubt settled over her. If Laban's words were true, which she could not trust for certain, might she truly find herself wed and in the home of her husband soon? How soon? Hope lifted her chest for only a moment. She would believe such a thing once she witnessed it.

4

Rebekah bent over the grindstone and gripped the wooden handle, turned the stone in a circular motion, and pressed the kernels of wheat between the top and bottom millstones. She'd been at the task long enough to cause her back to ache, and she stretched, trying to get the kinks to loosen. Three weeks had passed since her conversation with Laban, and he had not mentioned the subject of her future again.

She did not trust Laban.

Footsteps sounded in the adjacent house, and the voices of servants came closer. "There you are." Deborah approached and motioned her aside. "You look spent. Let me take a turn." She placed a woven mat beneath her knees and grabbed the wooden handle of the grindstone with both hands.

Rebekah sank onto the bench and breathed deeply. "The sun is warm today." She dabbed at the beads of sweat along her forehead with the edge of her head scarf.

Deborah glanced up at her. "I thought you would have Selima do this task today. Weren't you planning to go to the market with your mother?"

Rebekah shook her head. "My mother did not want my

company. I think she and Farah had plans they did not think I would approve." A sigh escaped before she could stop it.

"Perhaps they want to surprise you. If Laban has found a match for you, they could be buying gifts for your betrothal. You know how your mother enjoys surprises."

"My mother enjoys keeping things from me, if that's what you mean by her surprises." Rebekah gave a sardonic laugh. "Do you honestly think Laban has taken a single step toward seeking a husband for me? I think he has put it out of his mind."

"You do not know that for sure. Men don't always act in ways or at times we think they should."

The stones squealed beneath Deborah's hand. She paused to add more grain to grind between them.

"My father did. If I asked something of him, he gave it quickly and freely. Laban enjoys taunting me." She paced the wide outer courtyard, glancing toward the hills where she expected Laban to soon return from a visit to the flocks. "Perhaps I should seek help from Bethuel." If only her brother had stayed on at the estate, she could at least appeal to him.

"Bethuel lives in the hills for a reason, mistress. You know how Laban makes him feel."

"As though he has no use but to be a shepherd." She sighed. "But even in that Laban does not fully trust him. Laban left three days ago to inspect the sheep without saying a word to me. He only made those promises to placate me."

"You are assuming things."

"And you are making excuses for a deceiver!" She glanced quickly behind her, relieved that no servants stood nearby. Though her mother and sister-in-law were gone to market, Laban's concubine Refiqa, newly pregnant with his child, lay resting inside the house. "My brother can marry as many women as he pleases, but I must dangle like poor fruit on the vine." Though Laban was six years older than she, he had married Farah in his youth and taken Refiqa this past year. Already he had three young sons.

Deborah paused in the grinding, took the flour from the trough, and poured it into a clay bowl. "Here, add the oil and start kneading the bread. The others will be back soon, and unless you want to run off to the hills and live with Bethuel, we can only make the best of what we have."

Rebekah felt the rebuke in Deborah's tone. Deborah knew firsthand the shock of losing a husband and living ever since without one. Still, the words stung as Rebekah took the bowl to the cooking room and set it on the wooden table with more force than she intended. A thin crack appeared down one side. She uttered a curse. The bowl was one of her mother's favorites.

She searched the shelves for another bowl to replace it, glancing through the window as she did. A man's form appeared, striding toward the house, but on closer inspection, she did not recognize his gait. Laban walked with quicker strides, his hands swinging at his sides as though he was always hurrying to get somewhere, whereas Bethuel moved as though time meant nothing.

A neighbor, perhaps? One of the servants? The thought troubled her. Had something happened to Laban? Emotion surged, switching from anger to fear. She hurried from the cooking room to the courtyard to meet the stranger and found Deborah standing at the courtyard gate speaking to him.

"You are welcome to wait in the courtyard for Master Laban to return if you wish," Deborah was saying. "We will be happy to set an extra place for the evening meal."

The man shook his turbaned head and held up a hand. "No, no, but thank you very much. I have come to deliver the images Laban requested." He lifted a heavy sack Rebekah had failed to notice from her view at the window and handed it to Deborah.

"Images?" Rebekah stepped forward to address the man, ignoring Deborah's pointed frown. "What images did my brother order?"

The man looked at her, a gleam of appreciation in his eyes. Rebekah recoiled at his too-familiar look, suddenly aware of the pale blue head scarf that set apart her maidenhood. She dipped her head, keeping her eyes averted to the goatskin sack in Deborah's arms.

"Open it up and see for yourself. I stand by my workmanship. Laban knows where to come for the best quality." His chest lifted in obvious pride.

Deborah carried the sack to a bench to do as the man suggested, and Rebekah hurried to join her. She scooted close to Deborah, keeping her distance from the man, who followed them past the gate into the courtyard.

"Three images, as you can see," he said as Deborah pulled each one from the sack. "Carved of cedar and overlaid with gold. The finest quality."

Deborah turned each image over before placing them back in the sack. "We will be sure to pass them on to Master Laban." She turned to the man. "I trust the master has paid you for your services?"

The man nodded, though by his look Rebekah wondered if he had hoped to gain something more. Had Laban promised him something other than a simple merchant's order? The man eyed her, and she had to force herself to stand still and not shrivel beneath his open perusal.

"Why don't you take these inside, mistress?" Deborah thrust the sack into Rebekah's arms. She glimpsed her nurse's look, sensing her protectiveness. She was only too happy to comply. Deborah turned to the merchant. "Thank you for dropping these by. I am sure the master will stop at your booth after he returns to thank you himself." She crossed her arms, brooking no argument, while Rebekah slipped into the house. She waited just inside the door, until at last she heard his grunted thanks and his footsteps receding.

"Why would Laban order such images?" she asked when Deborah joined her moments later. "I know my brother would placate the moon and beg the sun to do his bidding, but since when does he keep household gods? Has he completely abandoned the God of Shem?"

Deborah shook her head. "I do not know, mistress." She eyed the sack with a hint of fear. "The God of your fathers, the God of Shem, is a jealous God." She met Rebekah's gaze. "Your brother is asking to bring trouble on this house."

Dusk deepened with an intermittent breeze, and the telltale howl of a jackal in a nearby thicket made the flesh prickle on Isaac's arms. The flap of bats' wings whooshed the air above his head. Familiar sounds. Comforting sounds. The cave at Machpelah had become a habitual stop on his return to Hebron from visits to the Negev. How was it that more than two years after her death, he could still grieve his mother as though her parting had been yesterday?

He rubbed the hair on his arms and pulled the cloak about him, the chill of the night air making him shiver. His father worried over his melancholy, comparing him too often to his untamed half brother Ishmael, who roamed the deserts of Shur and Paran with his many sons—a warrior, a fighter. Even Abraham's younger sons by his concubine Keturah carried a wild streak within them, inheriting their father's sense of adventure.

But Isaac had never known a desire to fight as his brothers fought or to hunt and kill as they did. While he did not share their sense of sport or hostile bickering, he did not fear the night sounds. Men might come to kill and steal and destroy, but Adonai controlled the wild beasts, and Adonai could be trusted to protect him.

He moved from beneath the protection of the oaks toward the steps leading downward to the cave's entrance. Darkness shrouded him now as he picked his way along, hugging the cool limestone. He stopped at the last step and sat upon it, wrapping both arms around his knees.

His mother had doted on him all of his life. An old woman by the time of his birth, Sarah had laughed often with him and taught him early to notice the world around him, the flowers and birds, the plants and trees, the way the water dripped into the clay cisterns and how wine tasted when held on the tongue. She shared her favorite dishes, the sheep cheese, and many spices she hoarded to flavor food just the way his father loved best.

How he missed her!

He stared at the large circular stone guarding the entrance to the burial shelves, protecting her remains from the jackals outside, the jackals she had feared.

"Do not worry, Ima. They cannot hurt you now."

He leaned back against the stone step and absently stroked his beard. Scratching sounds came from the distant recesses, probably a mouse of some kind. If he had brought a torch, he might catch the creature unaware and study it for a moment. But it was a skittish animal and would likely hide from the light as he was drawn to it, especially in the Negev, where the sun warmed his back, and where his own skittish thoughts could focus on Adonai and all the things he did not understand. Unlike here, where his thoughts grew muddled and grief overtook him.

"The days of mourning have passed, Ima." His voice echoed in the chamber, a sound that always made him pause. "I have no tears to give you. I only came to tell you"—his voice dropped to a whisper—"this is my last visit here. I must put aside grief and live the life I am meant to live."

Saying it aloud made it seem possible. He needed to face the future his father had planned for him, the future Adonai had promised him. And yet . . . he was afraid. He did not fear the jackals or the wild beasts his mother had feared but the people with whom he lived. He knew too well the sting of betrayal and the sudden way a man could turn against another.

The memory added to the grief he held too tightly. He had accepted the sacrifice, the purpose of God in his father's actions. But his mother had never fully recovered from the shock. Though she had lived on for several years, she had changed. Where Isaac had grown more submissive and accepting, she had grown fearful. Elohim's test had changed them all, and while his father passed the test with Adonai's acceptance and blessing, his mother had pulled inward, had withdrawn from everyone except her son, until death claimed her.

He had been her only joy, the only one to bring her comfort and laughter after that day. The memories only heightened his sense of uncertainty. His father said it was time to fill her place. Isaac needed a wife of his own. But he had no prospects, no women of kindred spirit in the camp who would understand him as Sarah had. Surely Adonai had a woman prepared for him. As He had made the first woman for the first man, surely He did not intend for the promised son to go without an heir.

Isaac pushed to his feet, frustrated with his insecurities, and turned to walk up the steps to the surface. He looked back one last time, bracing a hand against the wall. He should say something in parting, but there were no words left to say. She could not hear him from her place in Sheol, and he could not bring her back from there.

He climbed the rest of the steps and moved forward, following the shaft of moonlight now coming through a break in the trees. A stirring in the brush at the edge of the clearing made him turn. Twin circles of light looked back at him—a jackal or a large cat. He stilled, feeling the whisper of wind against his cheek, the breath of God at his back.

I am yours, Elohei Abraham. He had learned submission and trust through fear. Fear no longer bound him. Not fear of what God could control. Only fear of that which God gave free rein. Fear of men. Fear of relationships with those he did not trust.

He held the animal's gaze a moment longer, watching, waiting. The animal turned. A jackal. Ran back through the brush the way it had come. Isaac followed the opposite path toward his father's house in Hebron.

Voices, loud and boisterous one moment, muffled and angry the next, came from his father's tent as Isaac entered the compound. He continued walking, trying to blot out the sounds of his father's concubine Keturah, her animated voice rising higher against the booming insistence of his father.

"They are too young. You cannot send them away! I will die if you do!" Keturah's cries turned to sobs, and the tent grew silent except for her weeping. Isaac kept walking, weary of such exchanges.

He moved to the central area of the camp where the fire still smoldered and Keturah's older sons sat on tree stumps and large stones. Jokshan plucked a one-stringed lyre while Medan carved shapes from tree branches. Zimran, the oldest, was missing from the group, but nine-year-old Midian kicked debris into the fire, his actions threatening to put it out. He stopped at the sight of Isaac, his expression turning to a scowl.

Isaac approached and sat on a log opposite the boys. "You play a fine tune," he said, directing his gaze to fourteen-year-old Jokshan. "Perhaps it is time we built you a three-stringed lyre to increase your skills." He studied the youth—the square jaw, the intense dark eyes staring back at him, the dark brows knit.

"I don't need your help. I can have one of the servants build me whatever I want." Isaac sensed the boy's arrogance and sought a way to break the tension. Keturah's children were young enough to be his own, and with his father's advanced age, they rarely enjoyed the lessons or the discipline Isaac had learned at his father's knee.

Isaac moved closer to the boy and extended a hand toward the one-stringed instrument. "May I?" He waited, expecting refusal, but resisted a smile when the boy complied. He turned the instrument over and smoothed a hand along the wood's grain. "We could add strings to this one, but the sound would be better if the hole was bigger." He returned it to the boy.

Jokshan smiled, his teeth white against a tanned face. His heritage was darker-skinned than his father's Mesopotamian tones—more like that of his mother's Syrian ones. Normally a bit of a ruffian, Jokshan was one of the few of Keturah's children who also showed a softer side, one that Isaac tried to nurture. But the mother offered the boys even less discipline than his father did.

A commotion came from the tents, and Isaac turned at the ear-splitting screeches of Keturah's second youngest, Ishbak, whose little legs pumped hard and tried to outrun his oldest brother, but quickly failed. Zimran grabbed hold of Ishbak, whose wail pierced through to Isaac's heart. He stood, his blood pumping fast.

Zimran whipped Ishbak upside down and carried him toward the fire pit, then dangled him by one leg over the fire.

"You think you can steal from me and get away with it, you little beast! I'll teach you to take what belongs to me."

Ishbak's cries grew louder as Zimran lowered him, his hair nearly scorched by the low flames. "Abbaaaa!"

Isaac came up behind Zimran and pulled a blade from his belt, touching it to Zimran's neck. "Pull him away from the fire and release him. Now!"

Zimran did not move. "You will not cut my throat, *Brother*. You do not have the courage. And this one needs to be taught a lesson." Keturah's sixteen-year-old carried himself like a man and was too bold for his age, reminding Isaac of his older brother Ishmael and a time when he was the one taunted by the elder son of Abraham.

"Do not think me a fool, Zimran. You are not old enough to know what I will do. You have not witnessed what I will kill."

He breathed the threat into Zimran's ear, satisfied when the boy's eyes widened and he took two slow steps back from the fire. He released Ishbak, nearly dropping him into a heap. The three-year-old scrambled to his feet and ran, sobbing, toward his father's tent, where Keturah and Abraham had emerged, disheveled and angry.

"What is the meaning of this?" Abraham's vibrant voice boomed from his tent to the central fire. By now the camp had come to life as though it were day. Isaac sheathed his blade and let it hang in the pouch at his side.

"He threatened to cut my throat!" Zimran ran toward Abraham and fell to his knees. "Protect me from your son, Abba Abraham."

Abraham glanced up, meeting Isaac's gaze. Isaac gave his head a slight shake. "The boy is mistaken, Father. He was the one threatening Ishbak, dangling him over the fire by one leg until his hair nearly caught fire. I merely gave him a reason to stop his foolish behavior."

Abraham's shoulders visibly sagged at Isaac's words, and

Isaac hated the fact that they had to be said. But his father could not continue to ignore the behavior of Keturah's sons, or soon they would cause serious mischief and misfortune.

Abraham turned to Keturah, who held a sobbing Ishbak in her arms. She spoke something in the little boy's ear, and at his nod, she reached for Zimran's tunic, yanked him to his feet, and proceeded to whack his head with her free hand.

"What is wrong with you that you would do such a thing? He is your brother! Do you not know that your father will send you away for such a thing? You are a foolish boy." She smacked him again until the youth covered his face with his arms and fell to his knees again, trying to block her blows, sobbing like a child.

"I'm sorry, Ima! But he stole my new carving knife, the one I traded with the Philistines to get, and he won't tell me where he put it." The words came out through broken sobs, and he turned to Abraham. "Please, Abba, don't send me away!"

Something twisted in Isaac's middle at the plaintive cry, and he looked from his half brother to his father, seeing the telltale determined glint in his father's eyes. Memories jolted him, vague yet still carrying with them a sense of loss. Ishmael had been sent away along with his mother when Isaac was near Ishbak's age, and Ishmael not much older than Zimran was now.

"Enough!" Abraham's voice sounded weary, though for his age he still carried much strength. "Zimran, on your feet." He tapped the boy gently with his staff, allowing no argument.

The boy rose quickly from his crouched position while Keturah stepped back and wrapped both arms around Ishbak. A crowd of servants and Keturah's other sons looked on.

"Go to your mother's tent at once. You will stay there until I can decide what to do with you."

At his father's command, Zimran hung his head, shoulders

sagging, and walked with weighted steps toward Keturah's tent.

Abraham turned to the three-year-old. "Did you take Zimran's knife?"

The child thrust a fist to his mouth and nodded.

"Where did you put it?"

Ishbak pointed toward the fire. "It fell out of my pouch when Zimran turned me upside down."

Isaac's lips twitched, but he forced himself to hold back a smile. He moved closer to the fire, picked up a twig, and pushed the ashes around, searching for the small knife. Finding it, he dragged it away from the flames. Its carved wooden handle was scorched and ruined, the end already turned to ash. Only the blade remained.

"It's here." He faced his father, who had come alongside him. "Though it won't be much use to him now."

Abraham shook his head. "It would have been better if my other sons were all like you."

The quiet words surprised him. "They are young. You can still teach them obedience, as you so often taught me." Their gazes held, the memories passing unspoken between them.

"I am too old to teach them." Abraham's chest lifted in a sigh. "But you are right, of course. And soon it will be time to send them off, away from here . . . away from you." His look held determination mingled with a hint of sadness.

"Perhaps in a few years the timing would be better. The oldest is not even as old as Ishmael was then."

The promises had been for Isaac, not Ishmael, and neither Hagar's nor Keturah's children would share with him in his father's inheritance. It was understood from the moment of his birth, from the moment his mother demanded Hagar and Ishmael be sent away. Keturah's sons would fare no differently.

"When the time is right, then," his father said, his tone defeated. "I will not live to see their children or their children's children." He patted Isaac's arm. "But before I die, I will find a wife for you, my son, and perhaps if Adonai wills it, I will hold your children on my knee."

Isaac leaned forward and kissed each of his father's cheeks. "May it be as you have said, Father."

The older man returned his son's kisses and cupped an aged hand to Isaac's bearded cheek. "You understand why I took Keturah to wife?"

It was a question, yet Isaac waited, not sure his father really wanted an answer.

"Your mother did not disapprove." He looked beyond Isaac as though his thoughts carried him to another era, to the changes that had come between him and Sarah after God's test.

"My mother had many struggles," Isaac said at last. "She loved you until the end."

Abraham visibly relaxed at that, and he gripped Isaac's arm. "She was a good woman. The most beloved mother of you, and my only love."

The words were soft, and Isaac wondered at the admission. His father had never shared such personal thoughts with him.

"I think you are right that she loved me, but I do not think she ever understood or forgave me."

"I did my best to explain it to her." Isaac felt the familiar sense of defeat that he had been unable to keep his parents' marriage as close as it had been before that day—the day his father, in obedience to Adonai Elohim, had willingly bound him and laid him on the altar on Mount Moriah. If not for the startling voice of the angel of the Lord rumbling from the skies telling him not to slay his son, Abraham would have slit his throat and spilled his blood over the stone altar, giving back to God what God had given him.

"I know you did." Abraham's tone held sorrow and a hint

of regret. "I should have tried harder to convince her, but she would not speak of it to me."

In fact, Isaac's mother had refused to even look in his father's direction for a full year after the incident, until at last, through her servant Lila, she had suggested his father take another wife. For all of her hurt and anger at her husband, she could not bear to see him suffer and deduced that another wife could fill her place. Her only stipulation had been that any sons born of another wife could never inherit alongside her son.

"We cannot undo what is past, Father. You did what Adonai Elohim required of you. I too heard the blessings that came from above after He stayed your hand. My mother did not have that privilege, and her faith, though strong, could not rise above her grief."

"Her sense of betrayal, you mean." Abraham poked at the ruined knife with his staff. "I failed her one time too many." He faced Isaac and cupped one hand on his shoulder. "But I will not fail her in my promise. I will send your half brothers to the east, far away from you, where they cannot trouble you."

Isaac nodded, measuring the pensive look in his father's eyes. "When they are old enough to handle life on their own," he said, relieved at the nod of acceptance that followed.

"When they are old enough, they will go. After I have secured a wife for you from among my people." He slipped his arm through Isaac's and turned away from the fire toward his tent. "I will send Eliezer soon to Harran to the household of my brother's sons to get a wife for you there."

Dawn broke over the hills of Hebron, and Isaac emerged from his tent to the sound of finches, sparrows, and great gray shrikes chirping and warbling in the trees above. He glanced to his right, where the tent of his mother still stood like a monument to her memory. Someday he would bring a wife there, and she would bring life back into the camp and into his heart.

The thought stirred his blood as he moved away from the tents toward the central fire, where Eliezer's son Haviv sat blowing the steam from a clay mug.

He looked up at Isaac's approach and drank. "Care for some?"

At Isaac's nod, Haviv summoned a servant girl, who placed a similar cup into Isaac's hands. He sipped, the taste minty.

"Our fathers are in deep conversation already this morning." Haviv inclined his head toward Abraham's tent, and Isaac followed his gaze.

"My father wishes to send your father on a journey to his homeland to find a wife for me." Isaac accepted a plate of figs and flatbread from the servant and bit off one end of the bread, giving Haviv a pointed look. "I want you to accompany him."

Haviv swallowed his own bite of bread. "Your father's homeland is a long journey. We could be gone two months."

"I have thought of that, but your brother can watch over my interests while you are gone. It is time Nadab took on a little more responsibility for the flocks and herds." Isaac had been close to Haviv since childhood and had been grooming him to take Eliezer's place, anticipating the day when Eliezer would be too old to oversee their household. But with the increase in livestock and servants and household goods, the job needed more than one man to do it well, and it was time he tested Nadab's ability.

"You are afraid my father will pick a virgin who is not pleasing to look upon, is that it?" Haviv's right brow lifted, accompanying his smirk.

"I am sure your father's eyesight is still well and good. Consider the journey further training." Isaac gave Haviv a sidelong glance. The man had become more friend than servant in recent years, making him a valuable asset. "Besides, if there is more than one cousin to choose from, your father might need some advice." He took a long drink of the tea and wiped his mouth with the back of his hand. "I trust you to help guide his choice."

Haviv chuckled. "Don't think I do not see the gleam in your eye."

Isaac hid a smile, wondering what his bride would be like. That is, if one of his cousins would even agree to come to him. It would take a woman with a spirit of adventure to travel so far from her homeland. What would he do if she were unwilling to leave her parents? If no cousin could be found, what then?

He turned at the sound of voices coming closer, men and women emerging from their tents. An infant's cry came from across the compound as his father and Eliezer joined them around the fire. Isaac offered his father his seat, which he took with a grateful nod.

"Eliezer has agreed to travel to Harran to seek a wife for you among my kinsmen. He is bound by my oath not to take a wife from among the people who live alongside us. You shall not marry a foreigner but a member of my own flesh and blood." Abraham drew in a breath and slowly released it.

"What if the young woman refuses to come back with him?" The possibility had turned over in Isaac's mind more than once in the night, and he could not see a way around it. His father had married two foreigners, Hagar and Keturah, so why was it so important that he not follow in his footsteps?

"Adonai Elohei of heaven and of earth will send his angel ahead of Eliezer to prepare the way for him." His father's dark eyes held a look of certainty. "But if the woman refuses to come back with him, Eliezer will be free of the oath he has taken. If that happens, God will make another way."

Isaac finished the last of his drink and handed the cup back to a servant. "I want Haviv to accompany Eliezer on this journey, Father. With your permission, of course."

Abraham accepted food from the servant and nodded. "Whatever you wish, my son. Eliezer will take ten camels and six men with him. The woman will likely bring servants with her, so we will reserve three camels for the women. He will also gather household goods, jewels, and fabric to give in payment for the girl." He fingered a slice of soft goat cheese. "I thought we should look at your mother's jewels and choose something meaningful—a gift given only if the woman agrees to come."

Isaac ran a hand along the edge of his beard and nodded. His mother had owned many pieces of fine jewelry, gold and lapis lazuli being among her favorites.

"Take plenty of silver and gold to give as gifts to her family. They must be compensated for the loss of their daughter."

"It shall be as you say, my lord." Eliezer quickly finished breaking his fast. "I will get started right away." He glanced at his son. "If you are to come with me, let us get started in gathering what we need for such a long journey."

Haviv followed Eliezer toward their tents, and Isaac took the seat beside his father. "Perhaps I will save the most priceless jewels, the ones my mother favored most, to give the woman myself." He paused, reading his father's expression. "It would have pleased her, I think."

Abraham smiled and continued to chew a plump date. "Yes, it would have pleased her." His father regarded him for a long moment. "But if you truly want to bless your mother's memory—may she rest in peace—never take another wife. Love only one woman all of your life." He rubbed his mouth with a square piece of linen. "It is something I should have understood long ago."

The sound of children's voices drifted closer. Isaac caught sight of Keturah's sons making their way toward the campfire. "What did you decide to do about Zimran?"

Abraham glanced up at the flurry of boyish activity and sighed. "I will warn him to obey, to be kind to his brothers. Then I will send him to spend time with the sheep. The boy needs to work, and some time alone with the animals will do him good."

The children scampered closer, greeting Abraham and settling on logs spaced at various intervals around the fire pit. Isaac bid his father good day and headed off to find Haviv and Eliezer. He would oversee the things they planned to take on their journey, then he would gather his own things and return to the Negev. He had stayed in his father's camp only one night, but it was long enough.

❧❧❧

Isaac led a donkey loaded with his simple provisions south of Hebron later that afternoon. He hated the look of longing in his father's eyes when he made his excuses to leave, and Jokshan took a lot of convincing that he would return with just the right piece of wood to make a three-stringed lyre. He should have taken the boy to look for the wood and stayed to carve it, to teach him how to craft such an instrument. But a certain restlessness always came upon him when he was near Keturah's children, an impatience he did not feel among the animals of the desert.

He slowed as he came to an outcropping of rocks, tightening his grip on his staff. Robbers were known to waylay sojourners along this path, though they had never troubled him. Still, one could not be too careful. He urged the donkey to a faster walk and kept his eyes and ears attuned to his surroundings. The path took a bend, and he knew a cave awaited him up ahead.

Adonai Elohim, let the cave be free of bandits. He glanced at the donkey. *And free of lions and bears*, he silently amended on behalf of the beast. He edged closer, pounding his staff into the clay earth as he walked.

He breathed deeply, tasting the dry, sand-gritty air on his tongue, and glanced up the hill above the cave where the last of the trees stood sentinel against the encroaching desert. The donkey kicked up clods of red clay as it made its way up the incline a short way and settled at the mouth of the cave.

"There you go, girl," he said as he tied her reins to an acacia tree. He opened a sack and dropped a handful of grain onto the ground near her mouth. While she ate, he moved farther into the cave, checking to see if he was alone.

Satisfied, he returned, drew the donkey farther into the cave, and set about making a fire. He would settle here for the night and make his progress toward Beer-lahai-roi, where he would meet up with Nadab and see to the state of his father's newest lambs tomorrow.

He lay in the dirt near the glowing embers, grateful for the fire's warmth while the animal slept nearby. He closed his eyes, and his thoughts drifted. Sleep came fitfully at first as he fought to keep the dreams from haunting him . . .

His surroundings blurred, his sleep peaceful, but too soon a movement caught his eye, and he startled to see his father standing over him, one hand extended. Haviv and Nadab waited at the entrance of the cave.

"Come, my son. We must go." Abraham gripped Isaac's outstretched hand and pulled him to his feet. The donkey stood beside Haviv, its bundles flung over its sides. Haviv held a torch and turned to leave the cave, and Nadab followed, a bundle of thin twigs tied to his back.

"How did you find me here?" Isaac rubbed a hand over his eyes, still groggy, but quickly obeyed. He trudged after his father, whose feet seemed determined to follow his course, yet somehow weighted and plodding. "Where are we going?" It was not like his father to come after him when he set out alone for the Negev. What could he possibly want at this hour, and why were they traveling while it was still night?

"To a place God will show us." His father's look was shadowed by darkness, but the firmness in his tone allowed no argument. "Come."

Isaac fell into step beside his father, who moved ahead of the servants, taking the lead. They traveled in silence, the night sounds giving way to birdsong and the pink light of dawn. A mount rose above them in the distance, dotted with trees, growing ever closer as the sun rose higher in the sky. By midafternoon they reached the summit.

Abraham turned to Eliezer's sons. "Stay here with the donkey while I and the boy go over there. We will worship and then we will come back to you." He motioned to Nadab. "Isaac can carry the wood now."

Isaac lifted the bundle in his arms while his father took the torch from Haviv. They trudged ahead, Isaac's arms growing heavier with each step. His heart beat too fast as he blinked against the sun's glare. If his father planned on building an altar, where was the lamb for slaughter?

They walked a steady pace, the question bounding in and out of his thoughts until he could keep silent no longer. "Father?"

"Yes, my son?"

Isaac cleared his throat, swallowed, and tried again, a sense of foreboding nearly claiming his words. "The fire and the wood are here, but where is the lamb for the burnt offering?" His father had always come prepared for a sacrifice. How could he overlook something so important?

"God himself will provide the lamb for the burnt offering, my son." Abraham walked on, saying nothing more. Isaac's fear rose higher. His father had never been so closemouthed. Or determined.

Sweat broke out on Isaac's forehead when they reached a place that seemed to please his father. He set the wood on the ground and watched as his father built an altar, all without accepting his help.

What are you doing? The question begged an answer, but he could not bring himself to voice it.

When the last stone was placed on the altar and the wood put on top, Isaac looked toward the bushes, the trees, straining to see if God had truly sent the lamb his father expected. He turned to face his father, who stood above him now, a flaxen rope in his hands.

"Father?" He choked on the word.

Sorrow filled his father's dark eyes, and the fear Isaac had known since they left Haviv and Nadab paralyzed him.

"Hold out your hands, my son." His father's words came out hoarse. "Please, do as I say."

Isaac studied his father for a suspended moment. They both knew he could say no, could run off or fight his father's intentions. But in that moment, Isaac's fear lifted as clouds might drift from the sky, replaced by unalterable truth and a strange sense of peace.

And yet he also knew he was going to die at his father's hand.

He slowly lifted his hands, the wrists close together, so his father could bind them, then fell to his knees, allowing his father to bind his feet. Tears coursed down his cheeks. The news of his death would kill his mother. If only for her sake, he would not do this. But a deeper part of him sensed he was born for this moment. His life had been a miracle, and his death would be the ultimate act of sacrificial worship.

But what of the promise to his father? What of the descendants not yet born?

The questions flashed in his thoughts as his father somehow managed to lift him onto the wood, the sharp sticks poking into his skin. The pain would end quickly. His father would not let him suffer. But his humiliation could not be more complete. How could the son of promise be led like a lamb to slaughter? Was this how God provided, by asking a man to kill his own son? Had the Creator ever suffered such indignity, such pain and loss? How could He ask such a thing of a mere man?

Isaac could not meet his father's gaze, so blinded was he by his own tears, but he caught the glint of the blade as his father's hand lifted above his neck. He closed his eyes as the blade came down . . .

"Abraham! Abraham!" a voice like booming thunder called from above.

"Here I am!" The knife clattered against the stone as Isaac's eyes flew open. He blinked, trying to clear his vision.

"Do not lay a hand on the boy," the voice said. "Do not do anything to him. Now I know that you fear God, because you have not withheld from Me your son, your only son."

Isaac lay perfectly still as his father hurried to undo the knotted rope and helped Isaac down from the altar, then pulled him into his arms, weeping, their tears mingling.

Isaac rubbed a hand over his damp face. The action jolted him, and suddenly he was sitting beside the campfire in the cave, the donkey still asleep beside him, trying to wake from his stupor. The dream had not changed with the years, the memories as powerful now as they had been twenty years before. Would he never be free of them? And yet he knew it was the binding that defined him. The ram caught in the thicket nearby and offered on the altar in his place had been followed by the words of the Lord Himself, reiterating the promise his father had spoken of so often. And now it belonged to him as well.

He shook himself, wishing the memories were a little less vivid, a little less overpowering. He could still taste the tears that always accompanied the dream. Would the dreams continue when he took a wife? What would his bride say when he woke in the night, sweating and weeping?

He walked to the cave's opening, into the starlit night.

I will surely bless you and make your descendants as numerous as the stars in the sky and as the sand on the seashore.

He drew in a long, slow breath, rubbing the tears from his cheeks. "May Your will be done, Lord. I am ready."

7

Shouts, joyous laughter, and singing accompanied the grape harvest as men cut the heavy clusters from the vines, and women quickly followed behind with their woven baskets. Squeals of children coming from the nearby winepress matched the rhythm of their stomping feet as they squished the fruit between bare toes as fast as it could be harvested. A week of arguing with Laban about the images he had paid for and set up in the main area of the house had drained Rebekah's spirit, and she welcomed the harvest with a sense of relief.

"Let me empty that for you." A young man leading a donkey and pulling a cart stopped in the row where Rebekah and Selima worked. He lifted Selima's bucket and tossed the grapes into a larger one in the back of the cart, then did the same with Rebekah's.

"Thank you." Rebekah did not allow her gaze to linger. The man had stripped to the waist to work in the sun, and Rebekah felt heat fill her face at the sight of him. He paused as he set her empty basket at the base of the vine but did not move on.

"The pleasure is mine."

She heard the smile in his voice and glanced at his face but looked quickly away from his interested expression. She looked instead at Selima, who was watching her with wide, amused eyes.

"Yes, well, if you do not hurry, the others will overflow their baskets." She pointed beyond her to men and women from the village cutting the fruit from the vine. She turned to her work, but her heart gave a little flutter as he looked at her a moment too long. At last he grabbed the donkey's reins and moved forward.

"I will return," he said, looking back over his shoulder.

His smile made her stomach quiver. The man was too bold and much too interesting. Who was he? But she squelched the thought as a passing nuisance. He was probably a lowly servant, and Laban would want nothing to do with such a man, even if the man did choose to approach him.

Selima giggled when the servant passed out of earshot. She hurried to Rebekah's side. "Every man in Harran is attracted to you, mistress. You must admit, that one is comely to look upon."

Rebekah shrugged and returned to her work. "You think every man you see is comely." But she smiled at her servant just the same. "Get back to work before we lose daylight."

Selima obeyed, still giggling as she went. Rebekah tilted her head to accept the kiss of the early afternoon sun. Soon it would be too hot to continue in the fields, and she would have to set out food for Laban's workers beneath the shade of the trees in the nearby orchard. And in the days ahead there would be the continued work of setting grapes to dry in the sun and cooking the last of the fruit into honey. She would have little time to think of handsome young men who were too bold or too poor.

She jolted at a touch on her shoulder, turning to see who dared interrupt her concentration.

"They said I would find you here. How do you fare, my sister?"

"Bethuel!" Rebekah's heart lightened at the sight of her oldest brother, and she quickly abandoned the vine, falling into his embrace. "I was beginning to wonder if we would ever see you again. It has been far too long."

Bethuel patted her back and released his hold, keeping her at arm's length. "The sheep needed me." He smiled in that half crooked way she had always loved.

"I am glad you are here." She leaned closer. "Soon we must speak."

Concern etched thin lines along Bethuel's turbaned brow, and he studied her a moment as he thoughtfully stroked his beard. "Is Laban treating you well?"

She nodded, but emotion stuck in her throat. "I am well, but there is a matter we must discuss." She lowered her voice and glanced around, aware of too many people who might overhear, despite the singing and laughter surrounding them.

"After the evening meal then," he said, his gaze somber. She knew he would not brush her concerns as quickly aside as Laban had.

Daylight dimmed, and the workers in the vineyard bid their farewells, carrying heavy baskets of ripe fruit to their homes. Rebekah lifted her basket onto her head and moved behind a group of women, anxious to get home and speak with Bethuel. She had sent Selima on ahead to help her mother with the evening meal's preparations, though she would have preferred the girl's laughter to the company of the women of Harran and Nahor.

A soft breeze feathered the fabric of her head scarf against her face, and she had to pick her way carefully over the roots of the uneven vines. She stopped abruptly, nearly tripping headlong, as a man stepped from between the vines and stood in her path, blocking her way, a too-familiar gleam in his eye.

"What? Excuse me. Please, let me pass." Her heart beat faster as she suddenly recognized the man who had earlier taken her basket and loaded the fruit onto his cart. He was fully clothed now in a white tunic and striped cloak held together with a golden, jeweled clasp. This was no peasant worker, and by the symbol etched into his embroidered robe, she recognized him as a son of one of the elders of Harran.

"I had thought to do that. But your brother Laban had suggested I . . . shall we say, take your measure, before agreeing to a match. He assured me you were the most beautiful virgin in the land." He let his eyes travel the length of her. "I can see he is a man who speaks truth." A roguish smile lifted one corner of his mouth, and Rebekah felt her insides grow warm, her cheeks heating at his perusal.

"Please," she said, her voice weaker than she intended. "Let me pass. My brothers are expecting me, and if I am late, things will not bode well for you or for me."

He chuckled as though he found her quite amusing. "I do not fear your brothers' wrath, *betulah*. I am Dedan of Harran. I fear nothing." His fingers lightly grazed her cheek.

Was this man Laban's idea of a suitable match for her? What kind of a man would accost a virgin in the vineyard with dusk approaching? She stepped back abruptly, nearly tipping the basket from her head.

"You are a fool if you fear nothing. The wrath of the God of Shem be upon you if you do not move away and let me pass!" She raised her voice, hoping someone was still near enough to hear her. He had not stated his intentions, but weren't they clear enough? Any man who waylaid a virgin had only one desire, and she was not about to give it to him without a fight.

His laughter died as he studied her in the waning daylight,

his brows knit close in a frown. "You are a bold one, *betulah*." He stroked his beard. "I should enjoy taming that fiery spirit."

His tone made her blood run cold. Fear snaked its way up her spine, but she held his gaze without flinching.

He stepped forward, his breath fanning her face. "If I choose to take you, I will. If I choose to betroth myself to you, I will. Your brother has come begging, and now I can see why. He is weary of a sister who is too bold." His fingers drew a line from her temple to her jaw. "Though no one can deny your beauty." He leaned forward as though he would kiss her.

She clutched the basket and stepped back. He grabbed her arm. She jerked away and quickly lowered the basket to hold like a shield between them. He released her and stepped back, holding both hands up in a gesture of defeat.

"Do not act so worried, *betulah*. I only meant to steady you, to keep you from falling." He chuckled again as though he were quite pleased with himself. "You shall make a fine bride." He tipped his fingers to his head and saluted her, then backed away. "We shall meet again, *betulah*."

Rebekah stilled, her breath coming fast, not certain she could trust that he was gone. But a moment later, she shook herself, thrust the basket back onto her head, and fairly ran the rest of the way through the vineyard. Heart beating hard against her ribs, she did not stop until she reached her family's courtyard.

"I will not become his wife. You cannot force me."

The evening meal had ended, and Rebekah grew increasingly angry, unable to shake Dedan's actions from her thoughts. She stood now in front of Laban, arms crossed to still her nerves, while he reclined against plush cushions, smoking his clay pipe. Bethuel sat to his left, and she glanced between the two of them. "He accosted me in the vineyard."

Bethuel jumped to his feet. "He will pay for this." He strode toward the door, and Rebekah had to hurry to catch up with his long strides. It would cost him his own life to kill an elder's son.

She touched Bethuel's arm, halting him. "He did not harm me. He only frightened me." She smiled, assuring Bethuel with a glance she spoke truth. When Bethuel grudgingly took his seat once more, she faced Laban, who seemed not the least worried of what Dedan might do to her. "The man is a reckless fool, and I will not marry him."

"Since he has yet to ask for such an arrangement, I do not think you need worry about such a thing, my sister." Laban puffed on his pipe and crossed his ankles. "What makes you think he wants you?"

"He said as much." Rebekah felt the blood drain from her face. Had the man been merely playing games with her, lying to her?

"Did he now?" Laban looked at her for a long moment, his gaze thoughtful. "I did make a subtle inquiry but did not know they would take matters so quickly into their own hands." He puffed a few more times, letting his words linger in the air with the smoke. "It would seem Dedan acted rather rashly."

"You did not know he would be at the harvest pretending to be one of us? Or did he have your permission to look me over as though he were buying a donkey or a calf?"

Laban straightened, clearly resenting the accusation. "You need not trouble yourself so much, Rebekah. It sounds to me like the man was being shrewd. To marry a woman sight unseen would be risky for any man. Despite your beauty, my dear sister, not every man in Harran has been privileged to witness it firsthand."

Heat filled Rebekah's face as she recalled the man's too-familiar comments. "Elder's son or no, the man should not waylay innocent maidens and make them fear they will be taken advantage of. I cannot abide such a man. And if he does come to make such an offer, I want you to refuse him." She clenched her fists, looking first to Bethuel and pleading silently with him to take her side, then to Laban, who held her fate.

Laban grunted, set the pipe aside, and glared at her. "And what if that happens, Rebekah? What then? Will you remain an unmarried virgin in my house forever? An elder's son could give you the life you deserve. If you turn him down, where am I to go for a husband for you? You will not accept one from Ur or Nineveh or Babylon. Where else am I to look?"

"You have turned down perfectly suitable men for wealth. I am not the only one who has made this difficult." Rebekah could feel her insides quiver, but she stood firm, unwilling to let him see her fear.

"She need not wed a man she does not want," Bethuel said. "Father would not approve."

Laban grunted and sat again, his glare shifting from Rebekah to Bethuel. "How do you know Dedan would be so bad? All men are fools. She would learn to live with it."

"You are right in that, and I live with the biggest of fools right here!" Rebekah's voice shook despite her attempt to stay calm.

Laban rose once more, his expression moving from angry to dangerous. She took a step back but not fast enough to stop his palm from striking her cheek. Shame filled her as heat filled her face, but before she could move or think, she felt strong hands lift her at the waist and set her aside. In a flurry of angry words and flying fists, Laban was on the ground rubbing his jaw.

"You will not touch her ever again." Bethuel looked down on Laban, his expression frightful, menacing.

Laban scrambled to right himself, but he did not attempt to rise. Instead, he held up a hand as though the action would keep Bethuel at a distance. "Perhaps I acted rashly. But she needs a man who will keep her in line, and you know it." He looked up, but Bethuel's stony expression did not waver, and his hands clenched into fists.

"See to it that you do not lay a hand on her again. If I hear that you did, Brother, you will sorely wish you hadn't."

"You need not worry. I would not *think* of harming our precious Rebekah." He rubbed his jaw once more. "But she had better agree to a match soon."

Rebekah slipped quietly from the room, still feeling the sting of Laban's slap, wondering if she had deserved his wrath. She had spoken harshly. But had not his actions, Dedan's actions, caused it? Was she not allowed her anger?

She sank into a heap on her mat and hugged her knees to her chest. She really should learn to curb her tongue. She was far too outspoken. Would Laban hold it against her and make her life miserable when Bethuel returned to care for the sheep?

Abba, why did you have to go and leave me before we could choose a man for me to marry?

Her father would have cared what she thought. Her father would have respected her choices. He might have even allowed her to request a man she thought she could love.

Her father would never have slapped her.

She rocked back and forth, still shaking and cold. But it was too late now to undo what had been done and said. Bethuel was witness. But the look in Laban's eyes made her afraid. He had his own mind made up, and she sensed that when Bethuel left, Laban would try to force her into a decision she did not want. If she did not find a way to stop him.

Three days later, Rebekah spread the last of the grape clusters on a clean cloth to dry in the sun. The process would take several weeks, perhaps more, before the raisins could be pressed into cakes for storing. Too many days to think and fear what Laban and the elder's son might do in the meantime.

Constant movement seemed her only relief from the plaguing thoughts. She cornered one of the young servant boys to watch that the birds and flies did not swoop down to steal or spoil the grapes, then joined Deborah in the courtyard, where she stood over a large pot, boiling more grapes into thickened honey.

"I can stir that for a while. Your arm must grow tired." She extended a hand to the woman, fully expecting her to accept her offer.

Deborah's grip merely tightened, and she shook her head. "I am fine. But your restlessness is going to send us all to the hills. You have not been yourself since we returned from the vineyards."

Rebekah let her hand fall to her side. The tension along her upper back had turned into tight knots, and she had fought a constant headache since her argument with Laban. Her only consolation came in the fact that Bethuel had not returned to the hills.

"You need not fear Laban's greed, dear one. I have seen many men look at you with longing over the years. One of them will be worthy of you and be able to handle Laban as well."

"He would have to be a wealthy but humble prince to appease us both."

Deborah smiled and lifted the pot from the fire to cool on the stones. "Then the God of Shem will bring you a wealthy, humble prince. Get the jars and bring them to me."

"Such men do not exist," Rebekah said. She hurried into the house to do as Deborah requested, with a withering glance at Laban's shrine to his household gods.

The sun's rays angled downward by the time the task was completed, and Rebekah finally gave vent to her restlessness and escaped to the fields behind the house. She stopped near the edge of a low hill where trees blocked the wind from whipping the house with too much force. Down the rise a large well stood with steps descending to a river below. The well served both Harran and Nahor in Paddan-Aram, and she had made the journey nearly every day from the time she could hold a jar on her head and balance it without spilling. Already a flock of sheep had gathered there, and shepherds and shepherdesses waited for all of them to arrive to fill the troughs with water for the flocks. Hearty labor considering the size of the flocks. She looked on, spotting Bethuel's distinctive yellow and red turban among the other shepherds.

"You must not fear what is yet to come, Rebekah."

She startled at the male voice and grabbed hold of a tree trunk to steady herself. Turning toward the sound, she felt her knees grow weak at the sight of a man she did not recognize, a tall man whose garments shone brighter than sun-bleached wool.

"Do not be afraid of your brother Laban's plans for you. They will not succeed."

Rebekah's hand covered her throat. She tried to speak, but the words would not come. *Who are you?* She could not continue to look upon him, for the light of his garments nearly burned her eyes.

"I am sending my messenger to meet you. When he comes, you will know what to do." His words were like musical notes in her ears, and she wished he would continue speaking for the beauty of his voice. She closed her eyes against the light, leaning into the tree.

A moment later, the clouds passing over the sun made her look up. She was alone again, her breath coming fast, her heart pounding, wondering if she had imagined it all. In her fear of the future and her desperate need for control over Laban's actions, had she conjured a vision of an angel or a god?

She shook herself, feeling weak as a newborn lamb. She gripped the trunk of the oak with both hands and drew in several long, slow breaths. Her gaze turned to the well below, where the men and women now formed a line from the bottom to the top, pouring jar after jar into the trough to water the hundreds of thirsty sheep.

Do not be afraid of your brother Laban's plans for you. They will not succeed.

How did the man know of her brother or his designs for her? And how did he come and go with the wind? Surely she must have imagined it all.

Fearing the heat and the stress of the day was doing strange things to her mind, she turned and hurried back to her mother's house.

Deborah drew the head covering about her face and hurried from the house to the neighboring streets of Nahor. Emotion choked her, and she blinked, silently berating herself for taking Nuriah's comments so to heart. How often had she consoled Rebekah and Selima not to do that very thing? But the younger women did not have the history she shared with Nuriah, nor reasons to evoke the woman's hostility.

She picked up her pace and stayed to the side of the road as several young boys raced past, shouting and chasing a runaway donkey while men and women darted out of the animal's way. She should be back at the house working, but grief weighed her down, and for once she would give in to it. She must, or one of these nights Rebekah would hear her weeping upon her sleeping mat and ask too many questions. She had promised Bethuel. Rebekah could not know.

A deep sigh left her when at last she reached the city gates, and her feet took the road of their own accord as it curved and led to the well where the women would soon gather. Rebekah and Selima would come with the other women of the city to draw water, and she did not wish to be seen. She veered off the path toward the copse of trees that ringed the well on one side.

But as she knelt beneath an oak tree and allowed the tears to release at last, she could not help but berate the foolish choices that had brought her to this place. If she had never been betrothed to Samum . . . if he had not treated her as he did . . . if her father had agreed to Bethuel's first request . . . But then she would not have Selima or carry Rebekah's trust.

She sniffed and dried her tears with the edge of her scarf, then glanced up at the shaft of angled sunlight breaking through the leaves above her, touching her face like a warm caress.

O God of my master Bethuel, God of Shem and Abraham, what is to become of me?

She could follow Rebekah to her future husband's home, or Rebekah could release her and leave her at the mercy of her mother. If the girl knew the truth, she would choose the latter and never speak to Deborah again. Selima could also suffer her fate of rejection, something Deborah could not allow. Nuriah would not speak of it, lest she reveal her own weaknesses. Or would she? With Bethuel's death, there was nothing, no one, to keep Nuriah from twisting the truth and standing by a lie against Deborah.

Fear accompanied a sudden shift in the wind, the soft whoosh of the leaves displaced by the angry toss of branches above her head. In the distance, near the well, came the jangling of camels' bells, and the heavy footfalls of many beasts seemed to shake the earth. She pressed a hand to her cheeks, wiping away the remaining dampness, and covered her face once more, then walked to the edge of the tree line where she could get a better view.

A line of camels—she did a count and found ten magnificent beasts, each one laden with many sacks—slowly knelt, allowing six men to dismount their backs. She watched, fascinated, and crept closer. She stopped at the sound of male voices coming from the other side of the nearest camel.

"Paddan-Aram, city of Nahor."

At the man's comment, Deborah looked toward the city gates.

"We have reached the city where Abraham's relatives reside?"

"Assuming they still live here. Our last report indicated as much. Though they could live in one of the cities farther east."

"Pray let this be the place. And let us hope Abraham's relatives have daughters of marriageable age."

Deborah's heartbeat quickened with the words. Should she step forward, introduce herself, and tell the men they had found what they sought? But a moment later, one of the men—the older one by the slight warble in his voice—gave a loud cry, startling her.

"O Adonai, Elohei of my master Abraham . . ." His voice dropped in pitch on the last word, and she strained to hear the rest. "Give me success today, and show kindness to my master Abraham. See, I am standing beside this spring, and the daughters of the townspeople are coming out to draw water. May it be that when I say to a girl, 'Please let down your jar that I may have a drink,' and she says, 'Drink, and I'll water your camels too'—let her be the one You have chosen for Your servant Isaac. By this I will know that You have shown kindness to my master."

Deborah gasped, startled at the request. The circular well had many steps going to the spring below. To carry the jar down and up again with the many trips they would need to fill the stone troughs was more than any maiden would offer a stranger.

"Why do you pray for the impossible?" the younger man said. "A woman would need to be very strong and determined to carry water up and down the steps to fill the troughs."

The young man shared Deborah's sentiments. Perhaps she should just step from beneath the trees and invite the men to Laban's house, to save Rebekah the loss she must surely face when she did not do as the servant asked.

Disappointment filled her at the thought.

"Is not the master's God able to do the impossible? Was not Isaac's birth proof of this? Wait and see, my son, what God will do."

Shame replaced her doubt. Surely it was possible. Rebekah had a giving heart and a strong back, but this . . .

She moved just beyond the tree line at the sound of female voices drawing closer. Rebekah and Selima and the other girls from town approached, laughing and talking among themselves.

Deborah slipped away and circled around toward the city gates. She could not bear to watch the man's prayers go unanswered. She should not doubt Rebekah, but if she stayed, she would surely interfere and insist on helping and thwart the man's prayer before God could answer it. A prayer that was too big for any woman to fulfill. Abraham's servant was putting God and Rebekah to too great a test.

"Did you see those men?" Selima's girlish giggle followed the comments.

Rebekah gave her an indulging smile. "From the corner of my eye, without looking at them conspicuously, yes. And I suppose you did too." She lowered her water jar and dipped it into the flowing river, waiting as it filled to the top.

"The young one and the old one were looking at us." Selima filled her jar and hefted it onto her shoulder, following Rebekah back up the steps. "The young one is handsome."

"Interesting that you could notice such a thing in one quick glance." Rebekah smiled at the blush on Selima's cheeks as she steadied her full jar with one hand, her gaze on the stone steps. The trek was as familiar as her weaving, and she could make it easily enough, but after the rain they'd had the night before, the stones were slippery, and she took extra care to be sure-footed.

"And interesting that you did not." Selima's indignant tone made Rebekah laugh. Her maid noticed every young man they met either in the markets or in the streets. Except for the shepherds, who were usually too young or too old, it was rare to see one at the well.

"They are travelers. There is no sense in noticing whether they are handsome or not since it is certain they have not come to stay. Besides, he is likely already married." She glanced over her shoulder at Selima, noting the girl's pout. "Cheer up, Selima. One day we will both find men who are worthy of our notice and our dreams."

Rebekah put one hand along the wall as they reached the curve of the well, knowing the words were more hope than reality. She waited a moment for Selima to reach the top, then headed back toward the city gate. She stopped as she glimpsed the older man they had noticed earlier hurrying toward her.

"Please give me a little water from your jar," he said, stopping within arm's length of her. She read sincerity in his dark eyes, guessing him to be about as old as her father would have been had he lived.

She quickly lowered the jar to the ground and took a step back, allowing him to approach. "Drink, my lord."

He scooped water from his hand to his mouth. She looked beyond him, noticing the younger man Selima had mentioned watching, but his gaze seemed fixed beyond her. Rebekah hid a smile as Selima's face flushed crimson. Rebekah glanced back at the man and saw several other men sitting nearby among a pack of ten camels, looking exhausted.

How far had they come? If they had stopped at the well,

they obviously needed to water the camels, but one look at the empty trough told her they had not yet done so. The men would need to descend the steps of a well they did not know, perhaps not noticing the places where water could make the stones slick. One of them might fall . . . The thought troubled her. She knew this well and its unsteady stone steps. She could water the animals faster and more safely than a group of tired men.

She looked up as the man straightened.

"Thank you," he said. His look held kindness and deep appreciation. "You are most kind."

She gave a slight bow, then lifted the jar into her arms. "I will draw water for your camels also, until they have finished drinking." She did not wait for a reply but hurried to the trough and dumped the contents of her jar into it. One glance at the sky told her that dusk would soon be upon them. She would move quickly. She knew the exact spots to place her feet, and without Selima to distract her, she would easily finish before darkness fell.

She clutched the jar to her shoulder and hurried down the steps, one hand skimming the wall. Dipping the jar into the flowing river, she willed it to fill faster, snatched it back into her arms and onto her shoulder, and fairly flew up the steps. She hurried to the trough, the water splashing down over the lip of her clay jar into the stone enclosure.

"Mistress?"

She looked up at the sound of Selima's voice.

"Let me help you."

Rebekah lifted the empty jar to her shoulder again. She shook her head. "Take your water home. Mother will be waiting for it, and she will worry if I do not soon return." She hurried back to the steps, glancing behind her. "Tell her I am coming quickly. Do not tell her why."

Her heart beat faster with every step. It would take at least ten trips to fill both troughs. Would two troughs of water be enough to satisfy the thirst of ten camels?

Her feet landed in the soft dirt at the water's edge again, and she repeated the task, her legs carrying her to the surface once more. She had filled the troughs for Bethuel's sheep many times. Ten camels should be no different than a flock of sheep, should they?

She caught sight of the men watching her. Her face grew warm, whether from exertion or their perusal, she could not tell. The younger one did not strike her as overly attractive, as Selima seemed to think, but the girl probably wished Rebekah had let her stay to help, if only to glimpse the young man again. Silly girl! These travelers would be on their way by morning, and they would hear nothing of them again.

Then why did Rebekah feel so compelled to help them?

I am sending my messenger to meet you. When he comes, you will know what to do.

Her breath came faster at the memory of the strange man's words. Surely not. Was the old man a messenger? But no. She had merely imagined the encounter with the stranger and his comforting words in an effort to calm herself, to somehow feel she had some control over her brother's ambitious designs.

But she could not shake the thoughts, nor the urgency to hurry through her task.

After fifteen trips into the heart of the well and up to the surface again, her back ached and her legs felt like fire. She stopped at the trough where the camels had nearly emptied what she had filled, holding her last full jug on her shoulder to take home to her family.

She watched as the camels, one by one, turned away from the water to settle onto the nearby grassy knoll. The old man approached, and she willed her breath to slow, to wait for him to speak.

He carried a leather pouch in one hand and pulled out a

gold nose ring and two gold bracelets. "Whose daughter are you? Please tell me, is there room in your father's house for us to spend the night?"

Rebekah's heart did a little kick as the man offered her the bracelets. She extended her free arm, and he placed them over her hand. The gold felt cool against her hot skin.

"May I?" he asked, indicating the nose ring.

She nodded and waited as he slid the thick looped ring onto the side of her nose. The weight of the jewelry told her these were not mere trinkets. And it made sense that he might want to pay her for her work, but she felt awkward accepting the gifts.

He took a step back, and she knew he awaited her answer.

"I am the daughter of Bethuel, the son that Milcah bore to Nahor." She glanced beyond him for a brief moment at the waiting men and loaded camels. "We have plenty of straw and fodder, as well as room for you to spend the night."

Laban would be sure to agree once he saw the gold on her arms.

"I will send my brother to lead the way."

Despite the gifts and his kind manner, it would not look good for a *betulah*, a virgin maiden, to walk with a group of foreign men through the streets of Nahor.

She turned to go but stopped short at the man's voice. "Praise be to Adonai, Elohei of my master Abraham, who has not abandoned His kindness and faithfulness to my master."

Rebekah's heart held a strange warmth at the sight of the man bowed low to the earth.

"As for me, Adonai has led me on the journey to the house of my master's relatives."

What could this mean? Rebekah watched but a moment more, then turned, clutching her jar lest she spill the contents, and ran all the way home.

Laban entered the courtyard of his mother's home in Nahor, his mind churning, weighing his dwindling options. He simply must convince Bethuel to get Rebekah to agree to a match with the elder's son whether she cared for him or not. The man was willing to offer a costly sum to marry her, and Laban was tired of waiting for something better. While Rebekah's weaving did add to the family's wealth in a way he had not expected, he could not keep a virgin in her mother's home forever. He would be laughed off the council for such a thing.

He rubbed his temples, feeling the start of a headache, his third one this week. There was no doubt about it; he must act, and soon. He moved from the threshold across the spacious court and greeted Farah, who handed him his pipe and knelt to wash his feet.

"I trust you had a good day, Husband." She smiled, making her features almost pretty.

He grunted and sat on the bench to allow her to untie his sandals. His concubine Refiqa emerged from the house, and his chest lifted as it always did at the sight of her swelling belly. His son Tariq, by his wife Farah, raced from the house and hopped onto his lap. He laughed as he pulled the boy close.

"And what have you been doing this day, my son?"

The boy leaned in and kissed Laban's beard and whispered, "Mama taught me how to tell good plants from weeds. She let me use the hoe to dig them out."

Laban leveled a look at Farah, who lifted her shoulder in a shrug. "It is a useful task for a child, even for a son."

It was not the task that annoyed him so much as the way she challenged him with her gaze. He should be firmer with her, not allow such a one to tell him the way of things, but as with his mother and sister, he had no strength to fight against a woman's will. He would devote his time to Refiqa if Farah grew too wearisome.

The thought pleased him, and he smiled in Refiqa's direction and was rewarded with her coy response. But a moment later, the sound of running feet caught his attention. He looked toward the courtyard gate.

"Laban!" Rebekah shouted his name as she rushed into the court, winded. She quickly lowered the water jug to its niche in the stones and hurried to his side. "You must go to the well at once."

A thick gold ring hung from her nose, glinting in the setting sun. Laban startled at the sight. "Where did you get that?" He reached up to touch it.

She pulled it from her nose and held it out to him. Golden bracelets jangled from her arm. "A man at the well gave them to me." She drew in a few quick breaths.

"Come here. Sit." Laban motioned to a bench in the courtyard. He caught sight of Selima. "Get your mistress some water."

"Yes, my lord." Selima hurried to obey, drawing water from the jar Rebekah had carried home, while Farah poured water into a basin and swiftly washed and dried his feet.

Laban looked at Farah. "Finish quickly."

Farah retied his sandals while his mother and the servants crowded into the courtyard.

"Now tell me, who is this man, and what did he say to you?" he said, facing Rebekah.

"A man met us at the well and asked me for a drink. I lowered my jar and let him drink, but while he was drinking, I noticed he was not alone. Six men were with him, along with ten camels loaded with goods. They were kneeling near the water troughs, but the troughs were empty." She paused to take another drink and wiped her mouth with the back of her hand. "I considered how weary the men must be from their travels, and I knew the steps to the river could be wet and slick. They would not be as sure-footed as I, since I am used to carrying water from below, so I offered to water their camels as well." She dabbed sweat from her brow with her head scarf, her breath still rapid. "It took fifteen trips to fill both troughs and allow the camels their fill."

"You did all of this alone?"

She nodded.

Laban dragged a breath on his pipe, half irritated with her for taking such a risk by working alone with so many strange men close at hand, half intrigued by the gifts she held as evidence of their generosity. "They gave you these in payment for your work?"

She shook her head again. "I thought so at first, and maybe this is the case. But the man is a servant of Abraham, our uncle! He has been looking for us and wants to stay the night in our house. Of course, I told him we had plenty of room." She looked from him to their mother, then held his gaze. "You will not deny them."

He turned the nose ring over in his hand, weighing it. The piece must weigh at least a beka. "What kind of a man would I be if I denied hospitality to a relative? Why did you not bring him home at once?"

"What kind of a woman would I be if I led strange men through the streets of Nahor?" She straightened, lifting her chin.

He chuckled. "You will all be the end of me." The only way to live with so many women was to appease them. But he silently cursed his own weakness.

He stood, handing the nose ring back to Rebekah. "I will bring them home." He glanced at his wives and servants. "Hurry, prepare the stables and food for our guests. We do not want to keep such wealthy relatives waiting."

He ran all the way to the well.

⁂

Laban spotted the men Rebekah had described, some sitting, others standing beside their camels. All of them were near his age or younger, though one appeared to be about the age of his father before he entered Sheol. He approached the man and bowed low.

"Come, you who are blessed by the Lord," Laban said as he straightened and extended his hand, waving it toward the city gates. "Why are you standing out here? I have prepared the house and a place for the camels."

The older man bowed as well. "Thank you, my lord. You must be the relative of the young woman we met here."

"Yes, yes. I am Laban, son of Bethuel, brother of Rebekah, who watered your camels. We have plenty of room for all of you. Please, come."

He bowed again and led the group into the city, first to the stables to feed and bed the animals, then to the courtyard, where servants washed the men's feet. When the last foot was dried, Laban led them into the sitting room of his mother's house.

A low table awaited them, set with platters of bread and roasted fish with dill sauce, cucumbers and figs, and spiced wine in stone jars. Laban motioned to the men to settle on thick cushions along the floor beside the table and watched as the younger men obeyed. His brother Bethuel sat near the head, leaving space for him, while the women stood in the shadows at the edges of the room.

But the older man, the leader of the group, stood still. "I will not eat until I have told you what I have to say."

"Tell us," Laban said, taking his seat and motioning for the man to do the same.

He knelt instead beside the cushion on the hard floor. "I am Eliezer, Abraham's servant," he said. "The Lord has blessed my master abundantly, and he has become wealthy. He has given him sheep and cattle, silver and gold, menservants and maidservants, and camels and donkeys. My master's wife Sarah has borne him a son in her old age, and he has given him everything he owns. And my master made me swear an oath and said, 'You must not get a wife for my son from the daughters of the Canaanites, in whose land I live, but go to my father's family and to my own clan and get a wife for my son.'

"Then I asked my master, 'What if the woman will not come back with me?'

"He replied, 'Adonai Elohei, before whom I have walked, will send His angel with you and make your journey a success, so that you can get a wife for my son from my own clan and from my father's family. Then, when you go to my clan, you will be released from my oath even if they refuse to give her to you.'

"When I came to the spring today, I said, 'O Adonai, Elohei of my master Abraham, if You will, please grant success to the journey on which I have come. See, I am standing beside this spring; if a maiden comes out to draw water and I say to her, "Please let me drink a little water from your jar," and if she says to me, "Drink, and I'll draw water for your camels too," let her be the one Adonai has chosen for my master's son.'

"Before I finished praying in my heart, Rebekah came out with her jar on her shoulder. She went down to the spring and drew water, and I said to her, 'Please give me a drink.'

"She quickly lowered her jar from her shoulder and said, 'Drink, and I'll water your camels also.' So I drank, and she watered the camels also.

"I asked her, 'Whose daughter are you?'

"She said, 'The daughter of Bethuel son of Nahor, whom Milcah bore to him.'

"Then I put the ring in her nose and the bracelets on her

arms, and I bowed down and worshiped the Lord. I praised Adonai Elohei of my master Abraham, who had led me on the right road to get the granddaughter of my master's brother for his son. Now if you will show kindness and faithfulness to my master, tell me, and if not, tell me, so I may know which way to turn."

Bethuel cleared his throat and settled a firm look on Laban. "This is from the Lord," he said. "We can say nothing to you one way or the other."

Laban felt a moment of irritation that Bethuel spoke first, but he quickly squelched it. This man could pay far more for Rebekah than any elder's son. He glanced across the room, extending a hand toward his sister. "Here is Rebekah; take her and go, and let her become the wife of your master's son, as Adonai has directed."

The servant of Abraham put his face to the ground, and Laban sensed the man was praying. Silence settled over the room until the man rose to his feet. One of the young men with him stood as well, and the two walked toward the stables.

"We will quickly return," Eliezer said.

10

Rebekah's heart beat heavy and fast, her head spinning with Laban's words. A tremor rushed through her, and she wrapped her arms about herself to still the shaking. *Take her and go?* Just like that, without a word to her, without allowing her a moment to give her a choice? Could she do such a thing—leave her family and all she held dear?

Eliezer and the younger man returned carrying large leather packs and set them on the ground. Eliezer removed a golden necklace and draped it across Rebekah's neck. Circles of intricately carved gold inlaid with lapis lazuli and emeralds clung to a thick golden chain. She fingered each piece, counting seven large jeweled rings. Her mother had never owned anything so fine.

He returned to the sack and pulled from it a silver headdress, equally carved and bejeweled, along with golden earrings and a jeweled belt. Five exquisitely woven robes with matching head scarves were laid at her feet. She sank to a cushion on the floor, overwhelmed. She looked into the servant's dark eyes.

"I . . ." She swallowed and closed her eyes for a brief moment. When at last she looked at him again, his gaze held gentleness and kindness. She warmed to him, suddenly knowing he was a man she could trust. "Thank you," she said, unable to find any other words.

He nodded, returning her smile, then turned to retrieve more gifts for her family. Rebekah lifted one of the robes to examine the work—the close weave and the fine detailed stitches along each sleeve and the hem. A costly garment. Laban and her mother would be thrilled at her good fortune. She looked up to see their expressions, catching the gleam in Laban's eyes. She had judged correctly. No man in Harran or Nahor could have equaled this display of wealth or would have paid such a hefty bride-price, not even the king.

A sense of awe and fear rushed through her as twin emotions. The shaking started again as she pulled the robes to her, clutching them to her chest. Who was this uncle who could bestow so much or consider her of such worth? Would her cousin make a good husband? How could she go with this servant, despite these gifts, and marry a man she had never seen?

"My master is a fine man."

She startled, hearing Eliezer's voice. She looked up to see he had spoken to Laban.

"He will treat your sister well."

"I can see that he already has." Laban touched the soft fabric of one of the robes he had been given, a rich red and blue garment that rivaled her best work. He wore a new chain of gold about his neck and poured wine into a new golden goblet. He laughed freely, glancing her way. "Rebekah, my sister, you will have your wish, and I will have mine." He tipped his cup toward her and smiled, his gaze shifting to Eliezer. "Eat and drink, my friends, blessed of the Lord."

Eliezer and the younger man took their seats around the table, joining the others. But Rebekah could not force down a single fig or morsel of fish. She studied the garments and jewels in the lamplight for a moment more, then scooped everything into her arms and stood. As the eating and drinking and laughter continued among the men, she slipped out of the sitting room and moved toward her room, Selima at her side.

"Will you really go with those men and marry your cousin?" Selima's normally giddy tone was missing from the question, and Rebekah looked into her eyes, reading sorrow in their depths.

"You will go with me, of course. And your mother as well. You need not fear. I would never leave you behind." She gave what she hoped was a reassuring smile but felt a quiver in her middle that would not leave. "I could not go without you." Did Selima hear the waver in her voice?

Selima took a step closer. "Here, let me help you fold these and put them away."

Rebekah nodded numbly and moved to assist her. "I wonder what he is like."

Would he love her as her father had loved her, giving her the same freedoms he had given? Would she love him in return?

"Hopefully he is not disgusting or lazy." Selima made a face as she tucked the sleeve into place and laid the first garment in Rebekah's carved wooden chest. "Or has black teeth and smells bad."

Rebekah laughed. "If his teeth are bad, we shall give him mint for his breath, and if he smells bad, we shall insist he bathe." Rebekah considered the men she had met over the years, wondering whether Abraham's son would be like any of them. "If he is lazy, we will find others to do the work. He is certainly wealthy enough to pay his workers." She placed the garment in the chest. "But I doubt he is lazy. Wealthy men are not lazy."

"He inherited his wealth from his father." Selima placed the last garment on top and closed the lid, then sank onto Rebekah's bed.

"True." Rebekah removed the earrings first, then set the

pieces of jewelry one by one in a stone, fabric-lined casket. "But he has good men working for him, so he is likely to keep it." She sat on the bed next to Selima. "I cannot believe I am about to wed."

Selima put a hand to her mouth and giggled. "You are about to marry a prince after all!"

Rebekah smiled, and her stomach fluttered in anticipation. Though they had not signed an agreement yet, there was no backing out of this now. They had accepted the gifts and given the man their word. It was enough. She would go with Eliezer and his men some day in the near future and marry a cousin she had never met.

"We still have time here, though," Selima said, "to get used to the idea. Tonight was like the betrothal. You won't have to leave for at least six months. Maybe even a year." She yawned and stood. "Shall I get you some food from the cooking room? You should eat something."

Rebekah's stomach rumbled now, a mixture of hunger and anticipation. "You could bring me some dates and almonds. I couldn't eat fish tonight."

Selima nodded and left the room while Rebekah walked to the window and looked out at the dark sky.

What are you like, cousin of mine?

A thousand thoughts, images of rumors she had heard of her uncle Abraham during her childhood, stories of the Creator speaking to him and calling him to leave his homeland, filled her mind.

Adonai has called you to leave as well.

She stilled as the idea moved through her, seeing again the man who had spoken to her that day on the ridge. Laban's plans for her had not succeeded. She would be free of her brother's designs the moment she left home with these men, embracing a whole new adventure. Like Abraham and Sarah had done.

She shivered again, but this time from excitement and even

a hint of joy. She would marry the promised son of her aunt and uncle and move into a new future God was calling her to. She would go in faith and meet this cousin and become his wife.

***

Laban stifled a yawn as he bid the last of Abraham's men good night. He turned to head down the hallway toward his private room when his mother rushed toward him and clutched his arm.

"What good fortune this is, my son! My daughter will finally wed a man worthy of her status." She smiled, and he suddenly noticed the age lines at the corners of her eyes and how drawn her cheeks had become since his father died. "We must start at once to prepare the finest linens and collect wool from the best of your flocks to send with her. The betrothal should last at least six months, but a year would be much better." She moved away from him to pace the wide room. "We must whitewash the house and store plenty of wine at the next harvest for the feast. Surely Abraham's son will come to claim her and bring his household to celebrate with ours."

Laban shook his head, trying to clear the drowsy feeling the wine had produced. "There is plenty of time to talk of these things and prepare for the wedding tomorrow."

"No, no, you must listen to me now."

He had never seen her so enthusiastic.

"We must secure the promise from Abraham's servant to set a day for him to return for her. Normally, if they lived nearby, we could allow him to come with surprise and the sound of the ram's horn, but with such a distance to travel, we will need to plan, to clear some of the land for their tents." She leaned in closer. "You must take some of the coins I know you are hoarding and purchase the best quality wines and spices . . . plenty of spices . . ."

Her words ran like rushing water, and Laban blinked hard, awakening to her concerns. She was right, of course. There was much to be done to impress his wealthy uncle.

He placed a hand on his mother's stout shoulders, forcing her to stop pacing. "I will speak to the servant in the morning and secure from him what he plans to do. He may not want to wait a year—perhaps six months?"

"Ten months. We cannot accept less." She turned a decisive look on him, and he acquiesced with a nod.

"Ten months." He kissed her cheek. "Now settle down, Ima, and let me sleep."

The scent of toasted wheat rose from the griddle as Rebekah cooked flatbread for their guests the following morning. Deborah and Selima worked beside her while Laban's wives chopped dates and mixed them with water to cook into a syrupy mixture. Her mother bustled about, setting platters of cheese and olives on the low table. Several of Eliezer's men had begun to trickle into the sitting room, where Laban already waited.

"Shalom, peace and health to you, my brothers," Laban said, standing to greet Eliezer. "Come, eat and make your heart light." He motioned to the places they had taken the night before.

The men did as Laban requested, and Rebekah set before them a plate of the hot flatbread and a jar of warm date syrup.

"Send me on my way to my master," Eliezer said.

Silence followed the comment, and Rebekah stumbled, clutching the pillar between the two rooms for support. Her heart quickened its pace. So soon? The implication was clear that she would accompany him.

She slipped into the cooking room, out of sight of the men, to listen. Her mother moved past her to stand along the wall of the sitting room with a full view of their conversation.

"Let the girl remain with us ten days or so, then you may go," Laban said.

At the distinctive sound of her mother clearing her throat, Rebekah peeked back into the room where the men sat at the table.

Laban glanced at their mother, then looked back at Eliezer. "In truth, we will need at least ten months to prepare for a proper wedding celebration." He gave the servant his most charming smile, the one she had seen him use to coax even his enemies to bend to his will. The one he had used on her to convince her he had her best interests at heart, when in truth, he continually put her off to serve his own selfish ends.

Eliezer shook his head. "Do not detain me, now that Adonai has granted success to my journey. Send me on my way so I may go to my master."

Laban looked clearly troubled, his glance skirting from Eliezer to Nuriah. Rebekah saw the distress in her mother's eyes, making her own heart constrict. Once she left with the servant, she would never see her family again. Could she bear such a thing?

Her mother stepped closer to Laban, surprising her, and bent low toward his ear, but her words carried to Rebekah behind them. "We cannot possibly send her away so quickly! Is there to be no wedding? You cannot let them."

As her mother's only daughter, could she deny the woman the chance to dance and sing and meet her daughter's new husband?

Laban put a hand over their mother's where it rested on his shoulder. "We must do what is best for Rebekah, Ima. If this is of Adonai . . ." He let his words trail off.

Her brother Bethuel walked into the sitting room at that moment, his presence filling the archway. "Let's call the girl and ask her about it."

Laban and her mother looked up, startled at Bethuel's

comment. It was not like him to speak ahead of Laban or to assert his opinions so decisively. But Rebekah warmed to him now, knowing that he of all people cared what Adonai thought and what was best for her.

She waited several heartbeats, the room heavy with silence.

At last Laban cleared his throat, quelling their mother's response with a look. "Very well. Ima, go at once and bring Rebekah."

Her mother backed away, her chin lifted in defiance. "She is standing in the cooking area, listening. Call her yourself."

Bethuel spoke up. "Rebekah, please come into the room."

She suppressed a smile that he did not wait for Laban yet again. She smoothed the fabric of her robe, feeling the heat creep into her face as she walked. She stopped near Laban's side, opposite Eliezer.

"Will you go with this man?" Laban asked.

His look told her he wanted her to refuse, to side with their mother and stay the ten months needed to make all of the preparations, to secure all of the things she must have for her new home. A bride should not go to the house of her husband empty-handed. But this was no ordinary betrothal, and she knew with one glance at Eliezer and by the accompanying peace in her heart that she dare not stay. Such an opportunity might not come again. If Abraham should die before she could return, everything could change. She felt an urgency in the air, despite the disapproval of her mother and Laban.

She took a deep breath and glanced from one brother to the other. Bethuel's smile and nod of encouragement lifted her spirits, reinforcing her courage, assuring her that her decision was right.

"I will go," she said, meeting the servant's gaze.

Her mother's desperate cries followed her words.

11

Rebekah fingered the loom her father had given her, memories washing over her of working at it side by side with her mother and Laban's wives. She would miss the camaraderie, the laughter, the commiserating among the women on how to live with their men. Only Deborah and Selima would go with her to her new home, a new country where everything would be unfamiliar and challenging. She sighed and set about quickly breaking down the pieces of the loom, fitting them into leather sacks to pack and hang from the camel's side.

"So you are truly going." Her mother's plump body cast a shadow as she passed the threshold and crossed in front of the window, her tone holding traces of bitter emotion.

Rebekah could not bear to look up and meet her gaze, lest she give way to her own uncertain tears.

"Yes," she said, turning away from her mother to the wall where woven baskets stood. She hurriedly transferred skeins of dyed wool from the baskets into goatskin sacks and tied them at the neck. She looked up at Selima's approach.

The girl seemed to sense the tension in the room, stopping short just inside the threshold.

"Can you take these to the men, Selima?" Rebekah hefted the heavy sack of wool into Selima's arms.

"Yes, mistress." She glanced over Rebekah's shoulder. "I will be back for the loom." She hurried through the open archway while Rebekah looked to see if she had forgotten anything.

"I wish you would wait." Her mother took a step closer, within arm's length.

Rebekah faced her, surprised at her mother's sudden change of tone. She was not one to show emotion, nor had she seemed to care much for Rebekah's feelings. But one look into her mother's eyes showed Rebekah a side to the woman she had rarely seen.

"I know, Ima. I will miss you." Despite their differences, it was true.

Tears glistened in her mother's eyes, though she quickly blinked them away, and Rebekah stepped forward slowly, awkwardly, and pulled her into a warm embrace. "Don't cry, Ima." She swallowed, forcing back a sudden swell of her own emotion. "Surely we will see each other again."

She needed to believe their goodbyes were not permanent.

"You will not be back. Abram and Sarai never returned." Her mother stepped away from her embrace and crossed her arms, a posture she used whenever she was determined to get her way.

"Abraham and Sarah," Rebekah corrected, noting the scowl deepen along her mother's brow at the mention of their new names, "were not able to return, but they were much older. Surely their son will find traveling for a visit no hardship." She would not let her mother dissuade her. She mustn't!

"Why did he not come here himself to claim a bride? Why did not *Abraham* send the son with his servant?" Her mother whirled about, her back to Rebekah, another stance meant to show her displeasure, to elicit a change of heart. Rebekah was in no mood to placate her mother's pouts.

"I have more to pack." She walked past her mother into

her sleeping chamber, her heart beating fast. Such encounters always made her anxious. She did not wish to cause strife, but she could not go back on her word now, could not choose her mother over a husband.

A sigh lifted her chest, and she willed her racing heart to slow. She strode to the carved wooden chest that stood against one wall and lifted the lid. Selima must have already emptied it of the many new garments, along with the ones Rebekah already owned. The stone casket containing her jewels was gone from the low table, and her pallet was rolled up, waiting by the door. How quickly it had all been stowed for travel! Her pulse quickened again as she moved into the room, checking every corner, but nothing that could be packed onto a camel remained. The furniture would stay, as they had no way to easily transport it. Besides, Isaac would have his own tables and chests and more.

Isaac.

What would he be like? Her heart gave a little flutter at the simple intimacy of his name.

She turned at a touch on her arm.

"Everything is packed." Deborah came alongside her, a smile wreathing her face. "Are you ready?"

Rebekah glanced beyond her nurse, but there was no one in the hall outside. The room held an eerie quiet. "My mother?"

"Is out in the courtyard with the rest of the household. They are waiting to send you off. Laban has commanded food prepared for us to eat along the way. A canopy stands near the edge of the court, and your mother has retrieved your best robe." Deborah turned, extending a hand for Rebekah to lead the way to the courtyard.

"She is going to have a ceremony without the groom?" Rebekah stood unmoving.

Deborah nodded. "You can take the robe off before you mount the camel. Your family wishes to bless you, mistress."

She smiled, her expression reassuring. "Let them have this last moment."

Rebekah nodded, suddenly overcome once again with emotion. She looked over her sleeping room one last time, the memories short. She had not lived in this house in Nahor long. She had already left the house of her birth in Harran, and this room had little hold on her. Still . . .

"I will miss this place."

Deborah put a comforting hand on her shoulder. "As we all will. But a new adventure awaits us. A whole new way of life."

"Yes." The thought filled her with sudden excitement. "I am to be married." A surge of joy bubbled within her. "To a prince." She smiled. "Selima will be happy with that."

Deborah laughed. "Selima dreams of things too grand."

The sounds of music and voices of men and women filled the courtyard at Rebekah's approach. Her mother hurried to greet her, all traces of her tears gone. "Put this on. Quickly now. Eliezer wishes to be off, and you best not keep him waiting."

But by this very act of ceremony they were doing just that.

Rebekah did not say so as she clutched one of the new robes to her, stepped back into the house, and hurriedly switched from the one she was wearing. A moment later, she moved with graceful steps to stand beneath the canopy that Laban had used when he married Farah.

Silence settled over the court, and Laban and Bethuel stepped forward, each holding a goblet of wine in his hand.

"Our sister, may you increase to thousands upon thousands," Laban said, lifting his cup in the air.

Bethuel did the same, smiling into her eyes. "And may your offspring possess the gates of their enemies."

She knew what he meant. Enemies could be found in homes as well as foreign lands, and he had just blessed her and her children to conquer both. Her heart warmed to the thought, a little thrill passing through her.

"Let it be so!" The small crowd shouted the words together, and the sounds of flute and lyre and drum filled the air while her mother and sisters-in-law rushed forward. She hugged each one, unable to keep the tears at bay now. They quickly helped her switch back to her traveling robe and folded the wedding robe for the long journey to Hebron.

When the last goodbye was said, the last kiss accepted and given, Rebekah and her maids climbed onto the backs of the camels. She clutched the saddle as the beast rose, settling herself in for the long ride. The camel lurched as it started forward but soon fell into a steady rhythm. They would not stop for many hours and would not reach Hebron for several weeks.

She glanced behind her, waving to her family until they disappeared from view, then faced forward. Eliezer's men surrounded her and her maids, a wall of protection against thieves and marauders. She did not fear for her safety. But she could not help the pang of anticipation that grew with each camel's step closer to Canaan. She must know more about this cousin she was about to marry. When they sat about the fire later that night, she would ask questions of Eliezer and his son and the other servants. After all, a woman could not go into a marriage without knowing something about the man she was marrying.

⁂

Deborah did not allow herself to breathe deeply, nor did she lose her worry, until the camels came to rest the first night, many hours' distance from Nuriah's home. In the hurry of leaving, she had managed to avoid contact with the woman, who had enough things on her mind to keep her sufficiently distracted. Deborah felt momentary relief when she learned that she and Selima would accompany Rebekah, but the truth did not fully overtake her until she stood over the fire and smelled the scents of cumin and rosemary coming from the quick lentil stew filling the camp.

She glanced at Rebekah, whose wide-eyed look told her that she too was sensing the reality of her decision. Deborah stepped beside her and placed a hand on her arm.

"You made a wise choice to come." She studied Rebekah's face, hoping her own need to be free of Nuriah did not somehow show through her expression. But she could not contain the new feeling of joy that had started to rise from a place deep within.

Rebekah nodded. "I know." Her head lifted, and Deborah followed her gaze toward the low hill where the camels rested just over the rise. "Have you seen Selima?"

Deborah darted a look over the camp, her eyes finally settling on the women's tent. "She is probably in the tent, settling things." Though now that she thought about it, she had not seen her daughter since they set up camp, when Selima had gone to lay out their bedrolls and deposit their necessary items in the tent.

"I saw her leave the tent long before the stew was put together," Rebekah said.

Deborah glanced at the sky. The sun's orb suspended halfway between the horizon and its place in the west, nearly out of sight. The spring was more than an arrow's shot from where they stood, down the embankment where the land dipped away from the camp.

"If she went for water, she should have long ago returned."

Fear sent a prickly feeling up her spine. She looked around, the fear mounting. Where was she?

"Selima?"

Deborah turned at the male voice calling her daughter's name. She glimpsed Eliezer's son Haviv walking toward them.

"Why do you seek my maid?" Rebekah's worry matched Deborah's. And why was this man looking for her daughter?

"Is she not here?" Haviv's brow furrowed, and the concern in his eyes heightened Deborah's own fear.

"I saw her leave the tent, and I think she carried the jar to draw water." Rebekah dried her hands on a piece of linen and hurried to Haviv's side. "But perhaps she returned and slipped inside again."

Rebekah rushed to the tent while Deborah called to one of the men to keep watch over the stew, apologizing for the inconvenience. She hurried after Rebekah, Haviv a few steps behind her, but the tent was dark, as they first suspected.

"I'm going to check near the camels at the water's edge," Haviv said.

Deborah picked up her skirts. "I'm coming with you."

She felt Rebekah at her side, keeping her pace. When they reached the rise, they spread out their search in different directions.

"Selima!" Deborah's heart beat fast and hard. She could not come all this way to finally hold the hope of a better life only to lose her daughter! Emotion rose up, filling her throat. "Selima!"

"Selima?" Haviv's voice came from the distance, followed by Rebekah's high-pitched cry. But no answering response followed.

Had she been abducted by marauders? Had she fallen asleep among the camels? Ridiculous thought!

And then she heard Haviv's jubilant call. Deborah ran, following the sound near the last of the line of camels kneeling by the stream.

"Selima! What happened? We have been worried, and everyone is looking for you." Deborah fell to her knees beside her weeping daughter. "My child, what have you done?

Are you hurt?" She searched Selima's tear-soaked face, saw the way she rubbed her ankle with both hands.

"He kicked me." Selima motioned with her head to the camel at her back.

Realization dawned. A camel's kick could have broken a bone.

"Let me look."

A cloud passed away from the moon, giving them more light, and Deborah gently lifted Selima's robe from the offending limb. The skin was broken and purple and twice its normal size.

"I need to touch it to see if the bone is still whole."

Selima sucked in a breath and winced at Deborah's touch, but she did not cry again. "I am the biggest of fools."

"You are not a fool."

Haviv's voice startled them both, and Deborah leaned back and looked behind her, watching the exchange between her daughter and Abraham's servant.

"You are not used to these beasts. Many a man has been kicked who does not take care around them. I should have stayed with you and warned you."

"It is not your fault. I was stubborn and fat-headed to think I could manage out here near dark alone."

"Yes, well, speaking of dark," Deborah said, glancing at the sky and suddenly grateful for this man's presence, "we must get back before that man burns the stew and we all go to bed hungry. I will make you a poultice, and you will be well in a day or so."

"I can't walk."

Deborah opened her mouth to protest, but Haviv stopped her words. "Since it is not broken, I am going to carry you back to the camp."

Deborah watched her daughter's large eyes grow wider, as though she had never expected such a thing from him. She clutched her hands together and held them to her chin. "All right." Her voice was soft, and Deborah could see the interest and embarrassment in her expression.

He glanced at Deborah. "With your permission?"

Deborah nodded numbly.

"Put your arms about my neck, and I will lift you up."

Selima's breath hitched as he lifted her, and Deborah knew that she had gained freedom and found a man for her daughter all in one incredible moment.

12

Selima's injury forced them to stay an extra day in the camp, but by the end of the first week, the poultice Deborah had fashioned for her had almost healed the bruise. The sun had nearly set when they finally found a water source, and this time Rebekah gratefully thanked the men for watering the camels while the women set up the camp. Despite her growing affection for the beast she rode, she did not trust the animals and would not risk another injury, especially in the dark.

She settled now, enjoying the warmth of the campfire, and watched Haviv and Selima quietly talk. She smiled. Perhaps she and Selima had both found worthy men to love.

The thought made her pause, wondering. She knew so little about Isaac. She turned to Eliezer, who sat across from her, whittling.

"What are you making?" She had seen him carving something out of a tree branch earlier in the week, but this time he carved one of the bones taken from a bird they had snared and eaten.

"A flute." He looked at her and smiled. "I would sing, but my voice is as tuneless as Abraham's. It is better to blow air into something that can make a pleasant sound."

She laughed, finding the more time she spent in his company, the more she liked Abraham's servant. "Can your lord Isaac carry a tune?" Her heart fluttered as his name touched her lips. They would soon arrive in Abraham's camp at Hebron—within another week or so—and there were still so many questions.

Eliezer nodded. "Isaac's ear is quick and his tone the most pleasing in the whole company of men and women. But he rarely sings aloud for a crowd. Isaac is a quiet man." He flicked a thin shaving of bone to the ground, then looked up, meeting her gaze. "For you, he will probably sing many a song."

Rebekah's cheeks grew hot at the thought of a man singing to her. Such a thing happened at festivals in Harran where irreverent men in the public square would sing to the temple prostitutes. Men in Nahor sang when they had ingested too much strong drink. And on rare occasions, Laban and Bethuel had filled their home with pleasant songs. It was said that her grandfather had sung to the gods when their flocks did not miscarry and their crops produced food.

"Do you enjoy making music, mistress?"

Rebekah startled, realizing Eliezer had not stopped looking at her. She lifted her shoulders in a half shrug. "I can't really say I have had much opportunity. The songs of my people, the songs of the festivals, were not songs I cared to repeat."

"Isaac creates his own songs." Eliezer grew thoughtful. "He spends much time alone, often weeks at a time, in the Negev wilderness or traipsing after the flocks. He is a man of deep thought." He grew silent again, turning his attention to whittling his flute.

Rebekah shivered as the night breeze grew chill and the fire dwindled. Would Isaac share those thoughts with her?

"What else can you tell me about him?" She heard the

uncertainty in her voice, and she hoped Eliezer would not think she had begun to regret her decision to marry the man.

Eliezer sheathed the knife and dropped it into the leather pouch at his side, then carefully wrapped the unfinished flute in a wool cloth. He drew a hand over his beard in an obvious attempt to stifle a yawn, and Rebekah realized that the women should head to their tent so the men could sleep by the fire. Dawn came earlier each morn.

"Isaac is a quiet man, but do not take that to mean he is weak. He has an astute mind and is more aware of what goes on with Abraham's flocks and herds and possessions than Master Abraham is. Of course, he is much younger . . ." He chuckled and glanced beyond her as though seeing something from a different time, then looked at her once more. "He still grieves the loss of his mother. None of us expected to lose her so soon."

"But was she not already old when Isaac was born?" She had heard the tales of Isaac's miraculous birth. What kind of man must he be, chosen of God years before he was born?

"She was long past childbearing years, this is true. But Abraham still lives, and he was ten years her senior." He shook his head. "If not for the binding, she might be with us today . . ." His voice trailed off.

"Binding?" Rebekah's heart skipped a beat. "What do you mean?"

Eliezer gave his head a little shake as though to clear it. "I am sorry. I should not have said anything. It is not my place to share what happened. You will have to wait for Isaac to share it himself, if he will."

Rebekah stared at the man, her curiosity more than piqued. "This binding that you cannot speak of—it changed him? And Sarah?"

Sorrow etched Eliezer's brow, and he clasped his hands together between his knees. "Yes. Sarah and Abraham—they were never the same after that. It is why Abraham took Keturah, and why Isaac keeps many thoughts to himself." He looked at her. "He misses his mother because she lived for him, protected him, and listened to him. He trusted few others."

Not even his father?

But she did not voice the question. The image of Isaac somehow bound stirred her compassion, and she wondered what could have possibly happened to cause such a thing, and by whom.

Eliezer stood. "I am sorry I cannot give you more than that."

Isaac pounded the dry earth with his staff as he led his donkey, the heat of the desert sands still radiating beneath his sandals. Evenings at Beer-lahai-roi had been a balm, a respite, from the chaotic life in his father's camp in Hebron. Though he had only his father's shepherds to keep him company during such times, Isaac did not mind the solitude. He had learned well how to ration his water and food supply on treks farther into the desert, but he wondered not for the first time if his future wife would fare as well. Would she be a woman used to ease and means? Would she enjoy living sparsely, even where wealth abounded?

He crossed a dry wadi and looked up at the twin mountains that fed it where it wove through the sandy valley. The wilderness could both inspire and terrify a man, and from a distance it looked like a vast waste. But up close, Isaac found it fascinating, teeming with plants of all varieties, ibex and jackals, birds and snakes, rodents and insects, and colorful flowers. He enjoyed the study of the plants and determining how a man could survive against the elements. Somehow it seemed a foe more readily defeated than man.

Did that make him a coward? The question had troubled him too often of late, the answer always eluding him.

Am I only blessed because of my father's faith, because of his character and strength?

He lifted his face to the dimming sky, his heart yearning heavenward. Would he ever know God's favor on his own faith or merit alone? Was the faith of a man all that God valued? Or did a man need to earn His favor?

Surely his father's actions had proven his faith over and over again, from the moment he left his home in Ur until they walked together to the mount of Moriah. His father's obedience at Isaac's binding was an act of that faith. But was not Isaac's submission to that binding faith as well? Did God accept his submission the same as he accepted his father's obedience?

He closed his eyes, pondering the unanswerable. A breeze tickled his face, and he glanced at the sun, whose steady trek toward the west set its rays at an angle that nearly blinded him. He picked up his pace, strode past the wadi, climbed a low ridge, and came out into the field he often visited. Beersheba was not far now, but he would not cross the rest of the distance in the dark. Hebron, where his father's tents stood, would be another two days' walk from there.

He pitched his tent in the middle of the field and built a fire big enough to keep the jackals at bay. He looked to the horizon once more, and his heart stirred at the sight of approaching camels. He recognized the markings of his father's standard and counted the ten beasts Eliezer had taken with him to Paddan-Aram coming toward him—seven men and three women. So, Eliezer had been successful.

A strange sense of anticipation and awe filled him. What kind of woman would follow a servant to another land to marry a cousin she did not know?

Gratitude filled him, and he glanced again at the fiery

skies, the orange and yellow hues making the night brilliant and filled with promise.

He strode closer but stopped as the camels halted, still a fair distance away. One woman glanced in his direction, then quickly ducked her head. Her camel knelt, and she dismounted and spoke to Eliezer. His heart gave a little kick at the short glimpse he'd had of her. She was beautiful even from such a distance! Who was she? What was she like? Would she share his love of the desert, the music of nature? Would she understand his heart?

Hope surged as he watched, waiting. Soon he would know.

Part 2

Then the servant told Isaac all he had done. Isaac brought her into the tent of his mother Sarah, and he married Rebekah. So she became his wife, and he loved her; and Isaac was comforted after his mother's death.

Genesis 24:66–67

Then Abraham breathed his last and died at a good old age, an old man and full of years; and he was gathered to his people. His sons Isaac and Ishmael buried him in the cave of Machpelah near Mamre, in the field of Ephron son of Zohar the Hittite, the field Abraham had bought from the Hittites. There Abraham was buried with his wife Sarah.

Genesis 25:8–10

13

Rebekah's heart did a little dance within her as she waited for her camel to kneel, her eyes on the man in the field moving toward them. She lifted her leg over the camel's hump and walked toward Eliezer, who had dismounted his camel as well.

"Who is that man in the field coming to meet us?" She stole another glance, seeing he had stopped for a brief moment and then started walking again.

"He is my master," Eliezer said, smiling down at her.

She nodded, then pulled her veil across her face and secured it behind her ear, leaving only her eyes visible. Heat crept up her neck, and her heart skipped a beat at his approach. How handsome he was! Dark hair poked beneath a striped tan and blue turban, and his beard held strands of gray mingled with the black. Dark eyes probed hers as he drew near, and the hint of a smile lifted the corners of his mouth. She lowered her eyes, certain he could see her cheeks flaming beneath her veil.

"Isaac, my lord, how good it is to see you!" Eliezer stepped forward, and Isaac clasped the man's shoulders and kissed each cheek, treating the servant as an equal, a friend, rather than the servant that he was.

"I see you have had a prosperous trip."

At Isaac's words, Rebekah looked up again, hearing the rich timbre of his voice and seeing the twinkle in his eyes.

"Yes, we have. Adonai Elohei Abraham, the Lord God of your father Abraham, has given us great success."

Rebekah stood with hands clasped in front of her, listening as Eliezer recounted the tale he had shared with her brother of how God had answered his prayer at the well. She watched Isaac's reaction, unable to take her eyes from him, satisfied that he seemed taken with her as well in the way he kept glancing over Eliezer's shoulder to look at her, approval in his eyes. Relief filled her when at last the report had finished and Isaac seemed pleased.

She sensed Deborah and Selima at her sides, the three of them silent, waiting. At last Isaac broke away from Eliezer and approached.

"We will set up camp here tonight, then tomorrow we will begin the journey to Hebron where my father Abraham lives. Does that seem reasonable to you?"

She grew warm under his intense look, and she had to remind herself to breathe. She nodded, not trusting her voice.

He smiled, holding her gaze but a moment longer, then gave a little bow and backed away. She released her breath only when she realized he had gone to unload her camel. She hurried to help him, undoing the basket holding her robes and tunics from the leather straps that held it to the camel's saddle, while Isaac took her goat's-hair tent from its binding.

Tucking the sack under one arm, he offered a hand to take the basket from her. She reluctantly obeyed, then turned to remove the water jar and blankets from their clasps. She felt his presence beside her and glimpsed him watching her.

"You will not need the jar in the desert. There is no well or spring to draw from. But you can bring it if you like." He started forward, then motioned for her to walk beside him. "Come."

She fell into step with him, noticing the easy way he walked over the uneven ground, his stride sure, his posture relaxed.

"Did you enjoy the journey?" His question lifted her attention from watching each step among the spiny plants growing here and there in the field.

She nodded. "Yes, my lord. I have never done anything quite so bold."

He laughed. "Well, I for one am glad that you did."

She smiled, relieved at his pleasure. "I was only surprised that my uncle did not send his son on the journey with his servants. My family would have enjoyed the chance to meet you."

Isaac looked at her for a long moment, then he turned to watch the path once more. Had her comment offended him? Her heart skipped a beat, and she feared she had.

They continued several paces in silence until at last he stopped to face her once more. "My father's God told him to leave the land of his birth. He did not want his son to visit there and face the temptation to stay in Paddan-Aram." His look held a hint of sorrow. "He did not know that such a thing would not have been a temptation."

"Perhaps your father feared what he did not know."

His look grew thoughtful. "If my father knew me, he would not have feared. My father obeys Adonai. He does not always trust his son." He turned forward again, the only sound that of their sandals crunching dry earth and the voices of servants behind them.

They walked in silence until they reached Isaac's tent. He stopped a good distance away, several paces between his tent and where he set hers. Would he call her to him this night? Marriage customs normally dictated a betrothal, which by the gifts already given her had been accomplished back in Paddan-Aram. Would Isaac wait for a formal wedding ceremony? It was within his right to claim her even now, but surely he would wait until they reached Hebron and she was introduced to his father.

Did Isaac resent his father?

She helped him unroll the tent and pound the pegs, stretching taut the ropes.

"I will leave you to prepare the evening meal," he said when they finished. He gave a slight bow and held her captive with the strength of his gaze. "I am glad you came."

"Thank you, my lord." She wondered that her voice worked at all, so intense was the air that pulsed between them. He wanted her. She could read it in the subtle wink he gave her as he touched her shoulder. The contact made her knees suddenly want to give way. "I am glad I came too."

His gentle pressure on her shoulder was his only response, and then he released her and walked back toward his men.

⁂

The journey to Hebron took two days, and Rebekah chose to walk with Isaac part of the way, hoping she could learn more about him. He seemed to enjoy her company, and he pointed out various plants he had discovered along the way.

"Do you see the large flowers on that plant there beside the stream? Most flowers in the desert are small, but this one puts out large blossoms." He looked at her. "Do you know how it draws enough water to produce such impressive beauty?"

Her stomach fluttered, and she wondered if he spoke only of the flowers. He smiled and pointed to some large yellow blooms dotting the banks of what would normally be a dry wadi but now flowed with water from the recent spring rains. She looked where he pointed.

"Perhaps its roots go deep into the ground?" She had no idea if such a thing were true, but she warmed to the way his eyes shone as he spoke to her.

"I would have thought so too." He wound the donkey's

reins over his other hand, stepping closer to her. He leaned in as though his next words were a secret between them. "Until I studied the plant and dug into the ground around it. Do you know where it derives its nourishment?"

She shook her head, fascinated by the sparkle in his passionate dark eyes. "I have no idea."

His look held hers for the space of one, two, three heartbeats, and she sensed his growing fondness of this time with her. "The plant with the larger flowers steals its water from the smaller plant beside it. Do you see the smaller white flower?"

She followed the length of his bare arm to its fingertips, then past it to the flowers a short distance away. "Yes." Her words were a whisper.

"The smaller flower is hosting, feeding the one that takes from it. So the stronger host ends up looking weaker and becoming weaker because the second plant takes all the good from it."

"Does this not kill the smaller flower?"

Isaac shook his head. "You would think so, wouldn't you? But if the bigger killed the smaller, it too would die. Instead, the bigger keeps the smaller alive just enough so that it might live."

She smiled. "You draw much pleasure from such study." The thought pleased her.

"Yes. And I hope you might do the same." She grew warm at the intimate way he looked at her, and the deep tones of his voice drew her.

"I would like learning such things if you teach me."

He looked as though he might take her hand, but held back and simply smiled. "Such a thing would give me great pleasure."

He walked on, and she fell silent, already recognizing his penchant for introspection. They continued in companionable quiet until the sounds of an encampment grew close.

"We are here," Isaac said, stopping a moment to look at her. "This is my father's camp. You will meet his concubine Keturah and her six sons, along with the rest of the household. You will be mistress over Keturah, but take care not to use that against her. She will not take kindly to it." He paused but a moment, and she wondered if he could read the worry in her gaze. "Do not concern yourself with her too much. We will not live here long."

The servants and camels came to a stop behind them, waiting for Isaac to lead the rest of the way into the camp, whose black goat's-hair tents were visible just over the rise.

Isaac stepped closer, cupping her shoulder, his touch this time sending little sparks through her. "We will meet my father and hold a feast to celebrate your arrival. Then you will come into the tent of my mother." He paused, turned her to face him. "And become my wife."

His words turned her middle to warm liquid, and her heart quickened its pace.

"Tonight?" she managed through a suddenly dry throat.

He gave her arm a gentle squeeze, his look tender. "Tonight."

She nodded, suddenly wishing he would kiss her but knowing for certain that he would not do so until he had brought her to his mother's tent.

He stroked the veil near her cheek with one finger. "Do not fear me, Rebekah."

She lowered her eyes, feeling a swell of sudden emotion. "I won't, my lord."

She heard him sigh and lifted her head to look at him once more.

"Come," he said at last. "Let us go and meet my father."

14

Rebekah's hands trembled, and she fumbled with the lapis lazuli necklace that Isaac had given her that afternoon after they had briefly met his father, Abraham, and Abraham's concubine Keturah. Music of harps and flutes and the steady beat of the wedding drum filled the air outside her tent, making her nearly drop the precious piece.

"I can't do this." She held the strand of jewels out to Deborah, who took it in steady hands and clasped it behind Rebekah's neck. "I did not expect to be so nervous."

Deborah turned Rebekah to face her and cupped her cheek, coaxing her gaze upward. "There is every reason for you to feel so, my dear child. But none of them is valid. Not with the way Isaac looks at you. He will be a kind and gentle husband. Trust me in this. I know of what I speak." Deborah's dark eyes glinted with a memory Rebekah could not share, but she sensed that her nurse's past was not nearly as kind to her as her present.

"Was your husband . . . was he . . ." She could not finish the sentence, her words stopped by the shake of Deborah's head.

"It is not worth discussing. Not on your wedding night!" She straightened Rebekah's multicolored robe and the mantle over her head. "Are you ready for me to place the bridal crown over the veil?"

Deborah would clasp the fabric beneath the crown, encasing her behind the veil. Rebekah would see only through a slit where her eyes would be visible, a bride awaiting her unveiling by her husband. The thought made her palms moist, and she could not find her voice.

She nodded, telling herself once again that she had no need to fear. She felt Deborah's hands lift the veil in place, and her breath caused little droplets to appear on the fabric. She had already been given the ritual cleansing. She did not need to grow sweaty beneath the clothes! But her nerves were in tatters, and she could not still the shaking.

"There." The golden bridal crown rested heavily upon her brow, and she peered into the bronze mirror that Deborah held out for her. But she barely had a moment to examine her cloudy reflection before the music grew more intense, the beat of the drum picking up its pace. "It is time."

"Yes."

"You will be fine."

"I know." She believed it. She must.

She stepped from her tent to the crowd of people in Abraham's camp. A striped red and blue canopy stood near the campfire, and she spotted Isaac standing beneath it. Abraham sat on a large rock near Isaac's side, his weathered face beaming with pleasure. She slowly approached, Deborah at her side. She glimpsed Selima standing near Haviv and faintly wondered how long it would take for the man to ask for her hand.

But she could not think of that now, as the drum and the flutist drew her ever closer to where Isaac waited. When she reached his side, he took her hand in his and squeezed her cold fingers. His smile took her breath, and she longed to cup his cheek and touch her fingers to his bearded face. But she merely looked at him instead, wondering if he could feel the way her pulse jumped and soared at his touch like a bird in flight.

"My daughter, you do me and my son great honor this day by agreeing to become Isaac's wife."

Abraham's voice broke through her thoughts as the music came to an abrupt halt. She turned to face him, surprised to see him standing so close to them beneath the canopy.

"As you have come without a male relative to grant you the blessing, and as I have been informed your family has already bestowed such a blessing upon you before you left to come here, let me just say a few words before you two are joined together as one."

She bowed her head and felt Abraham's hand, still strong despite his many years, rest upon her crowned head. Her chest lifted, but the sigh would not release.

"Rebekah, my daughter, and Isaac, my son." He paused, his voice catching on Isaac's name.

She longed to look up, to see what passed between father and son in that moment, but she dare not move with Abraham's hand resting upon her.

"Be fruitful and multiply, as our God has commanded each of us. God has joined you together this day. His peace be upon you."

She heard another catch in his voice as he spoke the last word and wondered if his voice was affected by age or simply the emotion of the moment. As his hand lifted from her head, she met his gaze, seeing the moisture in his eyes.

"Thank you, my father." She smiled, though he could not fully see it behind her veil, and felt his approval in the look he gave her. Indeed, he was her only father now, and she prayed her actions would please him.

"If only your mother could have seen this day." He directed his attention to Isaac, and Rebekah looked at her new husband, seeing him nod.

"She would be pleased with Adonai's choice," Isaac said, looking from his father to her. His smile melted what little fear she had left, filling her instead with a new sense of desire to please him as well.

"Thank you, my lord." Her voice came out breathy.

Isaac squeezed her fingers again, and the music started up once more. "Come," he said, bending close to her ear.

She turned to follow, her heart beating faster with every careful step. Isaac crossed the campground, leaving the rejoicing crowd, leading her to a large goat's-hair tent on the edge of the ring of Abraham's camp.

"This belonged to my mother." Isaac lifted the flap and beckoned her to go ahead of him into the dark enclosure. He quickly followed, carrying a torch, then set about lighting two small clay lamps. He returned the torch to its post and let the flap fall, closing them in.

The tent was divided into several rooms, one of them a large sitting area with plush cushions scattered about. Her loom already stood in one corner, and as her eyes adjusted to the dim light, she saw that Isaac had taken care to have the items she had brought from home arranged in various places.

"I thought you would feel more at home here if you recognized some of the furnishings." He waved a hand, taking in the room, and she glanced to where he pointed.

"You are most thoughtful. It pleases me very much." She smiled, hoping he could see the pleasure in her eyes.

His look captivated her, and he did not move or speak for several beats of her already racing heart. What should she do next? Did he want her to pour him some wine? But she had no idea where to look for the flask.

"You are very beautiful," he said.

Her stomach did a little flip as his hands moved to take the crown from her head.

"But I cannot appreciate your beauty with this between us." He fumbled with the clasp holding the veil over her face, and in that moment she sensed he was as nervous as she.

She moved her hand to help, their fingers grazing, her breath growing still as he let the veil fall away. She felt her pulse throbbing in her neck and watched his Adam's apple move up and down. He traced a line along her jaw. "Yes, it is as I suspected. You are the most beautiful of women."

His smile made her knees grow weak, and when he bent to touch his lips to hers, she lost all sense of time and place. She had traveled half the world to get here, and the journey had been worth every step. God had given her a prince unequaled.

As his kiss deepened, she wrapped her arms around his neck and gladly returned it.

❧

Isaac rose up on one elbow, blinking at the light poking under the rolled-up sides of the tent. He shook his head, trying to remember when they had lifted the flaps, when he spotted Rebekah fully dressed and tying the scarf over her head. He smiled and wondered at the love that rose within him for this cousin, his wife.

Wife.

He liked the sound of the word and played it over for a moment, shaking off the last vestiges of sleep. He flung the covers aside. She turned, a dark blush filling her face as she looked down at him.

"You are awake, my lord." Her flustered state at seeing him in only a short night tunic the day after their wedding night made him almost chuckle.

"It would appear so," he said instead. "What are you doing?"

She was clearly dressed for a day's work. He should have told her last night not to worry about such things today.

"I thought I would draw water and help prepare the morning meal." Her voice sounded uncertain, and she glanced over her shoulder and then back at him again.

"There is no need today. Come, sit beside me." He smiled at her confusion, but when he patted the sleeping mat where she had recently lain, she obeyed.

"There is a need to eat, is there not? I would do my part, my lord."

He touched her cheek, stroked one finger down it. "I know you would, and you will. But this is our wedding week. We have seven days to get to know each other, and we are not allowed to leave this tent." At the surprised lift of her brow, he added, "The women will leave food for us at the tent's door, and at week's end we will join the others for a final feast."

"I see." She looked beyond him, and he wondered if spending seven days in his company might displease her. "What if we want to go for a walk together?"

He smiled into her eyes. "If such a thing would please you, I think we can sneak away without attracting undue attention."

"I would like that."

The thought seemed to cheer her, making his heart light. He knew just the place he would take her first, a lush valley where the spring bubbled over rocks and the trees plunged thick branches toward the heavens, offering shade and seclusion. He would carve a flute for her and teach her to make music at his side.

He scooted into an upright position, studying her. She sat slightly rigid, her back straight, as though she did not know how to relax now that darkness did not keep them in seclusion.

"You will not be needing this unless we travel." He gently pulled the veil from her hair and smoothed a hand along her dark tresses. "A married woman in the camp need not veil herself. Though you may tie your hair off your shoulders." He coaxed her to look at him, and the blush he'd found so becoming the night before only endeared her more to him now. He leaned in and kissed her cheek. "Does this displease you—spending so much time with me?" He hated the need to ask it of her, but if she truly did not wish his company . . .

"No, no, of course not!"

Her smile reassured him, and he let out a breath, relieved.

"I only . . . I did not know. Our customs are not so very different—there is a marriage week to be fulfilled—it is just that I am used to a house of brick with many rooms and much work to be done." She looked around, and he wondered how pale his mother's tent must be in comparison to her mother's house of stone.

"My mother's tent is the largest in the camp besides my father's." His tone sounded defensive and he knew it. Was he a child that he should pout? He shook himself for having such a ridiculous thought. Wealth could be expressed in many ways; he need not compare one to another to please her.

She turned back to him, her look chagrined. "Oh no, my lord, I did not mean . . . that is, your mother's tent is wonderful and large, and I am most comfortable. I just . . ."

He could no longer refrain from pulling her close, his lips tasting hers. "You have no reason to be sorry, Rebekah." He spoke in her ear, his breath lingering at her throat. He heard her breath catch and watched her pulse throb in her neck as he loosened the robe from her shoulders and moved to kiss her again. "We have a week where no one will interrupt us or question us and with no work whatsoever to keep us occupied."

"No work whatsoever?" She sounded incredulous, as though she had never experienced a day of rest.

"Only the work of discovery, of coming to know and understand each other." He could spend a lifetime getting to know this beautiful woman, and he determined in that moment that he would have none other. She was his and he was hers alone.

She offered a pointed look at the rolled-up sides of the tent, then sifted her fingers through his rumpled hair. "Shall I lower the flaps, my lord?"

He noticed a mischievous glint in her brown eyes and nodded, smiling. Her hips held a purposeful sway, and she glanced back at him as she pulled the ropes to lower the flaps again, encasing them in semidarkness.

She removed her robe, folded it gently, and laid it over a basket in the corner, then came to sit beside him. He took her hands in his and turned them over slowly, kissing each palm. "Tell me, my love, are you glad you came? Surely a woman as beautiful as you are could have had any man in Paddan-Aram." He pulled her closer to lie beside him, settling her in the crook of his arm.

"Not any man," she said, her voice soft. "If not for Adonai sending Eliezer, I might have pined away in my brother's home until it was too late."

He rose up on one elbow and searched her face. "Your brother would not seek a husband for you? What of your father? Surely he would have considered it long before his death."

She nodded, but her dark eyes grew distant, and he wondered at the flicker of sadness that clouded them. But a moment later, she looked at him with affection, her eyes clear. "My father did consider a man in Harran, but he was poor and could not give me what my father had always given. My mother would hear none of it, and my father died before he could secure someone else. Laban, his heir, kept promising to find a husband for me, but the few he considered were unworthy—men who did not treat women well and who had no reverence for Adonai. I could never have married such a man."

Her earnest tone and the smile in her eyes made his heart leap. Joy rose within him that Adonai had kept her for him, for surely she could have married years before if her father had allowed it.

"We are not so very different, my love." He intertwined their hands, her palm feeling perfect against his own larger one. "My mother, God bless her, never gave me the chance to marry. She would not hear of me taking a Canaanite wife, as my father had done with Keturah, or an Egyptian wife, as my father had done with my mother's handmaiden, Hagar. I feared she would be accepting of no one unless my father demanded it, but even then, I am not sure she would have listened."

The memories evoked a sudden sadness that his mother could not have been more trusting, that his parents could not have kept their love strong. Despite her faith, Sarah had struggled with fear, particularly fear of losing him.

"Your father has had three wives?" She already knew the answer, he was sure, but seemed to want to hear the response from him.

He squeezed their intertwined fingers and nodded. "My mother was his first wife and only true love. When my mother feared the promise would never come to pass, that she would never bear a son for my father, she gave him her Egyptian maid, Hagar, to be his concubine. Hagar bore him Ishmael. You might meet him someday." He paused, briefly wondering how his older brother fared.

"Does your father still see Ishmael?" She pulled him down beside her again, and they turned to face each other.

"No. Not that I'm aware of. But I do not spend all of my time in my father's camp. I have met with Ishmael from time to time over the years. He spends his days in the desert, one of my favorite places to live."

At the slight curl of her lip, he paused. "You do not care for the desert?"

"I do not know the desert." She smiled. "But I am willing to have you show it to me."

He sighed, again relieved at her answer, his fears of displeasing her slowly dissipating.

"My brother Laban has a wife of only five years and already has added a concubine."

He studied her face in the dim light, sensing the question she feared to ask.

"I am not like my father or your brother." He held her

gaze, willing her to believe him. For though she could not know the future, he knew his own strength of will. Unless God took her from him, he would not take another wife. He would not ever make her subject to all that his mother had suffered in sharing his father.

"You cannot know that. People change."

Her doubt did not surprise him. His own father had done the unthinkable in binding him when God had asked it of him.

"People do change, Rebekah, but God does not. But on God's righteous name, I promise you I will not take another wife or your maidservant or any other woman to be my wife while you are living. I could not do that to you."

The look she gave him shifted from doubt to awe, and tears quickly filled her eyes, spilling over. He brushed them away with his thumbs, took her face in his hands, and kissed her. "I would not have thought it possible in such a short time, but I love you, Rebekah. And no matter what the future brings to us, I will not break my vow."

"Thank you, my lord." She blinked several times, and he knew she struggled to halt the emotion. He pulled her close and rubbed circles over her back. "No man I have ever known would make such a promise. If I give you no heir, you may wish you had stayed your words."

"God has already promised an heir, and I am confident He will give it in His time." He held her away from him to search her face again. "I am living proof of His promise."

Her lip puckered, and he sensed she would cry again. On any other day he would let her fully express her emotion, but this was a day for rejoicing in the love they had found. There was no room for tears.

He bent to kiss her again, tasting the salt still hovering at the corners of her mouth. "Only you, my love. For all of my life, there will be only you."

He pulled her beside him, his kiss driving away any tears she had left.

15

Rebekah heard the sound of the water flowing over rocks long before it came into sight. Isaac reached behind him, grasped her hand in his strong fingers, and pulled her to his side as they drew closer to the trees, which hid the stream from view. Mating crickets sang their distinct song, and a jackal howled from someplace over the ridge. She shivered despite her attempt at bravery.

"Are we safe here?" She leaned close to Isaac's ear, grateful when his arm came around her waist. "That sounded close."

Isaac stopped near the opening of a copse of terebinth and willow and turned to face her. He drew her against him, his face near enough for her to feel his breath. "Do not fear the jackals, my love, or the animals of the night. Adonai is the only one we need fear. Even the wild beasts obey Him."

She swallowed, unable to escape another shudder as the jackal's howl sounded again. "I cannot help but hope those wild animals are able to hear Him when He speaks." She gave him a look, but his response was only a deep chuckle.

He brushed a light kiss on her lips. "Trust me," he whispered. He took her hand again and moved them both through the trees toward the ever-growing sound of the water.

Moonlight spilled over gleaming rocks along the water's edge, the spray dampening their faces as they approached.

Isaac led them higher to an outcropping of dry rocks where they could look down on the waterfall yet keep a safe distance from its edge. He sat, gently pulling her down to lean with her back to him. His arms held her close, and she laughed at the tickle of the water's mist on her legs.

"Look up," Isaac whispered in her ear.

She had been too intent on looking down, fearing they might fall or slip into the cascading water below. But she obeyed his words and lifted her head, her breath catching on the beauty of the starlit night.

"The stars are so close and so many!" She craned her neck, turning her head to look from one end of the heavens to the other. The sky stretched taut like the fabric of a black goat's-hair tent, and the moon sat to the left as though hung from a peg along heaven's tent walls.

"Well, we did climb up this hill, so we are closer than when we sit below among the plains." His breath tickled her neck. "This is better than being cooped inside the tent for a week, is it not?"

She could not suppress a little laugh that burst inside her at his mischievous tone and the way his breath moved the hairs on her neck. "Yes!" She leaned into his strength and let herself study the skies.

They sat in comfortable silence, and she listened to the night sounds and the water as it mesmerized her, lulling her into a state of relaxed peace. The jackal had long since moved beyond them, and she took comfort in Isaac's steady breath. She could not imagine a more comforting place or wanting to spend this time with any other man. How glad she was now that Adonai had kept her from marrying any of the men Laban had hoped to pair her with. Isaac's quiet strength and gentle laughter brought her greater joy than she had known in all her life. But there was still so much about him that she longed to know. Things he seemed reticent to share.

"How would you feel about moving to Beer-lahai-roi once our wedding week is past?"

His abrupt question pulled her thoughts back to her surroundings. She shifted, wanting to face him but unable to move easily on the narrow rock. Sensing her desire, he held firm as he helped her to turn.

"But come." He pulled her to her feet. "We can speak more easily in the clearing farther up the hill."

Her legs tingled, making her wobble slightly, but in the next instant he had stepped down from the rocky ledge and pulled her to safety. He grabbed her hand again, leading her up the incline. She pondered his question as they trudged higher and focused on her feet, trying not to get her sandals tangled among the protruding tree roots, leafy foliage, and fallen branches. At the top of the rise, he slipped both arms beneath hers and twirled her in the moonlight, laughing.

She laughed with him, unable to keep from smiling at his infectious joy. Did her presence truly evoke so much happiness in him?

"What is so funny?" she asked when he finally set her back on her feet.

He sank to the grass and tugged her down with him, then leaned back on both elbows, his gaze toward the stars. She looked in the same direction, appreciating anew the ever-changing celestial landscape. But a moment later she pounced on him, wrapping her arms about his neck.

"Tell me truly. Do you laugh because you think me funny or because you love my company?" She coaxed his head toward hers and sucked in a breath at the sudden intensity in his dark eyes.

"Need you ask?" His voice grew husky, his emotion startling. "The day you arrived was the happiest of my life."

She swallowed a sudden lump in her throat and wondered how the moment could move so quickly from laughter to tears. But the tears were not sad, and she knew a measure of relief that he already loved her beyond reason. She would go anywhere with him, do anything to please him.

She ran a hand along the soft hairs of his beard. "Would you move us so soon, my lord?" She would go to Beer-lahai-roi, to the desert, even to Egypt if he asked, but a part of her begged to know why he would leave his father's camp before she even had a chance to get to know the man.

He looked beyond her as though the question pained him. Something troubled him, and she yearned to know it.

She placed a hand over his heart, feeling its steady beat beneath her fingers. "Please, Isaac, what is it that causes the shadows to fill your gaze? Is there some problem with your father?"

Isaac's head gave an almost imperceptible shake, his look pensive. He drew a hand over his beard before resting it on top of her hand. He held her fingers in a gentle grip and sighed. "My father is a good man." He looked at her as though willing her to believe he meant every word. "But our relationship . . ." He glanced beyond her, letting the sentence die.

"Your father has other children," she offered when the silence grew too lengthy, needing to be filled. "Does he not have time for you?"

Isaac's attention snapped, and she sensed his thoughts had taken him far away. "My father would spend every moment with me. But you are right. He has another wife and six sons to occupy his time. His life is not as it was when my mother lived, when I was but a boy."

"What was it like when you were the only son of both father and mother?" She ached to understand the pensiveness that had come over him, to know the man and the boy he used to be.

He lifted her hand and kissed her fingertips. "They were days filled with much laughter. You must understand, my parents were very old when I was born, and my childhood was one of joy, though I will admit my mother's watchful eye never left me. She was . . . protective." He smiled and brushed a strand of her hair behind her ear. "I did not understand why they sent my older brother Ishmael away—I was only four at the time. I had looked up to him, and he used to play games with me. But my mother was always watching, forever watching, how other boys and girls in the camp treated me. I was the heir, the prince, and she would not allow me to be mistreated."

A wistful look crossed his handsome features, and Rebekah's heart stirred, hurting for the little boy who could not live as other boys would have lived.

"Did you have no friends?"

Some of the servants seemed close to Isaac the man. Did they romp and play as children?

He shrugged. "Haviv and I carried out a few mischievous pranks—when my mother was not looking, of course." He grinned.

"Of course." She smiled, sensing some of the tension had seeped from him.

He leaned back, stretching out on the grass, and tugged her to lie in the crook of his arm, their gazes toward the stars again. "My father and I have been through some difficult times," he said after another lengthy silence. "We do not speak of them, but we understand each other. My mother . . . she could never come to terms with my father's obedience to Adonai Elohim, to the lengths he would go . . ."

She waited several heartbeats, but he did not finish his thought. She felt the rhythm of his heart pick up its pace, and his breath came out in a strained sigh. What memories pierced him so deeply that he could not speak of them? Perhaps she had coaxed him too soon. They had a lifetime to discuss their pasts, to explain what lay beneath the surface of their thoughts. And yet, wasn't this what the wedding week was meant to accomplish?

She rolled onto her side, leaning on one elbow. "Can you not tell me, my lord? Are the memories painful?" Did his father do something to him? Discipline him against his mother's will? She could not begin to imagine . . .

He did not shift to face her, his eyes fixed on some point in the expanse above. "I will tell you, Rebekah."

She waited, watching deep furrows lengthen across his brow.

"I will tell you what it is that separated my mother and father, that keeps me choosing to live a life apart from my father." He turned at last, rising on one elbow to lean over her. "But not today. Not yet."

He traced a finger along her jaw, and she knew by the look he gave her that he was silently begging her to let it go, to wait for another time when he could trust her enough to share it. She nodded, saddened, yet grateful for the relief in his eyes.

"It is a hard story to tell," he said as his hand gently cupped her cheek. "The memories still invade my dreams."

Then why not share them and be rid of the memories?

But she did not voice the question. She somehow knew that saying even this much had cost him. Did he trust no one? How many in the camp knew what had happened to him? Was he keeping it secret from only her?

"I hope someday you will feel comfortable enough to tell it." She lifted both hands to sift through his hair, pulled him toward her, and kissed him, surprising them both at her boldness. She laughed, and he joined her.

"Thank you, my love." His smile took her breath. "Someday I will not only tell you, but I will take you to the place where it all began." He kissed her again, and she responded in kind.

❧

Rebekah smoothed the rumpled lines from her robe and tried to stifle a shudder as the beat of the wedding drum filled the camp. Flutes and lyres and the sounds of many voices took up the song of blessing, the one that marked the end of their wedding week. She waited at the tent's door behind Isaac's taller frame. He turned and reached for her hand.

"Are you ready?" His look held all of the love he had expressed to her in the past seven days, and the mirth in his smile was one she had happily come to expect.

"I am ready." Heat moved from her neck to her cheeks, and she almost wished for the veil of her maidenhood to hide behind.

He nodded once and touched her cheek. "You are beautiful, as always." He rested his hand on her shoulder and offered her a reassuring squeeze.

Loud cheers erupted as he emerged from the tent, and Rebekah heard the familiar sounds of boisterous back slapping along with Haviv's deep voice and Eliezer's mellow laughter. She waited, her breath shallow, until she reminded herself to breathe deeply. The male banter continued, but the voices grew more distant, and still she waited.

At last the music changed to a higher pitch, and the chatter of women's voices came close to the tent. She drew a calming breath, lifted the flap, and stepped into bright sunlight.

"There she is!" Selima's squeal made her laugh, and she caught her maid in a quick embrace. Deborah's arms came around her soon after, and Eliezer's wife Lila, his daughters, and even Keturah hurried to her side.

"When this last feast is over, I want you to tell me everything," Selima whispered after the women had ushered her to the central fire, set her on a cushioned seat beside Isaac, and brought trays of food for them to eat.

Rebekah glanced at Isaac, whose look held secrets shared and knowledge she knew she could tell no one. But she indulged Selima with a smile. "Perhaps not everything." At the girl's pout, Rebekah touched her arm. "But we will talk." She accepted the tray from a servant, then turned to face Isaac.

Plucking a date from the tray, she touched it to her lips, then placed it in Isaac's mouth. He accepted her offering, the symbol of a promise that she would do all in her power to keep him well fed. He chewed slowly as the music played around them. Women danced, twirling to the rhythm of timbrels and shaking of sistrums, but Isaac appeared not to notice. His mouth quirked in a knowing smile as he tossed the pit into the fire.

His hand closed over a thick piece of sheep cheese. He touched it to his lips, then held it to her mouth. She nibbled the end—his promise to provide for her from his flocks and herds. She took another bite but let him finish the large chunk, a joint promise to use each provision wisely.

Eliezer handed Isaac a golden chalice, and he took a long drink from the fruit of the vine. He touched his mouth with the back of his hand, then tipped the cup toward her. She drank as well, peeking over the rim to hold his steady, loving gaze.

"At last it is done!"

Eliezer's shout was followed by the long blast of a ram's horn. The singing and dancing and feasting would last until nightfall.

She felt Isaac's arm come around her, and she relaxed against his shoulder, smiling. She looked up and straightened at Abraham's approach. Isaac's arm fell away, and he stood.

"Father." Isaac offered Abraham the seat next to them, helping him settle before sitting beside her once more.

"Thank you, my son." He leaned forward, holding his staff, and looked at her. "And you, my daughter." He smiled at them both. "Now I can die in peace, knowing you have someone to watch over you."

Isaac bristled at his father's words, and Rebekah sensed that this was only part of the friction between the two men. "I hardly need someone to watch over me, Father." Isaac's voice was low, barely heard between them with the heavy music and laughter of the crowd.

Abraham patted Isaac's knee as though he were a small boy. "No, no, of course not, my son. I only meant that now I can rest, knowing that you have someone to share your life with, someone to continue the line of Adonai's promise." His smile was soft, but his face held a distant, pensive expression. "Your mother would have been pleased." He faced Rebekah, and she wondered how she could help strengthen the peace between father and son.

Isaac stiffened, though Rebekah knew his father meant only good.

"I should have liked to have met Isaac's mother," she said, holding Abraham's gaze. "You must have loved her very much." She slipped a hand in Isaac's and squeezed, hoping to breach whatever wall had so suddenly been erected.

"You would have loved my Sarah. She was a passionate, giving woman"—he glanced at Isaac—"albeit a protective one." His look grew wistful, and he smiled at something unseen. He shifted to face Isaac, his knuckles whitening on the staff. "She loved me well, even through our differences. I hope you both know half the love I had with your mother. None other compared to her or could replace her."

"I hope so too," Rebekah said before Isaac could respond. "Isaac has told me enough about her to know that I hope to please him as much as she pleased you." She smiled, hoping Isaac would not resent her interference. She was relieved when she caught the twinkle in his eye and felt the reassurance of his fingers encasing hers. "I trust that someday you can sit down and tell me about her as well, my father."

The lines on Abraham's face softened, and he released a deep sigh. He glanced beyond them, and Rebekah looked to where Keturah stood near her tent's opening, holding her youngest son in her arms. The woman was beautiful but much younger than Isaac's father, young enough to be Isaac's wife. Had Abraham's marriage to this lesser concubine bothered Isaac? Had Isaac suffered jealousy that his father would marry while he was forced to wait?

She glanced at her husband, seeing the slight tensing of his jaw, then looked again at Abraham and wondered if her father-in-law had any real affection for Keturah or her sons.

"At week's end, we will be leaving for Beer-lahai-roi, Father."

Isaac's words brought her gaze back to his, and she heard Abraham's quick intake of breath.

"So soon, my son?" Yet his comment did not indicate surprise, and his look held silent resignation.

Isaac ran a hand over his jaw, and his expression filled with sudden weariness. "It would be better for your sons to have you to themselves, Father. You have much to teach them, and Rebekah does not need to share her place with your wife."

"There is much you could do to help me," Abraham said. "I do not have the strength to teach them as I taught you."

The admission made Rebekah look to her husband.

"I am not their father," he said.

How many times had father and son had this discussion? Though Isaac was old enough to be father to each one of Keturah's sons, he obviously did not want the job of raising his brothers. Did he resent their entrance into his life?

"Of course not," Abraham said with sudden vehemence. "I take full responsibility for that. I had only hoped you might teach the older ones to hunt—"

"You would be better off entreating Ishmael to do such a thing."

Abraham gave his son a sharp look. "That comment is unjustified and you know it. You are as good a hunter as any of my men. And I have not seen Ishmael in years."

"Perhaps it is time you sought him out."

Abraham stared at his son, and Rebekah grew still at the

silent war going on between them. She searched her mind for something, anything, to say to help ease the tension, but could find nothing.

"I am old, Isaac. I ask for your help because I want to keep you near me. Is this such a hard thing to understand?"

Abraham's words drew Rebekah's sympathies.

"No, Father, of course not." She heard the words come out of her mouth but could not believe she had been the one to utter them. Heat infused her cheeks, and she could not meet Isaac's eyes, fearing she would see the disapproval she already felt from him. "That is, I do not see a reason why we could not stay for another week or so to help you." Her cheeks burned at the lift of Abraham's brow, and when she finally drew courage to glance at Isaac, she lowered her gaze, consumed by the fire in his dark eyes.

"I am sorry," she said, wishing she could run to her tent and hide. "I spoke without thinking."

The ensuing silence grew thick, churning her stomach. Indeed, she did not feel well and wished she could escape, yet feared that if she did so, she would add another insult to the offense she had already caused.

"I will spend some time with Zimran and Jokshan before we leave at week's end."

Isaac's tone sounded conciliatory, but Rebekah still could not look up at either man, and Isaac did not move to touch her, to reassure her that all was forgiven.

"But I cannot stay longer. I have sheep shearing at Beer-lahai-roi in less than a month."

The music momentarily stopped, and women hurried to spread the final wedding feast before them.

"Thank you, my son," Abraham said as he pushed himself up with the help of his staff. "We will talk again."

She watched her father-in-law walk away and turn toward his tent, though they had yet to eat of the feast.

"Will he be back to join us?" Rebekah looked at Isaac, praying she would see compassion in his eyes. But they were hard as flint and fixed on her with a look she had never seen.

"Do not speak for me again."

His voice was low but firm, filling her with shame. She had only meant to appease his father. Was that so wrong? And yet she knew by Isaac's reaction that she could not step into the role of peacemaker without offending one of them.

"I am sorry, my lord. Forgive me." She studied her toes peeking out of her jeweled leather sandals. "I only meant to ease the tension between you." Her words came out hoarse and strained, and she wished she could have this discussion in the privacy of their tent. Would he share her tent again this night? "Sometimes I speak too quickly."

She risked a glance at him, caught the faint hint of a smile lift one corner of his mouth. His eyes held sudden understanding, kindness even.

"I have noticed." His look held her captive, and she released a short sigh as his expression softened further. "But you do me harm when you make a decision without consulting me, especially when it contradicts what I have just said."

She swallowed, and the sick feeling churned once more inside of her. "I did not realize. I would never seek your harm, my lord. Not ever."

"My father does not like to see me leave. He would have me live in his camp until I take over all of his affairs. But he has already given me charge of his flocks and herds, and they require that I live where there is more space for them to roam and graze. All he has here are his wife and sons, and there is little I can do to help him in that respect. Nor do I want to."

It was more than he had said to her regarding his duties or his feelings for his half brothers, and she felt chastened, chagrined that he would tell her only because she had goaded him by her brash words.

"I should have respected your decision," she whispered. "I am used to my father indulging my opinion, and my brothers were no match for my wit." Her smile was rueful, and she wondered how much harm her father and brothers had done her by not being men of greater character and strength.

Isaac did not immediately respond, and she realized that she would have to adjust to his pensive and quiet moments, to his pondering and his comfort with the silence she despised.

Did she despise it? If nothing else, she needed to fill it, but she held her tongue, waiting, watching him.

"You will find I am a man of great patience, Rebekah, but a man without respect, especially respect from his own wife and for himself, is a man easily swayed by the opinions of others. And easily discouraged."

He paused, and she ached for him, wishing she had never opened her mouth to speak, had simply listened and learned. But it was too late to retract her words.

"I would earn your respect, Rebekah, but in the meantime, I would ask you to offer it freely until I can prove to you that I deserve it." He smiled and reached for her hand. "Can you accept that?"

"Oh yes, my lord! I already respect you a great deal."

What kind of man was this that he could be so gentle with her, even though she knew she had angered him?

"All is forgiven, my love." He kissed her fingers, then released them as platters of food were set on a smooth rock. "Let me concern myself with my father and the tension you sense between us." He motioned to the platter for her to take from its bounty. "Let us eat and drink and rejoice." He lifted the golden chalice in her direction and smiled.

She returned his smile with a tremulous one of her own and drank from the cup he offered her.

16

Rebekah rose the next morning and dressed quickly before Isaac was fully awake. Dawn had barely crested the horizon, but the other women of the camp would surely be up by now, preparing the morning meal. She glanced at his sleeping form, love for him rising within her. She would work hard, make him proud, and somehow repay the kindness he had shown her from the first day until now.

Lifting the clay urn by the neck, she hoisted it onto her shoulder and slipped beneath the tent's flap. Pink predawn light bathed the camp in its fresh, new glow. She spotted Selima emerging from the servants' tent and hurried to meet her.

"At last you are joining us again." Selima clutched her own clay jar, and the two fell into step as they walked up an incline and traveled a short distance until they at last heard the water of the stream rushing by. "So tell me, mistress, is he everything you thought he would be?" She stopped, her large eyes open, earnest. "Do you love him?" Her expression grew dreamy, and Rebekah laughed.

"You are impossible! I have only known him a week. How can I know all that he is so quickly? Even a wedding week is only time enough to begin to understand one another." She knew the words were true but could not stop the smile she had awakened with that morning.

"Oh, come now. I see the way he looks at you. Is he . . . that is . . ." Selima blushed and looked away.

Rebekah laughed again and lowered her jar to the bubbling water. "Some questions are not meant to be answered, my friend. You will just have to wait until Haviv takes you to his tent and puts all of your wild imaginings to rest."

Selima's color heightened further, convincing Rebekah that she had guessed correctly.

"Has he stated his intentions toward you?" Rebekah waited for the water to reach the top, then hefted the heavy jar onto her shoulder again, watching while Selima did the same.

"Not in so many words." A hint of a smile appeared. "But he has seemed quite attentive. I did not wish to say anything until your week had passed, but if he should ask . . ." She met Rebekah's gaze, her expression uncertain.

"If he should ask, I would happily allow you to marry him." They fell into step together again, balancing the jars on their shoulders.

"But who will serve you then, mistress?"

"You will, of course. As Haviv serves Isaac." She glanced at her maid, wondering what thoughts tumbled in her pretty head. "I still have your mother to help me, and I am sure Isaac has servants that will suffice." She felt almost guilty declaring their stations in such terms, but it was the truth, and she could not pretend otherwise. "But you are free to marry him if he asks for your hand. You have my blessing."

Selima nodded. "Thank you, mistress." They walked in silence a few moments, the morning sounds of chirping birds waking the rest of the camp as they approached. "If Haviv were to leave Isaac's employ someday, would I be free to follow him?"

It was an honest question for a slave, but Rebekah had

never considered Selima a slave, though in fact, her father had purchased both Deborah and Selima when the girl was still an infant.

Rebekah stopped at the edge of the camp to look at her maid, her friend. The thought of ever losing Selima or her mother had never once occurred to her, and she did not like the feelings such thoughts evoked now.

"Would Haviv do such a thing? Has he said as much to you?"

Had Isaac misread his overseer? Did Haviv have no desires to take over the duties of his father once Eliezer grew too old to continue them, especially once Abraham rested with his fathers?

Selima glanced around as though afraid someone would overhear them. "No, mistress, he has not said any such thing. But he is a restless sort, and so I have wondered if he would remain happy here."

Rebekah looked toward the waking camp, the scent of the fire and the first smells of baking bread reaching them. She breathed deeply, her heart warming to this place, and wished not for the first time that Isaac did not intend to leave at week's end. But she knew better than to ask him to reconsider.

"Perhaps Haviv is only as restless as Isaac is to return to Beer-lahai-roi and to begin the shearing of the sheep. Men do not like to stay near the tents and have little to do."

Though Isaac hadn't seemed to mind being secluded in the tent for a week with her. But a wedding week could not go on forever.

"Perhaps that's all it is." Selima giggled as though suddenly taken by a new thought. "He does seem to like me, though."

Rebekah glanced at her maid and caught her smiling. "Does he now?" They started forward again and made their way carefully down the incline. "Shall I speak to Isaac about this, or do you want to wait to see if Haviv acts first?" It was within her rights to seek a mate for her maids or give them to her husband as a concubine if she so chose. But Isaac had already said he would not marry her maids. A relieved little sigh escaped her at that thought.

"You would do that for me?"

Selima's delight brought a pang of regret to Rebekah that she had not considered to ever mention such a thing before.

"Of course." Rebekah lowered her voice as they neared the central fire. "I will speak to Isaac about it the first chance I get."

The end of the week came too soon, and Rebekah rose before dawn to make sure the last of their items were packed for the journey to Beer-lahai-roi. She and Selima had already been to the river to fill the goatskin sacks with water, and Isaac began taking down their tent as the first rays of pink brightened the eastern sky. She hurried now, baking flatbread over the three-pronged camp stove, then tucking the cooled loaves into sacks for the journey. They would eat as they walked or rode the distance from Hebron, south through the Negev to the oasis at Beer-lahai-roi.

"So you are finally going."

Keturah's sullen tone brought Rebekah's head up. During their stay in Abraham's camp, Rebekah had sensed the woman's dislike.

"I'm sure we will return again not too many days hence." She busied herself tucking the last of the loaves into the leather sack, then folded it closed. She lifted the hot oven from the fire and set it on the stones to cool. "I am sorry we cannot stay longer."

She met the woman's gaze but looked quickly away, pushing down the sudden anger that flared at her mocking look. She had done nothing to earn the woman's resentment, and she would not allow Keturah's bitterness to cloud the last few moments she had in Abraham's camp.

"If you will excuse me, I must finish packing." She hurried off, away from Keturah's scowl, taking the bread and oven with her. She found Selima among the donkeys and handed her the items to pack.

"Are we almost ready?" Rebekah asked.

Something in Keturah's manner had made her suddenly anxious to leave, though she wasn't sure what could have prompted the woman to act so sullenly. Ever since Isaac had returned from a hunting trip with Keturah's two oldest sons, Keturah had seemed eager for the week to end and for them to go.

"We are just waiting for the tents, mistress. Will we not break the fast with Master Abraham before we depart?" Selima secured the oven into one of the donkey's saddlebags and came to join her.

"Isaac did not want to take the time. We will eat on the road. He hopes to arrive in Beer-lahai-roi within two days."

They walked together back toward the area where Haviv and Isaac were rolling up the last of the goat's-hair tents.

She smiled when Isaac looked up, his tan turban held in place by the blue cord she had given him. It was just one of the many little gifts she planned to bestow on him from her weaving skills. There had been no time to make them before her marriage, but now she had a lifetime to give gifts to him.

"We will say our goodbyes and leave soon." He glanced at her, then at the sky.

She nodded and turned at Abraham's approach. Isaac hefted the tent in his arms and went to secure it to one of the donkeys' backs. Rebekah hurried to Abraham and knelt at his feet.

Abraham touched her bowed head, then helped her to stand. She took his hand and kissed it.

"Thank you, my father. I will miss you." A pang of regret filled her at the sadness in his gaze. "But surely we will return soon. And you must travel to visit us."

Abraham squeezed her hand, pulling her close into a fatherly embrace. Emotion rose at his touch. The faint scent of garlic clung to his skin as his strong arms held her. How she missed her own father in this moment!

"I will miss you too, Daughter. But my son has work to do, and he is restless to be off." He held her at arm's length, then released her.

"You must tell me more about your wife Sarah and Isaac when he was a boy next time we visit. I want to know everything about him."

He gave her a quizzical look, his white brows drawn together. Then a look of understanding dawned, and he nodded toward Isaac, who walked among the donkeys, checking to see that all was in readiness. "My son will have to tell you some of that himself," he said. "There are some things in a man's past that may take him a lifetime to share."

The look he gave her made a shiver run through her.

"Are you willing to wait for him to speak, my daughter?"

She nodded, though she wondered if her actions betrayed the lie in her heart. She did not want to wait a lifetime to understand her husband, to know what made him fall silent and introspective, to understand what had happened to cause the strain between father and son.

"Perhaps it will not take a lifetime." She offered the words on the altar of hope, knowing by Abraham's look that her hope was flimsy at best.

He patted her shoulder as they both turned to walk toward the waiting donkeys. "Be patient, my daughter. It is all we can do."

She looked at him, realizing that he too waited for Isaac to come to terms with his past. To perhaps forgive? To be reconciled to the life they had now, the life that was obviously not the same as the one they had known when Isaac was a boy? But Rebekah knew that one could not go back and relive what was past. One could only move on from where they were today.

"Thank you for seeing us off, Father." Isaac came up beside her and met his father's gaze. "We are ready to leave." He looked at her and tilted his head in the direction of the waiting caravan.

"Yes, my lord," she said to Isaac, then bowed to Abraham once more. "Shalom to you, Father. Until we meet again."

"Peace be upon you both." Abraham rested a hand on her head again, then transferred it to Isaac's.

Isaac embraced his father, kissing each cheek. "We will soon return," he said, taking Rebekah's hand.

Abraham nodded his acknowledgment, but she did not miss the hint of moisture in his eyes. Would he live to see them again? She prayed so.

But as Isaac turned her toward the donkeys and the men and women waiting to join them, excitement filled her. They were heading off to start their new life—together as husband and wife.

They arrived in Beer-lahai-roi two days later to the sound of merriment and the sight of a handful of goat's-hair tents spread beneath the date palm trees of the oasis. Isaac recognized the colors of Ishmael's standard flying above a large black tent at the center of the tribe.

"Will there be room enough for us here at this oasis, my lord?"

Rebekah's question brought him up short. He had not expected Ishmael to be here at this time of year, though he knew his brother often revisited the place.

"Ishmael does not stay long," he said, guiding her donkey to the shade of the trees on the edges of the grasses.

"The tents belong to Ishmael, your brother?" Her face held an eager wariness, as though she couldn't decide which way to feel about meeting his infamous brother. "He is a fighting man, is he not?"

He looked at her.

"The servants talk, my lord. I cannot help but listen." She smiled, and humor lit her expression.

He chuckled. "Of course. And yes, my brother is a fighting man—a skilled hunter. He is a restless man, never stays long in the same place."

"Why is he here?" She glanced around her as if she feared to ask the question.

Haviv and his brother Nadab had led the servants to the edges of the oasis, awaiting his orders. Isaac looked toward the tents of Ishmael, the sounds of laughter and gaiety carrying to them, as though Ishmael's clan were celebrating something important. Curiosity rose, and he longed to know the cause. Perhaps Ishmael would explain when they met.

He turned back to Rebekah. "Years ago, long before I was born, my mother discovered she was barren. As it is the duty of women to provide their husbands an heir, my mother offered her Egyptian servant Hagar to my father to wife. My father listened to my mother and Hagar conceived. But all was not well between my mother and Hagar after that." He rubbed a hand over his beard, silently vowing again to never take a wife other than Rebekah, whether she bore him a child or not. It was not worth the turmoil his father and mother had suffered.

"What does that have to do with Ishmael visiting this place?"

Frown lines creased her brow, and he bent to kiss them away. She gripped the edges of his robe and kissed his mouth but quickly pulled back. "Finish telling me first." She looked beyond him toward the tents, and he followed her gaze. Three men strode toward them, staffs in hand.

"It is said that Hagar scorned my mother once she knew that she was pregnant, making my mother feel worse than ever. My mother lashed back by treating Hagar with . . . less than kindness for the service she was providing my parents. Hagar should not have scorned my mother, but she did not deserve the harsh treatment my mother gave her in return."

He drew in a long breath and released it. He did not enjoy relaying such stories. His mother was a good woman, and he had tried many times to understand how she might have felt. But he could not help the hint of sympathy he felt for Hagar just the same.

"What happened to Hagar?" The men were drawing closer, and Rebekah's question sounded rushed, as though in an attempt to hurry his words.

"She fled. She ran off alone into the desert and nearly died of thirst and hunger. We think she was headed back to Egypt, where she came from, but when she discovered this oasis, she stopped, thoroughly spent. She had no strength to reach the dates in the tops of the palms or retrieve water from the well. She waited for death."

"How awful!" Rebekah pressed a hand to her mouth, the story clearly troubling her. "But surely that is not what happened, as Ishmael lives to this day."

"As does Hagar. She was sent away with him from my father's camp when I was a small boy. But that is a tale for another time." He gauged the distance, seeing the men were almost upon them. He recognized one of them as Ishmael's chief steward and looked quickly at Rebekah. "I will tell you the rest in fuller detail later. For now, I will tell you that this is where Hagar met the angel of the Lord and was told to return to my mother. The angel named Ishmael as he later named me, before our births. My mother always wished she had been allowed a visit from the Lord, but she did not hear from Him until many years later. I think Hagar's encounter changed all of them."

He touched Rebekah's shoulder. "Wait here."

Before she could respond, he strode forward, staff in hand, to meet Ishmael's servants.

* * *

Rebekah watched as Isaac conferred with the men from Ishmael's tribe, her heart beating thick with dread. What if Ishmael did not like her? During her life in Harran, she had heard rumors of the Ishmaelite tribes—men living in hostility to those around them. Though some of the stories contradicted each other, she wondered. Was Isaac safe from his brother—the brother who as firstborn should have been Abraham's heir?

She waited, trying not to fidget, her impatience rising. She strained to hear, but the men's voices were muffled and distant. They did not look angry, and in fact, the one man had smiled at Isaac's approach and all three had bowed to him, obviously recognizing him.

Her pulse skittered like a bird's fluttering wings, and she released a long-held breath when at last Isaac turned back toward her and the men left in the direction they had come.

"What did they say?" She jumped down from her donkey and rushed toward him.

He laughed, smiling into her eyes. "How impatient you are, my sweet bride." He placed both hands at her waist and gently lifted her off her feet.

She giggled. "Would you dance with me, my lord, here beneath the palm trees?"

"I would." His eyes held mischief. "But I will wait until we can join Ishmael's celebration." He set her down and bent close to her ear. "Or . . . you can dance for me later, alone."

She could not stop the blush his ardent words always evoked, but she playfully patted his arm, dispelling her embarrassment. "What does your brother celebrate? Does he welcome us? Will he . . ." She could not finish, the thought suddenly ridiculous. What did she care whether Isaac's brother cared for her? She was Isaac's wife. He would accept her, like it or not.

"Will he what?" Isaac lifted her chin to look into her eyes. "What troubles you, my love?"

"It is nothing." She shrugged. "Truly. It was silly to think of it."

"Obviously not." He waited, and she knew his patience would win her out.

She met his tender gaze, her resolve melting away. How could she think to keep anything from him? He read her thoughts too easily.

"I only feared that your brother might think you could have picked a better wife." She looked away, suddenly embarrassed again.

He tipped her chin toward him once more, and his eyes held hers for so long that she thought she might melt under the strength of his gaze.

"Never think such a thing. Promise me."

She nodded. "I promise."

He placed a gentle kiss on her lips. "What my brother thinks, what anyone thinks, does not matter. You alone are the one I love." He touched a finger to her nose. "Besides, you are wrong. My brother will love you." His smile reached his eyes, and he slipped his hand in hers. "But come. We must move and settle our tents, then we will go and meet my brother."

Rebekah's heart stirred with love for him, and peace settled over her. Isaac loved her. Isaac would protect her. Everything would work out fine.

❈

The sun had set over the camp, the evening meal was finished, and the remnants were tucked away before Isaac led Rebekah and a select number of servants toward Ishmael's tents. A large fire glowed at the center of the camp, and women danced, waving sistrums to the beat of timbrels and the melody of a reed flute, their colorful robes twirling about them as they circled the fire. A lone woman's voice rose above the din, clear and beautiful, her words poetic and joyous.

Rebekah took in the sight, mesmerized by the strange dance. This place was nothing like Abraham's camp. The women dressed in brighter colors—colors she would like to copy in her own weaving. Even the men wore bright sashes in their turbans, reminding her of the men of Harran.

The drumbeat quickened as they moved closer to the fire, and she glanced about, grateful for the press of Isaac's hand in hers. She felt Selima's presence close behind, and Haviv strode beside Isaac. They came to a stop near what could only be Ishmael's tent.

A man dressed in a colorful, flamboyant robe rose at their approach and motioned with his hand toward the drummer seated nearby. The music instantly ceased, and the man closed the distance between them. Isaac's hand fell away from hers as the two men embraced. Isaac kissed the man's cheeks, and he did the same in return.

Rebekah stood in silence, but her heart kicked over when Isaac turned and the man set his gaze on hers.

"This is my wife, Rebekah," Isaac said. "Rebekah, meet my brother, Ishmael."

"A pleasure."

Ishmael's intent look brought heat to her cheeks, and she quickly lowered her gaze, not liking the feelings he evoked.

"My, my, Brother. You have caught yourself quite a beautiful woman here. How did one such as you manage that?" Ishmael laughed, and Rebekah glanced up as some of the men in his camp joined him.

Were they mocking her husband? The heat increased, her blood pumping fast.

"God sent her to me. She is a cousin, a niece of our father's from Paddan-Aram." Isaac stepped closer, placing a protective hand at the small of her back.

Ishmael rubbed a hand over his bearded jaw, but the mirth did not leave his eyes. "How fortunate that you found her first."

His eyes held a gleam of interest she did not want. She returned it with a glaring one of her own.

"I daresay she has some spark in her as well. It's a wonder you can keep her in check."

"And where is the wife God has given you, my brother? I can see your sons sitting about. Perhaps she would like to meet Rebekah as well."

Of course, Isaac would expect her to sit with the women of Ishmael's camp, but Rebekah had no desire to leave his side. Not with this hostile brother mocking him. And yet she marveled at Isaac's ability to deflect the barbs.

"My mother chose a wife for me from Egypt, as you well know. Our father's God had nothing to do with it. But you would not agree with that, would you now, oh son of the promise?"

Rebekah stiffened at Ishmael's sarcastic tone, but Isaac did not flinch or seemed disturbed by it.

Is this the way you always greet your guests? She glared at Ishmael, but she did not speak the words.

A slow smile tipped Ishmael's lips. "I see I have angered your bride." Ishmael met Isaac's gaze. "I do not envy you the tongue lashings from that one." The two stared at each other a moment in silence, and Rebekah lowered her head, growing more uncomfortable with each breath.

She took a step back and crossed her arms, but his laughter only increased until he nearly choked with the humor of it all.

"I do not see what is so funny." She muttered the words, half hoping Ishmael could hear her but knowing her words were drowned out by his mirth.

She felt Isaac's hand at her waist, and he bent close to her ear. "If you speak, he will mock you," he whispered.

She met his gaze, expecting to read censure there, but he only acknowledged her with a nod. He knew what Ishmael was about but chose not to engage the man. Oh, that she could do the same!

"Come, Brother," Ishmael said, suddenly sober. "Join our celebration and tell me how you came about finding this cousin of ours." He motioned inside his tent, where a woman stood near the partition separating the men's open sitting area from the women's cooking and sleeping quarters.

Ishmael stopped near a number of plush cushions and bid Isaac sit, then waved the woman closer. "My wife," Ishmael said, as if that was the only explanation needed.

The woman looked Rebekah up and down, her mouth drawn in a strained line. Rebekah inclined her head once, acknowledging the woman, then glanced at Isaac. At his nod, she followed Ishmael's wife to the women's area. Selima followed, and Rebekah breathed a sigh, relieved for her maid's familiar company.

The evening wore on as the woman and her daughters served them fig cakes and wine, and though Ishmael's wife prattled on about the benefits of figs and their uses in healing, not just for food, Rebekah could not help listening to the male voices coming through the tent's partition. The men talked of sheep and the hoped-for rain, but Ishmael's mocking humor did not ease. Even his sons joined in the barbs, and Rebekah's skin prickled with every word.

Later that night as she rested beside Isaac, she could not

sleep and wondered how he could so easily put it all aside. She turned over once, twice, until he stirred.

"Is everything all right, my love?" His words were groggy, but he rose up on one elbow to look at her. "Try to rest. It will be morning soon."

"I cannot rest. How can you sleep after the way he treated you?" She could not shake the anger, even after Isaac had already assured her that Ishmael meant no harm. It was his way, and he wasn't likely to change.

"Ishmael has mocked me since I was a small boy, beloved. It is why my mother had my father cast him out. It is his hurt and anger that speak. Do you not see this?" His patient tone defused some of her anger, and she leaned into him, deflated.

"I am trying, my lord."

His arms came around her, and she rested her head against his shoulder.

"My very life usurped Ishmael's place as my father's only heir. And though my father loves him, Ishmael does not know it. Not in his heart where love is felt." He kissed the top of her head and stifled a yawn.

"I am sorry I woke you," she whispered, suddenly seeing Ishmael in a new light. All of the taunts and laughter now evoked a sense of pity, compassion even. "If only God could have chosen you both as sons of the promise and kept you both with your father."

"It was not meant to be," Isaac said, yawning wider this time.

He rolled onto his back, and she soon heard the sound of his even breathing as she pondered his words. Surely God had a purpose for Ishmael too. Only one could be heir to the promise, but God had spoken to Ishmael's mother and called him by name. Surely . . .

But Ishmael did not recognize what Isaac seemed to see so clearly. He was too blinded by his bitterness.

17

Rebekah followed the sound of the lone flute, its minor tones drawing her feet forward—a swallow in search of its mourning dove. The grasses where the sheep grazed were coarse, picking through the open sides of her leather sandals, but she walked on, a basket on her arm, and spotted Isaac sitting in the shade of a terebinth tree playing the haunting melody.

How he made the flute sound so much like the actual birds he mimicked, she could not begin to tell. The skill was one she admired, but since Ishmael's departure, the solitude Isaac sought to craft the flute not only confused but troubled her.

"There you are." She wove her way among the sheep and approached his side.

He set the flute among the grasses and looked up, his mouth tipping in a welcoming smile. "You were looking for me?"

"I have not seen you in days, my lord. Perhaps you enjoy the time alone, but I do not."

In the three months since they had settled in Beer-lahai-roi, she had rarely joined him in the fields. She'd been too busy with dying, spinning, and weaving the yarn from the wool he had shorn, supervising the servants, and showing specific women how to extract the dyes from the henna trees, pomegranate peels, nuts, and crocuses.

He patted the ground beside him and reached to take the basket from her. She handed it to him and settled her skirts around her.

"I planned to return home this evening," he said, lifting the basket's cloth cover and peering inside. "What did you bring me?"

She laughed. "Your favorite seasoned bread and some thick chunks of the sheep cheese I've been hoarding. I made it the way your mother used to. And some date cakes of my own creation."

Eliezer's wife Lila had gladly shared Sarah's recipes with Rebekah when they had stopped by during the sheep shearing several weeks back, but she enjoyed trying her hand at new dishes when they had the spices or fruits on hand to do so.

Isaac gave her a mischievous smile and lifted the contents from the basket. He bit off a hunk of the bread, then tore a piece from the other half and handed it to her. "I daresay my mother would be proud of your skills." His look grew more serious then, as if the mention of his mother still carried the weight of sadness. "As am I."

She felt the heat of a blush fill her cheeks, suddenly shy at his compliment. "Thank you, my lord." She looked at the bread he had handed to her and nibbled the end, then met his gaze.

Silence settled between them, broken only by the sounds of the sheep rustling the grasses, bleating here and there, and the birds squawking in the air above.

"Why do you prefer to spend so much time here, rather than let the servants stay with the sheep?" The question had burned within her during his absence.

He glanced at her, then looked into the distance where the sheep grazed.

"I am sorry, my lord. Perhaps I should not have spoken."

He looked at her and smiled. "Of course you should. I fear

that sometimes I am not the husband to you that you need." He glanced beyond her as if his admission were too painful to face. "I am used to often being alone."

She waited, knowing he wanted to say more, wishing he did not ponder every word he uttered. "What do you do when you are alone besides carve new instruments or study the plants in the desert?"

A sigh escaped him. "I think about God." He turned penetrating eyes on her. "I pray to understand Him through the things He has made. And I study the details of all that grows, and even the things that don't."

Her heart stilled with his words, and she wondered that he should be so introspective. "Has God met you here?" She glanced around, imagining she could see Him hovering nearby.

He shook his head. "Not in person. Though I have heard His voice."

Awe filled her and her eyes grew wide. "What does His voice sound like? And when did you hear it?" Why had he never told her this before?

"It was a long time ago. When I was a young man." He looked beyond her again, his dark eyes clouded as they often were when he shadowed his feelings.

"Do not pull away from me, Isaac. Please." She took his hand in hers. "Tell me." She rubbed circles along his palm and felt his breath release.

The silence grew so deep she searched to fill it, finding and discarding more thoughts than she could count, most of them not worthy of utterance. At last he intertwined their fingers and looked deeply into her eyes.

"I intended to tell you the story when I could show you where it took place."

"But I long to know it now. Please do not continue to withhold it from me, my lord. I can tell that it troubles you, that you wake in the night with a start and your breath comes too fast." She pulled his hand to her lips, kissing his fingers. "I would help you, but how can I do so if you will not confide in me? Should not a marriage be based on trust in one another?"

He nodded his agreement. "Yes, of course. The story is so long ago. It should not matter to us now."

"But it does. It is why you spend so little time with your father, is it not?"

He looked at her intently, and she feared he would not answer, but at last he gave a defeated sigh. He stood and pulled her up beside him, the food left beneath the tree. "Walk with me."

They moved together as one, his hand clasped tightly to hers. He said nothing as they passed several lambs that barely noticed their presence, until at last he came to one of the few rams among the flock. He stopped at its side, placed a hand on one of its horns. The ram stilled and lifted its head, and then as though recognizing Isaac's touch, it turned and looked at him.

"I owe my life to God, and to such a ram who took my place." He faced her, releasing the ram's horn. "Years ago, before my father married Keturah, back when my mother and father were happy together, when our home was filled with joy and laughter, God spoke to my father. At least that is how he tells it. I do not know. But I do not doubt him because God spoke to him again later. That is when I heard His voice."

Rebekah's breath caught. He gripped her hand, and they walked farther among the flock, Isaac touching a ewe here and a newborn lamb there.

"God told my father to take me up to a mountain, three days' journey from where we lived, and to offer his son, his only son whom he loved, as a sacrifice there on the mountain."

"The only son whom he loved? You?" Her heart kicked over at the hurt that flickered in her husband's dark gaze.

He nodded. "So he took me, along with Haviv and Nadab,

three days' journey to Moriah. When we neared the place God had told him about, my father left the servants and took only me farther up the mountain." He paused, ran a hand over his beard, and she knew the memory still pained him. He blew out a breath. "I carried the wood and my father carried the torch, but there was no ram to offer as the sacrifice. So I asked my father, 'Where is the lamb for the sacrifice?' and he said, 'God Himself will provide a lamb.' I did not understand until he had built the altar and then came toward me with the rope he had strapped to his belt."

Rebekah's pulse thumped harder, and she could not keep the horror from her expression. "What did you do?"

Surely he'd fought back. Told his father no. Run away. But as she searched his gaze, she knew he had done none of these.

"I knew in that instant that my father intended to bind me like an animal and place me on the stones and wood. I would die on that mount without ever seeing my mother again, without ever loving a woman or fathering a son. Either my promised birth had been a cruel joke, or God would bring me to life again. But I knew without question that my father intended to kill me. I could have stopped him, for I was stronger than he. But I did not have the will to do so. He would prevail because I would let him."

"But . . . why? Why not run away at least?"

Her own father's face flashed in her mind's eye, and she could not fathom him ever doing such a thing to her. She would have fallen at his feet and wept, begging him for mercy. Did Isaac plead for such a thing? She had heard the tales of child sacrifice on the altars of foreign gods and could never understand how a god could request such a thing. And how on earth could a father ever justify killing his child?

"Because I knew that God had commanded it. My father's heart was breaking with every step we took up that mountain. He was determined to obey what he did not understand, but he did not like it. His hands shook as he bound me. I could have overcome him with little effort."

But he had not made that effort. Rebekah tried to wrap her mind around the thought, but the horror of it still overpowered any rational conclusion. "What happened?"

"He tightened the rope around my hands and feet." His cheeks darkened as if the memory still shamed him. "And he lifted me onto the wood. The branches poked through the fabric of my tunic, stinging like nettles . . ." He choked and looked away. "I wanted to beg him for mercy, but my throat closed tight against the need to weep. I closed my eyes for the briefest moment, and when I opened them again, my father stood over me, weeping, his knife raised above me. 'Forgive me, my son,' he said, and then he readied the knife at my throat, raised it again, and quickly lowered his arm.

"I waited for the pain I knew would come, knowing my father would make the cut swift and deep so I would not suffer. But a loud boom startled him, and he dropped the knife in the dust beside the altar."

Rebekah released a breath she had been holding, though her heart continued to pound.

Isaac squeezed her hand. "That's when I heard His voice. He called to my father, saying, 'Abraham, Abraham!' My father called back, 'Here I am.' And the voice said, 'Do not lay your hand on the boy or do anything to him, for now I know that you fear God, seeing you have not withheld your son, your only son, from Me.' That's when we found the ram in a thicket. My father sacrificed the ram in my place."

Isaac had circled them back to the tree where the basket of food still lay. A trail of ants had found a piece of the cheese he had dropped, and Rebekah would have snatched it up and brushed it off if not for the pressure of Isaac's hand in hers.

He turned her to face him. "So now you know."

"Thank you for telling me." She touched his cheek. "Not

every man would submit to such a thing. Not every man would be a willing partner to what God intended."

"My mother did not see it that way." The shadow passed before his eyes once more. "Things were never the same after that. She could never forgive my father for putting my life in such danger."

"I might feel the same if it were my son," she said, suddenly wondering if God would require any other sacrifices of Isaac for their own future children. When they had children . . . Why had she not already conceived? She squelched the worry as he bent to kiss her.

"Then you can understand the struggles my family has faced since that day. It is why my father took Keturah, why my mother, though she loved him fiercely, could not forgive him."

She nodded. "Have you forgiven him yourself?" She sensed the truth but wanted to hear it from him.

He looked beyond her, and she feared she had lost him to his thoughts. At last he leaned down and scooped up the basket, brushed the ants from its side, and placed it in her arms. "I would like to think so, beloved. It is one of the many things I ponder when I am alone, when I am seeking God's face."

She reached up to kiss him again. "I shall pray that you find the answers you seek."

They walked in silence until the camp was within sight, then Isaac bid her home and returned to gather the sheep.

The morning before the Sabbath many weeks later, Rebekah awoke with the familiar monthly pains, sequestered in her own tent where she would wait out the week of uncleanness. A week she had seen every month since her marriage and now feared would spread on into a future of uncertainty. Surely she was being foolish to fear so soon. But she could not help herself.

She forced herself to stand, though she wanted nothing

more than to stay abed and moan in self-pity. Isaac would not come to her until her time had passed, and she would eat alone with the women of the camp. She would work as she always did, but she would not have the privilege of his touch, and she desperately needed him now.

The rustle of the tent's fabric door brought her out of her melancholy, and she walked to the basket where her garments lay folded into neat piles. Deborah poked her head around the corner from the sitting area into her sleeping quarters.

"You are up. Good. Let me help you with that." Deborah chose a fresh tunic and robe, then proceeded to help Rebekah dress.

Silence stretched between them, but Rebekah did not care to fill it.

"You are quiet today."

"There is nothing to say." Rebekah blinked against the sudden sting of tears, surprised at how bitter she sounded.

"Obviously there is or you would be able to say it."

"Am I so quick with my tongue that my silence means I finally have something worthy to say?" She looked at her nurse and did not like the sardonic smile touching her lips.

"My dear Rebekah, you are very seldom at a loss for words." She tied the belt at Rebekah's waist and bid her sit while she pulled the ivory comb from the basket of hair ornaments. "What troubles you?"

Rebekah winced as Deborah worked to pull through her tangled mass of dark hair. "How long did it take . . . how long were you married before you carried Selima?" She needed reassurance that there was nothing at all to fear.

Deborah twirled a strand of Rebekah's hair into a loose knot and pinned it atop her head. "Every woman is different, dear one. You have barely been married six months. You must put a child out of your head. Then it will come when you least expect it."

"Isaac's mother did not see it that way. She waited twenty-five years to bear him." She tilted her head to meet Deborah's kind gaze, her heart stirred with affection for her. "I will die if I must wait that long, Ima." She rarely used the motherly term for her servant, but Deborah had always been like a mother to her. Somehow the word slipped out unintended.

Deborah's smile held compassion, and she touched Rebekah's cheek. "Isaac is the son of the promise, is he not?"

Deborah waited and Rebekah reluctantly nodded.

"Did not Adonai promise Abraham many descendants through Isaac?"

Rebekah conceded the argument with another nod.

"Then what do you fear?"

Rebekah looked away. "I don't know. I just thought it would happen by now. And with Isaac . . ." Tears grew thick in her throat. "He can be so hard to talk to sometimes. If I had a child . . ." She let the words go unsaid.

"You think a child would replace the love you desire from your husband?" Deborah's gaze held no reproach.

"I do not know. Perhaps." She shook her head. "But I know Isaac loves me . . . it is just that I want to please him. He will make a good father. I know it."

Deborah smiled and took the pot of kohl from the cosmetic basket. She picked up a long, thin tool to apply it to Rebekah's eyes. "And in God's good time, he will be the father you so desire. Be patient and trust Him."

Rebekah lifted her head, allowing Deborah to dab the paint to the edges of her eyelids, just enough to enhance her appearance and make her dark eyes appear larger, brighter. "I am trying." And failing miserably. "But you never answered my question." She crossed her arms and met Deborah's gaze.

"What question was that, mistress?" Deborah shrugged as though she could not remember, though Rebekah knew for sure that she did.

She squelched her irritation. "How long did it take you?"

Deborah was silent for so long that Rebekah turned to face her, reading uncertainty and perhaps fear in her gaze.

"I did not wait long." She looked away, and Rebekah knew the answer was not complete. She touched Deborah's arm.

"Tell me what it is that you keep from me." She tried for a commanding tone, but the words came out more as a request.

"Some things are not meant to be shared." Deborah turned from Rebekah and hurried to the tent's door. "I must see what Selima is up to. Forgive me."

Rebekah stared after her, determined to discover what Deborah kept so secret.

18

Deborah managed to avoid another confrontation with Rebekah the rest of the day, though she knew her mistress would not allow her to keep silent for long. The time had come to speak the truth, or at least what she would tell of it. She could not tell all. What mother would admit to such a thing when it could shame her only daughter?

She stiffened her back even as she stirred the stew for the evening meal, listening to the voices of women fussing at children and men laughing where they sat in groups around the fire.

Please, Adonai, let Rebekah's tongue be quieted and her questions kept to herself.

She might be a servant, but she did not need to reveal everything just because her mistress wanted to know. Nuriah had not told Rebekah. Why should Deborah demean herself so?

She turned at the sound of rushing feet, startled by Selima as she came up beside her, breathing as though she had run halfway across the camp. She set the water jar in the dirt beside the fire and bent over, hands pressed to her knees to draw in air. "There you are, Ima."

Deborah set the stirring stick aside and cupped her

daughter's shoulders. "Slow down, my daughter. Sit and drink." She dipped a clay cup into the water and handed it to Selima. "Now tell your mother before you upset the whole camp."

Selima straightened and glanced quickly over her shoulder. "Haviv is back, and he and Nadab . . ." She paused, placed a hand over her heart. "They are fighting over me!" She sighed as though this was the best thing in the world, but Deborah's heart sank with the news.

"Fighting over you? Surely you are mistaken, my daughter."

They had clearly waited too long to give Selima in marriage, and now her imagination was running away with her.

"I am telling you the truth, Ima! I heard them."

"And just how did you overhear such a conversation? They did not throw fists at each other in front of you, did they?" She touched her chin and studied her daughter.

In her conversations with Lila, she knew the brothers did have their differences, but everyone knew it was Haviv whose heart was bound to Selima's. Nadab could not possibly want her too, unless he should do so to spite his brother.

"I was hidden by the tree line, and they could not see me from their place at the crest of the hill. I went to draw water at the wadi when I heard them."

"What did they say?" Deborah took the cup from Selima and refilled it. "Drink."

Selima obeyed, and the two walked to a corner of the cooking tent where the women were few.

"Nadab had just returned the day before Haviv did."

"Yes, yes, Rebekah told me that Isaac had sent them to check on different flocks and herds. In opposite directions."

"Perhaps they were already at odds before they left?" Selima's eyes grew wide, but her voice dropped to a whisper.

"They do not always get along. It is the way of brothers. Laban and Bethuel were no different." She thanked the God of Shem, blessed be His name, that her only child had been a girl, despite the circumstances of her birth.

Selima's look grew thoughtful.

"So, finish your thought, my girl! Your mother's bones grow old waiting for you to finish." She rubbed the small of her back to emphasize her point.

"Nadab said he had come back to ask Isaac for permission to marry. And Haviv says, 'Good, good, I am happy for you, Brother.' And Nadab says, 'I'm glad you feel that way, Brother, because I am asking to marry Selima.'"

"Is there another Selima in the camp?" Deborah scowled, trying to think, but could not recall another girl or woman that shared her daughter's name.

Selima paused and slowly shook her head. "No. I do not think so. In any case, Haviv says, 'Selima? My Selima?' He called me his, Ima! And then Nadab says, 'As far as I can tell, she is not yours yet, Brother. I thought you should know that Isaac is considering my request.'"

"He already asked Isaac?"

"That's what he said."

"What did Haviv do?"

Selima sighed. "I wanted to sneak closer to see, for all I could hear were grunts and the sounds of flesh against bone. I think Haviv struck Nadab. Do you think he will kill him?" Horror filled her gaze and she covered her mouth, swaying as though the thought had suddenly dawned on her.

Deborah caught her arm. "Brothers have killed each other over such things before. Was not the first murder done because of jealousy? The God of Adam, blessed be His name, banished Cain for killing Abel."

A sob escaped Selima's lips.

Deborah's grip tightened. "Come, my daughter. We must run to Isaac and tell him. Perhaps he can stop their fighting before it is too late."

Rebekah picked up the camp oven and hung it from a peg inside the women's cooking tent. The buzz of female voices filled the area, rising and falling as the women hurried to and from the central fire, taking food to their men. She turned at the sound of Selima's excited chatter as Selima and Deborah rushed past her toward the place where Isaac sat. What on earth?

"Deborah, wait!" She hurried after her maids, who did not stop despite her call. Something was wrong. She joined them as they came to a halt near Isaac's seat and bowed low.

"My lord, forgive us," Deborah said, rising to face Isaac. "But you must hurry to the wadi and stop Haviv and Nadab before they kill each other."

Rebekah gasped, and she looked to her husband.

Isaac began walking, acting more quickly than Rebekah had ever seen. "What are they fighting about?" he asked as the three women gathered their skirts and hurried after him.

"Nadab told Haviv that he had asked you for permission to marry my daughter, while everyone knows it is Haviv who has his eye on her. Why should the boy do such a thing?"

Deborah's comment would have made Rebekah smile if the situation weren't so grave.

Isaac did not respond, but his pace increased, and all three of the women had to run to keep up. They came at last to the outskirts of the camp, to the rise overlooking the wadi, where they spotted Nadab squatting in the dirt and no sign of Haviv.

Isaac slowed his approach and stopped at Nadab's side. "Where is your brother?"

Nadab tilted his head toward the wadi, and Rebekah raced Selima to the edge of the rise to look down at the moving water below. Haviv sat a good distance away, his back to them.

Selima started down the rise, but Deborah caught one of her arms, Rebekah the other. "Wait," they both said at once.

Selima resisted, but at Deborah's stern glance, she stilled. "Why? I must go to him to see if he is all right."

"And destroy the man's pride? It is already bruised. Come." Deborah pulled Selima away from the wadi, back in the direction of the camp.

Rebekah glanced once more at Haviv, who appeared to be fine, and followed. They walked in silence until they were out of earshot of the men.

"Why wouldn't you let me go to him, Ima? He needs me!"

"Yes, of course he needs you. But what man who is thinking straight wants a woman to see his defeat? They did not kill each other. That is enough. Let Isaac sort out the details between the brothers, and when Isaac comes with an offer from one of them, you will marry him and be done with it. If he gives you to Nadab, you will be glad you did not rush to comfort Haviv." Deborah's words came out winded, and Rebekah touched her arm.

"There is no longer a need to rush. Let us catch our breaths on our way back to camp." Rebekah turned to Selima. "Your mother is right. Listen to her."

"But I don't want Nadab."

"Pouting does no good, Selima. Pray. Trust Adonai to give you the man you want. Did He not do so for Rebekah?" Deborah looked at Rebekah, and the two exchanged a smile.

Selima nodded. "Yes. But it is very hard to wait for God to act."

Rebekah placed an arm around her maid's shoulder as they reached the edge of the camp. "It is even harder to wait for men to act. Pray, Selima. God works faster than men."

The words silently chastised her. She had her own praying to do and only hoped her words were true.

⁂

Isaac paused at the threshold to his tent, suddenly realizing that Rebekah could not join him this night. He had seen the shadow cross her face when she served him the morning meal two days ago, a reminder that her time was upon her. There would be no child this month, and despite his reassurances, the knowledge seemed to trouble her more with each passing day. Adonai must have something to teach them with the waiting, but Isaac's comments to that extent did not bode well with her. Why could she not simply trust?

He took the torch from its stand near the entryway and lit a clay lamp to carry inside. He turned at the crunch of stones behind him.

"May I speak with you, my lord?" Moonlight revealed the concern in Rebekah's eyes. "I would not ask if it were not important."

He studied her a moment, longing to pull her close, to touch the softness of her hair and to kiss the worry from between her eyes, but he did not broach the distance, unwilling to defile either of them simply because he could not restrain his desires. Only the foolish did such things and did not respect Adonai's plan.

"I cannot invite you inside—"

"No, I understand."

"Perhaps a walk?" He took the torch to light their way behind the row of tents where the trees grew tall and proud beyond them. He came to an outcropping of rocks, brushed some loose branches aside, and bade her sit. "I am glad you came. I assume you are curious about Nadab and Haviv."

"Yes." She folded her hands in her lap and looked up at him. The worry lines decreased, and her eyes held deep interest.

He set the torch in a crevice between two rocks, then braced himself against the trunk of a terebinth tree. "They did indeed fight over your maid Selima."

Her expression grew serious and she nodded. "She wants to marry Haviv."

Isaac rubbed a hand over his beard, contemplating this new piece of information. "Why would Nadab try to take the girl from his brother? Everyone in camp can see the way the two look at each other."

Nadab appeared more interested in mocking his brother and purposely inciting his wrath. The boy needed a woman to ease some of his wild streak.

"It is hard to say, my lord. Nadab may be jealous of Haviv. You do give Haviv more authority and responsibility." Rebekah shifted and smoothed her robes.

"Haviv is older. It is his right."

"And Selima is my maid. I can give her to you if I wish. They have no right to fight over her."

"I do not want your maid." He looked at her hard. "I have told you this."

She lowered her gaze, and he berated himself that he had hurt her.

"I am glad, my lord. Forgive me. I look too often for reassurance."

"There is nothing to reassure. I want only you, beloved."

She looked at him and he smiled, relieved to see her relax. He straightened and walked a short distance up the path, then turned back to her. "Her betrothal must be sealed at once." He leaned one hand against the tree trunk and looked at her. "Shall I give her to Haviv?"

Her smiled warmed him, and he had to fight the urge to take her hand, pull her into his arms, and hold her close.

"I am glad that you value my opinion, my lord. Haviv seems to be a worthy man. Selima would be pleased. But Nadab should also be given a wife. He has waited too long to choose one."

"I agree. But that decision should belong to his father and mother."

"Will Nadab cause trouble if he does not get his way with

Selima?" She placed both hands on the stone seat, her bearing stiff as if ready to pounce on Nadab should he even think to do such a thing.

Isaac wondered the same. He could not have these brothers continue to fight. "Nadab will respect my decision. If he does not, I will send him back to my father's camp."

She tilted her head, her look thoughtful. "That might be wise even before he can respond. Give him time to let his anger cool." She looked at him, sudden alarm creasing her brow. "Or plot his revenge. How much time does it take a man to get over a woman he loves?"

He regarded her. "To hear my father speak of it, he never does. But Nadab does not love Selima."

Had God's test never come, the love between his father and mother would not have been strained. He shook the thought aside and glanced at Rebekah, seeing compassion softening her gaze.

She rose and took a step closer. "I wish I could change the past for you, my husband."

He shook his head. "You cannot change the will of Adonai, my love. And we cannot keep Nadab from his anger. One of them will go away from this perhaps hating the other. They cannot both have her."

He studied her, finding her changing expressions far more interesting than the turn of a leaf or the intricate carvings in the bark of a tree. He suddenly wondered how he could traipse into the wilderness to be alone, away from her, to study the created things and how they grew, when the most amazing of all creatures stood before him within arm's reach.

"I will send word to Eliezer and Lila to seek a wife for Nadab." He closed the distance between them, bending his head toward hers. "I hope you know, dear wife, that I want desperately to kiss you right now." His breath fanned her face, and she laughed.

"And I wish you would, dear husband." She gave him a coy smile, then took a step backward. "But the teachings of Adonai—we do not want to break them." Uncertainty flickered in her gaze. "We must not do anything to anger Him."

Her worry sobered him, and he stepped back a pace as well. "No, of course not."

Though they had no written code or law that commanded they do one thing or another, the teachings of their ancestors Seth and Eber had given them plenty of instructions to follow. Were not the sacrifices themselves proof of the need to obey?

Shame heated his face that he had come so close to leading them both astray. To touch a woman in her uncleanness, even the most chaste kiss, might cause Adonai's disfavor. And though a sacrifice might be enough to cover their sin, Isaac knew better than to purposely disobey. He would do nothing to cause Rebekah to fear or to blame him for incurring God's disapproval.

"We should go back," he said, suddenly anxious to return her safely to her tent. He picked up the torch and motioned for her to go ahead of him. "When your week is passed, we will travel to Hebron together with Nadab to secure a wife for him. In the meantime, we will see to it that Haviv and Selima are wed."

19

Rebekah walked with Selima to the wadi the next day, trying to determine how to tell the girl of their decision. "I suppose there is only one way to say it."

Selima joined her at the river's edge, where they both dipped their jars and returned them to their shoulders. "Do you have good news, I hope?"

Rebekah leaned closer and lowered her voice. "Isaac and I have decided on a husband for you. We are giving you to Haviv this night."

Selima stopped midstride and faced Rebekah with an expression that seemed to change quickly from awe to excitement to worry. "This night? But, so soon?"

"It could not be helped, Selima. It is safer this way."

Though Rebekah had thought they might wait until week's end, Isaac had met her when she emerged from her tent that morning and proclaimed the wedding would be best completed now. He had spoken to Haviv after their discussion the previous eve and feared what Nadab might do if the girl was not safely in Haviv's arms by nightfall.

The thought spurred Rebekah to move back toward the camp. "Come. We have much to do."

Selima hurried to catch up with her. "Am I really to wed Haviv this night?" A giddy laugh escaped her lips. "I had hoped . . . When he found me with the injured leg, I think I loved him at once." Her eyes lit with delight. "There is so much to be done. Will we have a big celebration? Will you make the special fig cakes as part of the meal?" She paused in her chattering and stopped again.

Rebekah turned back, reading worry in Selima's gaze. "What is it?"

Selima's face flushed several shades of red, and Rebekah did not need her to speak to know what had entered her mind. She closed the gap between them. "You have nothing to fear. Haviv is a good man."

Selima nodded, but when she did not speak after several moments, Rebekah turned toward camp again. "Come. Isaac is going to announce your wedding at the morning meal."

She glanced back and smiled at Selima's stricken look. This was a good decision. It was time Selima had a man to please instead of her own wild imaginings. The reality would be nothing like what she had dreamed of in her infatuation with handsome and wealthy men.

It was time the girl faced that fact.

Isaac found Nadab still abed long after dawn had risen in the sky. He bent to rouse him and was greeted with a groan and a muttered curse. "Let me sleep." But as the man opened his eyes, he seemed to think better of his words. "Forgive me, my lord." He pushed himself to sit up, quickly closing his eyes again, and put a hand to his head. "Is it morning already?"

"How much wine did you drink last night?" Isaac glanced around the tent, looking for a jar of water and a cloth to dip in it to ease the man's headache, but the tent was sparsely furnished and the jar nearly empty.

"Not much." Nadab let his head flop back on the cushion and raised an arm over his eyes. "Am I late for something?"

Isaac sat back on his heels, studying the younger man. Nadab had always been the reckless sort, and perhaps more hotheaded than he should be. How well would he take the news Isaac was about to deliver?

"I need you to arise and shake the stupor from your head." Isaac walked to one of the tent walls and lifted the sides just enough to let light filter inside. He turned back to Nadab, relieved that the man was at last sitting up.

"You have come to a decision." Nadab's tone held resignation. "You are giving her to Haviv."

Isaac squatted at Nadab's side, searching the man's beleaguered expression. "Yes."

Nadab ran both hands over his face and shook his head as though trying to clear it. "I should have known. Haviv always gets his way."

"She is better suited to Haviv."

Nadab stared, unblinking. "You cannot know that."

Isaac stood, turning his back to Nadab. "You do not love her as Haviv does."

Silence followed the remark, and Isaac faced Nadab again, but Nadab would not meet his gaze.

"What do you want from me?" Nadab's tone did not hold its usual respect. Definitely time to send him to his father.

"I am sending you to my father's camp for a time. You will serve him until we can work things out between you and your brother."

Isaac offered a hand to pull Nadab to his feet, but he refused it. He rose of his own accord and walked to the chest where the nearly empty water jug sat, poured a small stream into his palm, then splashed the water onto his face and beard. He shook his head, letting the small droplets fly where they would, and faced Isaac again.

"What if I do not want to go?"

His eyes held a glint of something Isaac had not seen in him before. Resignation, yes, but resentment also lingered in the narrowed eyes and the slight clenching of the chiseled chin.

"Go anyway. Let your father seek a wife for you, and then we will discuss your return."

Nadab stepped away from Isaac and crossed both arms over his chest. "I do not need my father's help in choosing a wife. I am capable of choosing a wife on my own."

Isaac looked at his overseer and lifted a brow. "You might want to rethink those words."

Nadab's gaze still held defiance, but when Isaac did not flinch or look away, he at last lowered his head. "Forgive me, my lord."

Isaac watched the man for a moment. His rigid posture, despite the bowed head, belied the sincerity of his words. But Isaac chose to ignore what wasn't said. "Do as I ask and go to Hebron. Speak to your father and marry a wife. Things will improve when you do."

He turned and walked out of the tent, hoping Nadab was quick to obey his words.

The week ended with a sense of excitement. Saddlebags were packed, and Rebekah gave Selima last-minute instructions on caring for the household in her absence. "Don't let the servants grow lax in their work. The men still need feeding, and the garments still need to be finished for the Syrian caravan that should come through within the month." She touched Selima's arm. "I am counting on you and Haviv to keep things in order."

Selima's color heightened at the mention of Haviv's name, and she glanced toward the donkeys, where Isaac spoke with the girl's new husband. She nodded, her eyes wide with too much responsibility, and Rebekah feared the girl was still too young and inexperienced to handle all that was required of her in their absence.

"I will do all that you have said, mistress. I won't let you down." Selima's eyes took on a dreamy expression as she glanced once more in Haviv's direction.

"Marriage suits you well," Rebekah said, trying to draw the attention back to the task at hand. Perhaps she should leave Deborah with her daughter after all, to oversee things. But Isaac had been insistent that if Haviv should be his chief overseer, Selima must learn to do her part at his side.

Selima looked back at Rebekah and gave a sheepish grin. "Haviv is so wonderful. I cannot believe I am so blessed!"

Rebekah stifled the urge to sigh, suddenly wanting to hurry and leave. She grew weary of Selima's exuberance and the way she always managed to bring any conversation around to focus on herself. Perhaps in time Selima would mature.

Rebekah looked at her maid and forced a smile. "We will be back within the month. I will expect a full accounting of all that I have given you to do. Do you understand?" She hated talking down to the girl but at the same time wondered if anything she had said was getting through to her.

"Oh yes, I understand, mistress. I will do all that you have said. When you return, all will be well."

Selima looked so hopeful that Rebekah nodded, praying that her trust in her was not misplaced.

The journey took two days. Abraham's camp at Hebron came into view the morning of the third day as the sun fully crested the eastern ridge of the earth. Isaac stepped beside her and helped her dismount, then tied her donkey securely to one of the surrounding tree branches. He moved to walk into the camp but paused when she placed a restraining hand on his arm.

"What is it?" His look held concern, and she stepped closer, slipping her arm in his.

"I don't know. I'm . . ." She glanced toward the camp, where the sounds of women and children mingled with the scent of smoke from the fire. "What if Eliezer cannot find a wife for Nadab? And what if Haviv and Selima don't manage well without us? If Keturah does not control her sons, I don't know if I will be able to hold my peace. And—"

The words rushed out of her, but he placed a restraining finger on her lips. "Hush now. Slow down." He smiled, patting her arm. "You did not tell me you had so many worries about our visit. And here I thought I was the only one who wanted to throttle Keturah's sons." He laughed, and she joined him.

"She is not raising them well, and that is the truth of it." Rebekah sighed and glanced around, afraid one of them might be within earshot even now. She rose on tiptoe to reach his ear and whisper, "Do you suppose your father is too old to notice?"

Isaac kissed her cheek and leaned close. "Probably. In the future they will not be near to trouble us, so he probably does not think that his wife's teachings will make much difference."

"But surely he teaches them of Adonai." From what little she knew of her father-in-law, she could not imagine him neglecting that truth.

Isaac nodded, straightening. "He does. But he does not have the stamina to teach the things he ought. The sacrifices mean little to a boy who always gets his way."

She looked into his eyes, held captive by the intensity in his gaze, and knew that despite his mother's doting, Isaac had not been spoiled like Keturah's sons.

"You will make a good father." Her heart yearned toward him in that moment. Could he read the love in her expression? How she wished she could give him the news that he would be thus blessed.

He bent low, his lips hovering over hers, his dark eyes probing. "And I could pick no better woman to bear me sons." He kissed her, a gentle touch that lingered until she felt herself melt in his arms. He slowly pulled back, the fire igniting in his gaze. "How you tempt me, dear wife." He smiled, and she wrapped her arms around his waist.

"I wish we could spend every moment together. I would leave everyone else to be with you."

She knew in that instant how much she wished he would agree. To escape the men and women in both camps, to go together into the wilderness and be everything to each other. They would need no other. She would fulfill his every desire, and he would be all she needed.

He looked at her, and she sensed he would not soon forget her words. "We will visit the wilderness soon, beloved."

"Just the two of us?" A little thrill rushed through her.

He smiled. "Just the two of us."

20

Rebekah's arms ached from working the millstone, the pain and stiffness moving to her neck and back. She tuned out Keturah's endless chatter and wished for the hundredth time that the woman would stuff a date in her mouth and be quiet, or go off with her unruly sons into the fields to glean the wheat. Instead she had chosen to stay with Rebekah and Lila to grind the threshed wheat and prepare the bread for the evening meal.

"It has been good to have you with us this past month," Lila said, bending close during a short lull in Keturah's monologue. "Does Isaac plan to make Hebron his home from now on?"

Rebekah met Lila's gaze, admiring the peace the woman displayed. No lines along her brow betrayed her cares, and even her smile reached her eyes. "Isaac has not made any firm decisions. We had only intended to stay to help see Nadab settled with a wife, but plans do change sometimes."

Lila nodded, but Rebekah glanced at Keturah's too-interested expression and determined to hold her tongue. She did not trust Abraham's wife, and the less she said, the better.

"It is good that Nadab agreed to marry," Lila said, her eyes flickering with the slightest hint of sorrow. "I hope they are content with each other."

"Too bad for you that he didn't choose one of Abraham's maids." Keturah's unwanted comment and sarcastic tone made Rebekah cringe, but Lila did not seem ruffled by the woman's words. "Don't think I am not aware of your true feelings in this."

Lila faced Keturah. "We appreciate your recommendation of a wife, Keturah. I am sure your cousin will make a fine wife for our Nadab."

Rebekah rolled her shoulders and straightened, trying to ease her tense muscles. Did Lila really believe that Keturah's Canaanite cousin would make a good wife for Nadab? But Nadab had wanted nothing to do with the maids in Abraham's camp who worshiped Adonai. The thought saddened her. How hard for Eliezer and Lila to watch a son follow the way of their pagan neighbors. Had the man married the girl out of rebellion because he had lost Selima? All the more reason Rebekah was grateful they had given Selima to Haviv.

"Isaac has done a good job overseeing the wheat harvest."

Rebekah turned at Lila's attempt to change the subject. "He enjoys God's creation and seems to have a knack for caring for things that grow from the earth."

"Eliezer tells me that this is the biggest harvest they have yet seen. Adonai has surely blessed your husband."

Keturah noisily stood and gathered the ground flour in her skirts, then took it to the cooking tent to be kneaded into bread.

When she was out of earshot, Rebekah released a deep sigh. "That woman gives me a headache." She glanced in the direction Keturah had gone. "I am sure she does not take kindly to talk of Isaac or his accomplishments."

"I'm sorry. I should not have brought it up."

"No, do not worry. She would have made things worse talking of Nadab and his bride."

Lila nodded, her dark eyes clouded. "It is hard to watch a

son harbor such resentment. But nothing his father or I can say will mend the rift between him and his brother. Even his sisters and older brothers here in the camp are distant from him."

"I am sorry for you."

If only she had given Selima to Haviv when they first arrived from Paddan-Aram. The girl was surely willing enough. Then Nadab would not have been tempted to usurp his brother's place.

"It is not your fault. When a man matures, his choices are his own. He must decide whether to love or hate, whether to hold resentment close to his heart or to forgive. Not even Adonai will force such a choice on us." Lila lifted the sieve in one hand and sifted the wheat, the soft flour separating from the hard outer shell and floating onto the wide woolen mat.

"He does not force us, but I daresay He is pleased when we love and forgive rather than hate." Rebekah looked to make sure Keturah was still visible through the open sides of the cooking tent. "Though some are harder to love than others."

Lila chuckled. "You will find no argument from me where that one is concerned." She met Rebekah's gaze with a smile. "Sarah was much different."

"Tell me about her." Rebekah's heart gave a strange tug, the longing for her own mother suddenly vivid and strong. How she would have enjoyed knowing Isaac's mother, sitting beside her at the loom or fretting together over the men they loved.

Lila smoothed the mound of flour with one hand, then tossed another handful of ground grain into the sieve. "Sarai—Sarah as you would have known her—was a strong woman. She was beautiful and loving, very giving to those of us who lived in Abraham's camp. Her only failing was her impatience in waiting on Adonai to fulfill His promise of a son. But then, twenty-five years is a long time to wait."

Rebekah nodded. "How hard that must have been for her."

She had heard the stories of Isaac's promised birth and imagined more than once what his mother must have gone through.

A pang touched her heart. Would she be forced to wait as well? But that was ridiculous. They had only been married seven months.

"Indeed it was." Lila looked beyond their grinding area toward the trees circling the camp. "But of all the trials she faced waiting for Isaac to finally be born, they were nothing compared to the pain she felt, the betrayal she imagined, when Abraham nearly sacrificed his own son. She was never the same after that."

Lila's gaze swung back to meet hers. "You must understand, Sarah loved Abraham." She lowered her voice, glancing toward the cooking tent as though fearful that Keturah might overhear. "Even to the day she died. But she could not look at him again without seeing Isaac bound with rope and laid on an altar, and though Isaac would tell you he did not scream or beg for mercy, Sarah often woke in the night screaming after that day. I think if Adonai had put her to the same test, she would not have passed it."

Rebekah paused in turning the millstone, Lila's words resonating deep within her. If Adonai were to put her to such a test, could she lift a hand against her son? She shuddered to think it.

"Why do you think God asked such a thing? After all of those years waiting for the promised son, then to ask his father to sacrifice him? It makes no sense." She still cringed whenever she imagined the story, and a sense of horror filled her every time Isaac woke with a start, coated in sweat.

"Who can understand the mind of Adonai?" Lila shrugged, but by the look in her eye Rebekah knew she had pondered the question much.

"Surely you have an opinion. Did Abraham ever explain it to Sarah?"

Lila's smile was sad. "He did. Many times. He had almost convinced her too."

"Convinced her?"

"Of what he believed. He told her that if God had wanted him to kill Isaac, then God must have intended to raise the dead, because Isaac was the son of the promise. All nations would be blessed through Isaac. So even if he had died, God would have raised him to life again." Lila laid the sieve to the side and lifted the four corners of the mat, pulling the flour into a neat bundle to add to the evening's baking. "He could not have done what he did without believing that."

"Sarah did not agree with him?"

Surely Isaac's mother trusted Adonai. The stories told of her extolled her for the faith that allowed her to bear Isaac when she was long past bearing age.

Lila shook her head. "No . . . that is . . ." She blew out a breath. "Sarah always struggled with the idea of the promise. Her faith was never as strong as Abraham's, though she did have such faith. She just could not see as far into God's plan as he did. She could not imagine Isaac rising from the dead because she could not imagine him dead in the first place."

"That makes sense." Rebekah looked behind her at the sound of female voices coming closer. "The women have returned from the field."

Lila glanced in the same direction, then tilted her head toward the sky. "The sun will be setting soon. We can finish the grinding another day."

Rebekah scooped the last of the wheat kernels and poured them back into the clay jar. They had enough flour ground for the flatbread that would accompany the evening meal. But as she worked alongside Keturah in the cooking tent a short time later, she could not help but wonder why Abraham had taken the woman to wife. Why not work harder to mend things with Sarah? Or had Isaac's mother grown so inward, so focused on Isaac, that she could no longer see her husband? Had the woman traded the love of her husband for the love of her son?

She vowed in her heart that she would never do such a thing. Isaac was such a perfect match for her. Even a beloved son would not change her feelings for him.

❊✢❊

The time in Hebron lasted longer than Rebekah expected or appreciated. Though she enjoyed Abraham's company, she quickly grew weary of Keturah. Three more months had passed, nearly a year since her marriage, and still she had no child. And Isaac had yet to keep his promise to take her to the wilderness, where she could be completely alone with him.

She strode to the field where she knew she would find him among the sheep, determined to convince him to leave Hebron. She spotted him near the water's edge, his arms draped around a young ewe.

She stepped closer. "Is she hurt?"

Isaac was stripped to the waist, the ewe dripping wet in his arms. His skin glistened from the sun and water, and her heart yearned to feel those strong arms wrapped around her.

He looked up, struggling with the ewe, and rubbed his hand over its gray wool. "She followed her mother too far from the flock and fell into a mud pit. It has taken the two of us"—he nodded toward one of his shepherds—"half the morning to find her and clean her up."

Rebekah glanced at the sky. The spring rains had brought a recent downpour, which would have filled the wadis and low-lying places. "I am sorry to hear it."

She stepped closer as he moved from the stream and set the ewe among the grasses. The lamb shook the water from its coat, spraying Rebekah's skirts. She laughed, and Isaac drew up beside her and lifted her in his arms.

"What brings my beautiful wife to visit me here today?" He kissed her cheek, his breath tickling her ear.

She smiled, warmed by his nearness. "I was missing you." She lifted her head and glanced above her at the blue expanse. "And the camp can be stifling sometimes." She did not want to complain, not after seeing such delight in his eyes.

Isaac's look grew thoughtful. He undid the girdle at his waist and pulled the tunic over his chest, then walked over to a low-hanging branch and retrieved his robe. He came toward her again, tying the belt as he walked.

"You are finding Keturah difficult?" He draped an arm around her shoulder and walked with her among the sheep, stopping to inspect one here and there, allowing her time to frame her response.

"I find her difficult, yes. She harbors anger toward you, I think." She looked up as his gaze swept over her. "Must we stay here, my lord? I would not begrudge you time with your father, but I daresay even that is strained with Keturah's sons always underfoot."

Isaac drew in a slow breath and released it, then ran a hand over his beard. "I have been trying to give my father more time, beloved. I know I promised to take you to the mountains. I did not expect my father to need me so."

"He has Eliezer and Keturah's sons."

"Eliezer is a servant, though a beloved one. Still, I am his heir. My father is planning to send Keturah's sons away soon."

"Even the young ones? They are just children!" The thought appalled her. "How would they fare without their mother?"

"Not the youngest sons. The two oldest, Zimran and Jokshan."

"But they are barely men."

"They are old enough and trouble enough. This is why Keturah is angry. She wants to go with them, to take all of her sons with her. My father has refused her." Isaac paused and turned to face her. "Try to be patient with her, Rebekah. We will leave here soon enough, after the rains have passed. But we will return again from time to time. You must learn to get along with her."

The quiet reprimand stung.

"Do you think I have not tried? She is sarcastic and unkind in her comments. She treats Lila with contempt. She is worse than Laban's wives combined."

Though in truth, Laban's wives were nothing like Keturah. They had always deferred to her as Bethuel's only daughter.

"I did not mean to offend, beloved." He touched her cheek, drawing her eyes to look into his. "I do not know how else I can help you. We cannot leave until the rains end. Please try to find something good to like in her."

Rebekah lowered her eyes, humbled by his earnest plea. She had not truly tried to like Keturah. She had only kept a list of her failings, letting them mount up, knowing she would soon be free of the woman. But if they were not going to leave for at least three more months . . . The thought grated, but she could manage to avoid confrontation for at least that long.

"I will try, my lord. But she does not make it easy to do so." She leaned in close. She could learn from his example. Surely she could be kind to Keturah, if only to please him.

21

The spring rains turned to summer's drought, and the seasons passed too quickly. Isaac and Rebekah moved from Abraham's camp in Hebron to Isaac's favorite Negev near Beer-lahai-roi. Keturah's sons grew to manhood, and Abraham sent them with gifts to the east, away from Isaac, until the last remained. Keturah finally gained Abraham's permission to leave and accompanied her youngest to settle in the mountains of Horeb.

Abraham grew old and came to live with Isaac and Rebekah. And still Rebekah remained barren, her worst fears realized. The trips to the mountains alone with Isaac did no good, the herbs Lila and Deborah prescribed brought about no child, until Rebekah despaired that she was destined to bear a child in her old age like Sarah had done. The thought brought little comfort.

Rebekah rose stiffly from the small stool where she sat before the loom, setting her work aside. Her time had come upon her again, and the very thought brought a pang of emotion so strong that her throat ached from unshed tears. She should be used to this by now, be resigned to her plight, but after twenty years of waiting, she could no longer hang on to her fragile thread of hope.

She moved from the weaver's tent into the sunlight, searching the camp for some sign of Isaac. He would be in the fields or with the sheep most likely, unless he had stayed to keep company with his father, something he did more often since Keturah's leaving.

She walked across the compound beneath the swaying palm trees toward Abraham's tent, the summer's heat warming her beneath the soft linen head scarf. The tent's sides were rolled up, and she saw Isaac sitting with his father, their voices too far away to hear their conversation. At her approach, Isaac stood and came toward her.

"What is it?" His look held concern, and she knew he could read the emotion in her face.

"I must speak with you, my lord." She glanced toward Abraham, whose interest had piqued as she neared his tent, his lined face wreathed in a smile.

Isaac looked from her to his father, and for a moment she feared he would ask her to stay and visit with him. "Father, if you will allow it, I will return to you this evening."

Abraham grew serious, and he nodded his understanding. "Take all the time you need, my son. I know you have much to attend, and it is time I rested these old bones." He reached for a large cushion and did not attempt to rise to move into the sleeping area, but just leaned back on the pillow and closed his eyes.

Isaac led her away from the tents to walk among the trees, their sandals creating soft footfalls among the grassy knoll.

"What troubles you, beloved?" He stopped near one of the largest date palms and turned to face her, his turbaned brow knit with concern.

"You once made a vow to me . . ." She paused, unable to hold his intense gaze. "I do not want you to break it."

He waited for her to finish her thought, but she could not speak past the lump in her throat. She looked at him, silently begging him to read her heart. His eyes were dark, probing, and she could not stop the tears at the compassion in his gaze.

"You fear I will take another wife?"

She nodded. "Is it not obvious that I am barren? Nothing I have tried has brought about a child, not the herbs in Deborah's medicines or Lila's remedies, and even time alone with you has not given what we desire. If God has promised you an heir, as He did through your father, perhaps I am the one to blame. Perhaps the promise is not meant for me."

He placed a finger on her lips, making no attempt to keep from touching her in her uncleanness.

She took a step back. "Please, my lord . . . We must offer a sacrifice . . . We must not displease Adonai . . ." Her words broke off, and she put a fist to her mouth to stifle the urge to weep. Had she somehow already sinned in such a way as to cause her barrenness? If Isaac took another wife, they would know for certain, they would confirm that she was at fault . . .

"I will not break my vow to you, Rebekah."

His quiet words coaxed her to look at him again.

"I will die without an heir before I take another wife while you live. And I pray that you will live long after I rest with my fathers. We have many years ahead of us, beloved."

"It has already been twenty years since our marriage!" Her tone held the edge of despair. As a young woman of twenty, newly married, she had expected, had dared to hope, she would not be like Isaac's mother had been. Now her fortieth year was nearly upon her, and though she was still far from middle age, she had lost all hope.

He took her hand in his and held firm, despite her attempt to pull away. "Adonai will not fault me for comforting you, my love. He is a God of mercy and patience, and His love is everlasting."

"But I am unclean." Her voice dropped to a whisper.

"And now I am too until evening. But are we not all unclean in His sight?"

His soft touch on her chin made her shiver, but the feeling was one of relief and joy.

She dried her tears with the edge of her scarf. "What are we going to do?"

If he would not take another wife, they would have no children—unless God intervened and granted their hearts' desire.

Isaac looked into the distance, then pulled her close until she rested her head on his chest. She felt his steady heartbeat and his even breathing. His tender action made the tears surface again, and she wept in his arms. He held her still until at last she quieted.

"This is what I will do for you, my love. For us." He tipped her chin to look into his eyes. "I will take you to the mountains again, to the mount where my father bound me, and there I will pray."

He held her at arm's length, and his tender gaze stole her breath. In all of their years together, he had never taken her there, despite his early promise to do so. They had not spoken of his binding since the day he told her the story soon after they had wed. Even when the dreams haunted him. Even through the strained relationship with his father. She had known he would deal with the matter in his own way, in his own time.

Was now the time? Would the journey there free them both from the burdens that held them?

"Thank you, my lord." She smiled, though the effort was tremulous.

He bent closer and placed a soft kiss on her lips.

"When do we leave?" she could not help but ask, amid the swell of hope rising inside her.

He gave a smile in return, but it did not reach his eyes, and she knew in that moment that this trip would cost him more than a simple prayer. Would he sacrifice his memories and pain on God's altar?

"When your time has passed. Then we will go." He turned in the direction of the camp.

As she watched him go, she saw the slightest sagging of his shoulders, and she suddenly wished she had not laid her troubles at his feet. But if not his, then whose? She had no other choice.

Isaac dug his staff into the earth, each step of the climb up the mountain harder than the last. He glanced behind him to be sure Rebekah followed close, but she did not notice his struggle as she tried to avoid the brambles and sharp weeds dotting the rock-hewn path. The area was one that wild gazelles and goats and jackals trod at various times of the day or night, but there was little evidence that men had spent much time here. Had God somehow preserved it since that long-ago day when his father walked with him here?

He had been glad of Haviv's company on the three-day journey, and grateful Selima was not heavy with child and was able to accompany Rebekah. Deborah had been more than pleased to spend time with her three young grandchildren. And Isaac needed Haviv's support, though in truth, he sensed that Rebekah would have been pleased to be alone with him. She had her wish now, as they had left the other couple where they had camped the night before. Only Rebekah would join him as he walked farther on. He could not bear to share the memories with another.

He reached the top of the ridge before she did, and his heart gave a little kick at the sight. He moved closer, each footfall heavier, until he came to the rock-hewn altar, its rough construction only partially broken down, the stones having barely shifted with the passing years. He clung to his staff, the effort sapping what little strength he still possessed. The night had not passed easily—his sleep restless, the dreams unceasing—and he awoke long before dawn, unable to risk closing his eyes once more.

"Is this it?"

Rebekah's soft voice held a reverent tone, and he turned, catching the awe and horror mingled equally in her large, luminous eyes.

"Yes." He forced a steady breath and took her hand. "Come." He managed to lead them closer until he stood at the edge where the trench around the altar was no longer visible, the winds of time having filled in his father's painstakingly slow attempts at its construction.

The wood had burned with the ram who had taken his place, and the only evidence of its having been used in the sacrifice was the blackened stones scarred across the altar's top. Rebekah reached a hand to touch the surface and lifted a coated finger to her lips. She sniffed, then kissed the spot and bent to rub it clean in the surrounding grasses. She faced him and slipped her arms around his waist.

"This is a sacred place," she said, resting her head against his chest. "This is where you heard God's voice."

He closed his eyes and let her words register in his heart. He heard again the urgent thunder clap, the trumpet sound of God urgently calling his father's name, insisting he stay his hand. The voice that had saved his life. Adonai, who had never intended his death, only his father's obedience.

The truth hit him with a force that made his knees suddenly weak. Then slowly, as if waking from a dream, he disentangled Rebekah's hold on him and sank to the earth at the base of the altar.

O God, Elohim Adonai Eloheynu Echad, my Creator, my Lord, my God, my King. You did not abandon my soul to the grave. You did not intend to see my destruction that day.

His hands splayed before him, his mouth tasted dust.

Forgive me. I have blamed my father, I have blamed You, but I did not understand. I did not see . . .

Emotion rose, a deep well within him begging release, until he could no longer hold back the tears. He was vaguely aware that Rebekah had knelt beside him, heard her tears mingling in a duet of sorrow with his own.

Bitterness rose like bile within him. *Father, what have I done to you?*

He had not forgiven him soon enough, had allowed his mother's anger to harbor his own. How had he not known it before now? Guilt came in waves, but as the wind shifted, he sensed it taking the pain with it.

I am not worthy.

And yet God had spared him. God did not hold his sins against him.

He rose to his knees, studying each stone his father had carried, had laid one atop the other. Their symmetry did not match, but they had remained fitted together well and strong as though they were meant to remind him, to help him see the truth in the testing. What he had considered betrayal had carried a far deeper meaning, and he sensed he would not understand it fully in this life. But it was time he faced his past and accepted the lesson it carried.

"You are worthy of honor and glory, Adonai." He whispered the words, his voice hoarse against his spent emotions. He looked at Rebekah, her eyes bright as though their shared grief had somehow changed her as well. "You have given us Your promise, that all nations will be blessed through the seed of this woman whom You have given to me." He reached for her hand and gently squeezed. "And now, O Lord God, please hear my prayer and grant this desire of our hearts, grant the answer to what You have promised. Give my Rebekah a son."

He lifted their joined hands toward the heavens, then

released her fingers and raised both arms over his head in praise. Peace as he had never known filled him, and he felt the feather-light touch of joy in his spirit. Rebekah's voice rose beside him in the quiet cadence of song, its clear tones making even the birds stop to listen. Isaac joined her, the song new yet familiar, one he had learned as an adult yet had known all of his life.

A song of praise to Adonai.

Part 3

Isaac prayed to the LORD on behalf of his wife, because she was barren. The LORD answered his prayer, and his wife Rebekah became pregnant. The babies jostled each other within her, and she said, "Why is this happening to me?" So she went to inquire of the LORD.

The LORD said to her,

"Two nations are in your womb,
and two peoples from within you will be separated;
one people will be stronger than the other,
and the older will serve the younger."

Genesis 25:21–23

The boys grew up, and Esau became a skillful hunter, a man of the open country, while Jacob was a quiet man, staying among the tents. Isaac, who had a taste for wild game, loved Esau, but Rebekah loved Jacob.

Genesis 25:27–28

22

Rebekah sat up with a start and clutched her bulging middle. The action roused Isaac, and he rose up on one elbow, his heart beating too fast. "Is it the babe?" The question seemed ludicrous even to his untrained mind. What else could it be? "What can I do?"

She stroked her sides and whispered cooing sounds, but even through the thin sheet, he could see the babe's kicks causing her skin to move as though a war were being fought within her.

"He is a strong one." She winced, and his heart constricted with her agony.

"Is it painful?"

She nodded, then shook her head. "Not painful in a way that I fear he will be born too soon," she said through a clenched jaw. "But he does not sleep. Even in the day"— she gasped—"it is as though he cannot find a comfortable position to rest." She turned her face to him, and he could make out the tears through the dim light of the flickering oil lamp. "I don't know what I'm doing wrong. Is God punishing me somehow?"

He drew her as close as the babe would allow and pulled her head against his chest. It was a question he had asked himself many times in the months since God had seen fit to bless them. Never in his years had he seen a woman so torn by pregnancy. Keturah's sons had caused her little distress, and Selima seemed to birth children on top of one another without a struggle.

Why, Adonai, have You given my Rebekah such grief?

"It is not your fault, beloved. I only wish I could take this from you and carry it in your place."

She laughed, though it came out garbled by tears. "You would look mighty strange, a man carrying a child within him." She cradled her belly and spoke softly. "There, there, my sweet child. Rest now and let your mother sleep."

She snuggled closer against him, and within moments he heard her soft breathing. She seemed to rest better in his arms, and he gladly allowed it if only to give her peace but a moment. But his own sleep was long in coming, and he worried not for the first time what kind of son would be born to him, what kind of son could bring such turmoil.

Rebekah paced the confines of her tent, her legs barely carrying her from one side to the other. She pressed both hands against her protruding middle, stroking and speaking softly, quietly begging her unborn son—for surely it was a son—to still long enough to give her a moment's rest. Since she had first felt the stirrings of his life, he had not ceased to shift and kick and roll until she thought she would scream for the frustration of it! Why was this happening to her?

Neither Deborah nor Selima, nor any other woman in the camp, had experienced such agony so early in her pregnancy. The pains didn't come upon a woman until her travail, which for Rebekah was still two months away.

A little cry escaped her, and she stuck a fist to her mouth to stifle the sound. It would only frighten the camp if she screamed as she wanted to. And she feared, always feared, it would somehow harm the babe.

She sank onto the cushions, spent from her pacing, but the movement within her would not cease.

Oh, Adonai, what wrong have I done?

If only He would answer.

Unable to sit still, knowing the only way to get any relief was to walk, she rose on shaky legs and left the tent, making her way to the edge of the tree line where Isaac's altar stood. Should she ask Isaac to offer a sacrifice on her behalf? Perhaps God would relent, allow the babe to rest, if she humbled herself in that way.

She stopped at the altar's edge and rested a hand on the blackened stones as she had done at the altar on Mount Moriah. God had heard Isaac's prayers for her there and granted the request for this babe. Oh, but she had never expected the result to be so hard!

She gripped the stones for support and sank slowly, awkwardly, to her knees, faintly wondering if she would be able to rise again with the burden of the babe so great. But she must humble herself, must do *something* to seek God's favor if she was to find peace.

She braced her hands on her folded knees, unable to lean close enough to touch her forehead to the dust as she had done that day on Moriah, and prayed that the One Who Sees Me would notice her here regardless of her posture, would somehow once again show His great mercy.

Oh, Adonai, why is this happening to me?

She waited, hoping against hope for an answer. But as the shadows lengthened and she could no longer kneel in her awkward position, she rose, defeated. Perhaps God did not hear the prayers of a woman.

She brushed the dirt from her robe and bit back the urge to weep. She must strive for strength to endure until the day came for his birth. There was nothing else to be done.

She moved away from the altar, then turned back for one more look and was startled at the sight of a man not unlike the one she had seen many years before, when Eliezer had come to take her to Isaac. The thought brought a swift pang of fear to her heart, and her knees nearly buckled beneath her.

"My Lord," she whispered, wondering that she could speak at all.

His look held such kindness, taking her fear and causing it to still within her.

"Two nations are in your womb," he said, his gaze never leaving hers, "and two peoples from within you will be separated; one people will be stronger than the other, and the older will serve the younger."

With that he vanished from her sight.

She blinked, not certain his presence had been real, and yet knowing it was. As with the first visit of the Lord many years before, she had not imagined this.

Two nations are in your womb.

No wonder she suffered so. There were two, and already they fought within her.

The older will serve the younger.

The thought troubled her. Such was not the way of things. And yet, was not Isaac the younger of his father's first two sons? God had chosen the younger. She must tell Isaac. And she would not forget God's word to her.

❖

"Praise be to the God of Abraham, blessed be His name! What a red, hairy son you have!"

Deborah lifted the child, wriggling and slimy, and Rebekah opened her eyes for a brief moment to gaze on her firstborn before another contraction bore down on her. The baby's cry split the damp night air, a joyous sound amid the ripping of Rebekah's insides as she pushed, seated on the birthing stool.

"Look, his brother has hold of his heel." Selima rested both hands beneath her, ready to catch the twin as Rebekah pushed. "He is almost out, Rebekah. Two more good pushes."

Rebekah groaned and cried out and fisted both hands while she bit hard on a linen cloth. But at last her months of anguish ended in a gush of baby, blood, and water. She leaned back against another maid's strong grip, sweat clinging to her.

After the women had cleaned her up, Rebekah moved to the softer bed of cushions and settled among them. She breathed deeply, in and out, relief flooding her that the ordeal and the many months of turmoil were finally past.

"Let me see them."

Deborah moved closer to her left, holding a cleaned, red, and hairy infant to her face, his angry fists clenched and his lips puckering in indignation in the dim light of the birthing tent.

Rebekah laughed at the sight of him. "Surely you have been the one causing most of the fighting within me all these months, little one." She met Deborah's motherly gaze. "He shall be Esau, my red and hairy one."

"And what of this child?" Selima's sturdy arms lifted the most beautiful child she had ever seen. "Your little heel grabber."

Joy filled her at the sight of him, and she took in the light brown skin and hair and the mewling mouth that looked for sustenance without a sound. Love for him surged in an instant, and she wondered how he had fared against his twin during their preborn battles.

"He shall be Jacob, he who grasps the heel." She held out her arms to take him from Selima. "My son." The words sounded as foreign as the truth that two sons of hers had now been born into the world. "You must tell Isaac that his sons are safely here."

Isaac. The thought of him made her warm with contentment, and she felt a strange glow fill her that his prayers for her, for them, had at last been answered. How good of him to take her to the mount of his suffering, to pray for a mere woman's request. And God had answered!

She looked up at the sound of the tent flap rustling. Isaac stood in the opening, moonlight bathing him in its ethereal light.

"What have you named them?" He took their firstborn from Deborah's arms, laughing at the child's boisterous, flailing arms and urgent cries. "I think he wants his mother." But he sat in the chair beside her and held him on his knee just the same.

"His name is Esau, and his brother is Jacob. If you agree, my lord." She lifted Jacob from her breast and handed him to Deborah, who switched boys with Isaac and handed Esau to Rebekah. Her milk had not yet come in full, but Esau suckled as though by working hard enough, he could force his own nourishment.

"He is an insistent one." Isaac held Jacob, but his eyes were focused on Esau. "Perhaps he was the cause of your misery." He smiled down at Jacob, who seemed completely docile and content to be held on his father's knee.

"They've been fighting to divide into separate peoples from the start." She smiled at the memory of God's messenger speaking the words of their future to her only two months before.

"Perhaps you are right," Isaac said, holding Jacob closer to his heart, but he did not look at her.

He had never fully accepted her vision, though she had spoken of it often enough. Why did he not believe her?

"In any case, they are here now." She looked down at Esau at last content in her arms. "You will be a strong man, little one." She glanced at Isaac, and he nodded his approval. "But your brother will be stronger." She looked away as she said the words, unwilling to face Isaac's response, fearing she would lose that approving smile.

"Thank you for my sons," he said, letting her comment stand silent between them. "And they are good names you have given."

She looked at him, relieved at the genuine love in his gaze. She smiled her response, letting the soft sounds of the newborns answer for them both.

23

Deborah moved among the tents, feeling the breezes of early fall lift the tree limbs up and down like waving arms. She cinched the scarf closer to her face and continued on, all too aware of the effect the chill had deep in her bones. She still walked upright and did not creak and groan like Lila and Eliezer or Abraham, but the signs of aging were close on her heels.

Life had fallen into a gentle rhythm since Keturah's parting, and Abraham often spoke to Deborah as she passed his tent, when the men were not around. She approached the broad awning now, where Abraham sat beneath a flapping overhang.

"Greetings to you, my daughter," Abraham said as she came to kneel near his side.

That he called a servant his daughter had at first made her think he had surely lost his eyesight, but after years of his so doing, she had warmed to the affection the word carried.

"And to you, my lord."

"You will never consent to call me Father, will you, faithful Deborah?" He smiled and patted the cushion near him, bidding her to sit. She complied, releasing a sigh at the effort.

She smiled, looking into his wrinkled face. "I'm afraid not, my lord. I am but a servant. But Rebekah is pleased to call you such."

They had had the same conversation more times than she could count, and the realization that his memory was not what it used to be always brought sorrow. But she did not show him what lay hidden in her heart.

"Rebekah is busy with those two grandsons of mine. She has little time for an old goat like me." He fingered the staff Isaac had long ago carved for him, examining the intricate lion's head at the slight curve in the top. "My son thinks I am like a lion. Ach! Those days passed long before he was born." He looked into the distance as though time had slipped backward and he could see what no longer existed.

"You are still a lion at heart, my lord. You are strong in your faith, in the God of Noah, of Shem, of Eber, and now Elohei Abraham, the God of Abraham." She picked up a cushion and looked at the threads, though she felt his eyes on her.

"It is your faith that has endeared you to my family, Deborah. You have passed that faith on to your daughter and grandchildren. You are truly blessed."

His words warmed the dark places in her heart, where the doubts lived. She looked at him but could not hold his gaze as the familiar shame surfaced. Shame she thought long past.

"I only hope Adonai Elohei accepts my faltering faith, my lord. I am unworthy of His notice." She looked down at the cushion again and played with a loose thread, wishing for a bone needle and thread to mend it. She expected him to agree with her or at the very least question her statement.

Silence followed her remark until at last she glanced up, fearing he had fallen asleep and not even heard her comment. But his clear dark eyes were focused on her.

"We are all unworthy, my daughter. It is only because of God's great mercy that we are not consumed." The lines around his eyes softened as he continued to look at her. "But I sense there is a reason you have made such a statement."

She studied the cushion, surprised at the intense emotion suddenly coming over her in waves. It had been years since she and Bethuel had spoken in confidence, since he had learned of her plight and taken her in, protected her. She had told no one of the circumstances of Selima's birth, not even Rebekah, who had at last given up asking. But something in Abraham's spirit reminded her of the kindness of Bethuel, and she did not realize until this moment how she longed for a confidante to replace him.

But could such an old man as Abraham, a man who had loved three wives, be trusted with a lowly servant's secrets?

"Will you tell me what troubles you, Deborah?"

"It is an old tale, one that does not matter any longer."

And in truth it didn't. It only mattered when Selima was still a maiden. Now that she had a husband, even Rebekah could not turn Selima away, though the news might cause a rift between them, just for the length the secret had been kept.

"Sometimes the oldest tales matter the most because the longer they are held within us, the more pain can gather to them."

She looked up at that and searched his aged face. Compassion etched his smile, though the lines around his eyes held sadness.

"You speak from experience, my lord?"

He laid the staff across his lap and folded his hands. "I have made many a mistake in my lifetime . . . many a mistake."

He lifted his head and looked across the circle of tents, where a woman chased a young toddler away from the fire and others took up their daily tasks and moved in the direction of the various tents for weaving, spinning, grinding, and the working of clay and straw. She should join Rebekah in the weavers' tent, but it was understood that time spent with Abraham was time well given.

"But my God has been ever faithful to forgive, to restore, to mend what was broken."

"How so, my lord?"

Everyone knew Sarah's heart had never quite mended after Isaac's binding. Keturah might have remained a servant if it had.

He looked into her eyes and patted the place over his heart. "He is faithful to heal in here, where faith lives. He would have restored and strengthened Sarah's faith in me, in Him, if she had allowed it. Our God does not force His will on us. We must receive and request it." His gaze grew intense. "What is it from long ago that you need our God to restore, my daughter? Tell me."

Deborah looked quickly around her, making sure they were alone, then scooted slightly closer to him. "I fear to tell you, my lord. I have feared to tell anyone since Rebekah's father Bethuel. He took the secret to his grave, though his wife looked at me sometimes as though she knew. Rebekah did not know, and I could not bring myself to tell her. I was relieved when she brought us with her here, away from Nuriah's scornful glances."

"So you have carried the burden alone all these years."

She nodded. "But it is really not so big a burden. It happened so long ago, I barely remember it now." She lifted a hand as though to brush the words away like a pesky insect. She should leave before she said more.

"But you do remember. Does the memory bring pain, my daughter?"

Deborah leaned away from him, searching her heart. She closed her eyes, the memory of that day flashing in her thoughts.

Samum, a wealthy merchant of Harran, had won the right to marry her, tearing it away from Bethuel, who had been her friend from childhood, the man she had always hoped to marry. But Samum had convinced her father, then had gone away for so long she feared he would never return. And when he did, he'd had no patience to wait until the wedding tent and took her forcibly among the olive groves near the outskirts of town. When her pregnancy was discovered, rather than take her to wife, he divorced her quietly, leaving her to live in shame. If not for Bethuel taking her in after Selima was born, to help Nuriah nurse Rebekah . . .

She opened her eyes, but the memory would not leave. Did she still feel the pain of Samum's betrayal? Of her father's shame at the condition Samum left her in?

She rolled her shoulders, suddenly realizing how stiff they were, and met Abraham's solemn gaze. "You are right, my lord. The memory has brought pain until this day." She swallowed, determined to at last be rid of the thoughts.

"I was betrothed years ago to an unworthy man who first left me waiting for three years, then suddenly returned and took me before our wedding night, and he divorced me when he found out I had so quickly conceived. We discovered later that he had taken another wife in the three years he was gone and no longer wanted me. My pregnancy was the excuse he needed to be rid of me." Tears stung her eyes that the man could do such a thing. "I bore Selima in my father's house and nursed her there until Bethuel discovered what had happened and took me in as a nurse to Rebekah." She held Abraham's gaze. "Bethuel and I should have married years before. He wanted me. We had grown up together. But my father chose Samum instead."

Abraham stroked his beard, his look thoughtful, introspective. "A man who does not care for his wife and child is a foolish man indeed. You were not to blame in this, Deborah."

"But Selima was born without a father, without a home."

"It seems to me that my nephew took care to see that this was not true." He shifted, and she could tell that the conversation had wearied him.

"You should rest, my lord." She plumped the cushions and placed them around him.

He nodded, and she wished she had not spoken of such weighty topics with a man whose strength was so limited.

"Were you ever with Bethuel?" He held her with a look that brooked no argument, that would allow no lies.

She shook her head. "No, my lord. He would not betray his wife in that way." She glanced beyond him. "Though in truth, we were one in spirit, in companionship, more than he ever was with Nuriah. He confided in me. He trusted me. Though he never touched me in that way."

He closed his eyes, and for a moment she thought he had fallen asleep. But several heartbeats later, he opened them and nodded. "My daughter, be at peace with your past. Your husband betrayed you, but Bethuel protected you. Sometimes a man does foolish things and a woman takes the blame for them. Stop taking the blame for your husband or for Bethuel. Live in faith and trust Adonai, my daughter. Let Him heal your heart."

Tears filled her eyes as his words washed over her.

He placed a veined hand over hers and squeezed. "We are often harder on ourselves than we need to be. Our God is just, but His heart is also filled with mercy." He closed his eyes again, and she knew the conversation was at an end.

"Thank you, my father," she said, noting his smile at her use of the endearment. She suddenly realized that the pain where the memories lived was not as intense, the worries of the past eased with Abraham's words.

"May you be blessed, my daughter. Your past is over. Let it rest in peace."

She left him with a lighter heart than she could have imagined.

24

Rebekah stopped her work, letting the shuttle on the weaver's loom grow still, then stretched and rubbed the crick in her back. She glanced at Deborah, but the woman's head was still bent where she knelt over another loom, threading colorful red strands through the brown and yellow and green already taking shape beneath her skilled fingers.

The summer's heat seemed to grow more oppressive with each passing year, and she feared drought would ruin the crops Isaac had taken such care to plant. A crop failure would make them rely more on the game Isaac and Esau hunted, but even the wild animals would grow scarce if a famine ensued.

She kneaded the knot at the back of her neck and walked through the tent's opening, grateful for even the slightest breeze. The sun glared down on her, and she shaded her eyes to better see the rows of black goat's-hair tents and the open circle of stones separating several campfires among them. Jacob walked toward her, the carcasses of two young goats flung over his shoulder. She smiled at his sure stride, heard his clear whistle as he drew nearer.

He dropped the goats at her feet, his smile wide, and bent to kiss her cheek. "Are you ready to help me?"

She looked into his dark eyes and had the sudden longing to thrust the tan turban from his head and ruffle his hair, as she had done so many times when he was but a boy. How quickly those days had passed! And now he stood before her a man, yet not quite a man, in his fifteenth year. So much had changed in him, in her.

"Of course I am ready."

First they would skin the kids, then clean and dry the skins and sew them together to hold milk or water or wine. She retrieved two large clay pots from her tent to hold the meat and fat and led him to the area outside of the circle of tents, where a wide stone slab had been set up for this specific purpose.

"Your father did not mind parting with these?"

Isaac had been training the boys to care for the flocks since they were old enough to wield a staff and sling. But it was Jacob who had taken to the task, who enjoyed the times of solitude with the sheep, as Isaac had so often when he wasn't tending the fields of grains or going off to the wilderness to hunt.

"My father enjoys a good goat stew." Jacob's grin showed white, even teeth, and a hint of mischief was in his dark eyes. "And if you help me to season it just right, he will think Esau succeeded in a great hunt."

Rebekah searched Jacob's face. "Does your father even know you took the kids from the flock? You know he will want an accounting."

Jacob shrugged. "My father trusts me, Ima. He knows we need to eat."

"There are lentils and barley to fill our bellies. We don't need to kill the goats and sheep unnecessarily."

Isaac had indulged both boys too often. But it was clear to her that he more often favored Esau. Esau who had followed Isaac's love of the wild and of the game that came from a successful hunting season. The boy who carried Ishmael's rebellious streak. And yet if the angel's words were true . . .

"He has told me more than once that I am free to choose from the flock for special occasions. And this is such an occasion." His grin left no doubt to his mischief making.

She laughed despite the silent urging within her not to. "What foolishness is this of which you speak? There is no day to remember, no festival, no sheep shearing." She forced her lips into a scowl.

He looked at her and winked, but unable to hold himself back, he burst into laughter. She knelt beside Jacob and held the legs of the first goat, watching her son deftly skin the hide with all the skill of a craftsman. She beamed at him, love for him surging from a place deep within her, a place only Isaac used to hold.

"You will make a fine shepherd one day, my son. Your skills exceed the finest among the men in the camp." Her chin lifted, and she could not keep the pride from her tone. "But what possible excuse did you give your father to allow meat on such an ordinary evening?"

Jacob continued to carve the goat into serving pieces like she had taught him, pulling the best of the meat and the fat from the bones. He tossed the last of the second goat into the clay jar and lifted the bigger jar in one arm. "The servants met us in the field as we were with the sheep. They have dug a new well, and my father is pleased. Is this not reason enough to celebrate?"

She shook her head, wanting to smack the smirk from his tanned, handsome face. "You mock me, my son."

"Never, dear Ima!" He scooped the carcasses in his other hand and tossed the bones into the fire pit, then lifted the second jar, one on each shoulder.

"You look like an awkward woman. Let me take one of them." She extended her arms, but he shook his head.

"Go gather your spices and meet me in the cooking tent. Let Selima or one of the other women tend to the hides."

She ought to correct him, should not allow him to lead her when it was clear he still needed her guidance. But the coaxing look in his eyes made her hesitate. "I should not let you talk me into these things."

He strode toward the cooking tent, and she fell into step beside him. "But I need you to chop the spices and measure the right amounts. If you are off tending the hides, who will help me? No one makes the stew to my father's liking as you do."

He glanced over his shoulder at her, and she could not stop the smile he elicited. But the brief encounter also brought a stab of sorrow to her heart. Jacob had her love, and he knew it. But he was not so secure in Isaac's favor.

Though Isaac gave both boys freer rein than she would have liked, it was Esau who brought the pride to his eyes and the smile of affection to his lips. A smile Jacob received far less often.

She glanced ahead where Jacob had already entered the cooking tent and hurried aside to enter her own, where she stored the spices that she saved for when she especially wanted to win Isaac's attention. Something she sensed her son needed now far more than she did.

❧❧❧

The campfire crackled as the sparks flew upward, and Isaac's laughter followed something Esau had said. Rebekah sat near her men, satisfied that the stew she and Jacob had put together had met with such approval.

"Well, Brother, you should spend more time in the cooking tents with the women. Your skills exceed even theirs." Esau rubbed his mouth on the back of his sleeve, making Rebekah cringe. How many times had she taught him to use a linen cloth? But it was the mocking tone toward his brother that troubled her more.

"I will take that as a compliment and not the insult you intended." Jacob leveled his gaze at his twin, and Rebekah glanced from one to the other before meeting Isaac's concerned look.

Had he not noticed before now the way the two bickered? Did he not see that Jacob needed his support and Esau needed his correction?

"Think what you want." Esau picked at a tooth with a fingernail and spit the remnant of food into the dust. "I do thank you for the fine stew, though. Almost tasted as fresh as the real thing."

"I could not tell the difference, my son." Isaac's comment seemed to soothe the sudden flash of hurt and anger that had filled Jacob's dark eyes. But Isaac's focus on his son did not last. He turned to look at Rebekah. "Your mother has always been able to turn the most common meal into a feast, and even the toughest meat into tender, seasoned game." Isaac's look held the affection she'd come to love and appreciate, but she did not want his attention now. She wanted him to praise Jacob, not her. To build their son's confidence to help him become the leader she knew he would soon be. And to ease Esau into accepting a lesser role . . .

The older will serve the younger.

The memory of the words was never far from her thoughts, and the turmoil of her pregnancy and the twins' birth as vivid as though it were yesterday. But it was the vision and God's voice, the stunning revelation, that she silently treasured above all. Had Isaac forgotten what she had told him? But of course not. She had surely reminded him often enough.

She looked at Esau, who sipped a cup of barley beer and quickly drew Isaac's focus to the tale of his recent trek into the nearby hills to hunt gazelle.

"The gazelles were as skittish as hares and as hard to find as a partridge in the hills." Esau laughed, and Isaac seemed fully engaged in his tale. "But I figured out a way to trap them next time. And I got plenty of practice with my bow." He leaned back and smiled, and Isaac said something in response.

Rebekah studied Jacob, yearning to go to him, to remove the pensive look from his face. If only she could openly declare God's choice to both sons and boost Jacob's confidence and pride.

She drew in a lengthy breath and slowly let it out. She waited a moment more, then walked away, unable to watch her husband engage one son at the expense of the other. She must do more to make up the lack. Surely Isaac loved Jacob. Had she somehow favored this son too much, causing Isaac to swing toward Esau's side? But no. Isaac loved the wild, the beauty of the desert, the thrill of the hunt, and Esau shared his passion, nothing more. Jacob shared his father's private pondering, but perhaps they were too much alike in this. Did Isaac wish himself to be more like Esau and less like Jacob?

She shook her head to rid it of the troubling thoughts and turned toward her tent to ease the throbbing that had begun just above her brow. But she stopped abruptly at the splintered cry that came from across the compound. Running feet accompanied the sound, and she stood stricken as one of the servants rushed and knelt at Isaac's feet.

"My lord, you must come at once. Your father . . ."

"What has happened to my father?"

Rebekah's heart stilled, and she met Isaac's gaze above the servant's head. But in her heart she knew before the man spoke the words.

"Your father Abraham has just now slipped into Sheol."

25

Rebekah at his side, Isaac looked down at Abraham's still form inside his father's large tent. The servants had washed his body for burial, and a runner had been sent to summon Ishmael.

"He looks peaceful." Rebekah reached for Isaac's hand and intertwined their fingers, squeezing gently. "He lived a good, long life, old and full of years."

Isaac nodded, aware of the lump in his throat. Tears had come earlier when he had slipped away alone. He had led his father's camp and handled his interests for many years, so the loss was not one of leadership, only of companionship. He had come to appreciate the man since the day God had spoken to his heart on the mountain where he had prayed for Rebekah, for himself.

"I am glad you had time with him after Keturah."

Rebekah's soft words brought his thoughts around. He shifted to look from his father to her.

"As am I."

She smiled, her expression soft, compassionate.

"We lost many years in misunderstanding. I am pleased that Adonai gave us time to make up for it."

She nodded and leaned her head against his chest. "He

loved you fiercely, you know. As you love Esau." The last came out breathy, as though she feared to say it.

He stiffened at the insinuation. "As I love you and Jacob as well." He cringed at the defensiveness in his tone. "Are you suggesting otherwise?" He faced her, searching her eyes for the truth. "You know that I love you."

She nodded, but the action seemed hesitant, as though she did not completely agree. "I know you love me." She breathed the words against his chest. "I fear it is Jacob who is not certain of your love, as you once wondered about your father's for you."

Her words were sharp arrows, tearing at scars now healed. Was it true? He looked away, seeing again his father's still form, and was suddenly reminded of his loss, of the man who had taught him obedience but whose own obedience had made Isaac question his love.

"Jacob knows I love him." He winced at his harsh tone. "I have taught him everything I know."

"Not everything."

He looked at her again, reading more in her expression than he wanted to dwell on just now. "He does not care for the hunt. I cannot make him do what is not in his heart to do. My father wished me more like Ishmael, but we were not the same. What do you expect me to do?"

His anger rose with the question. He knew what she wanted, what she said she had heard from God long ago. But he had not heard it, and in looking at his sons, he struggled to believe it.

"You could teach him to lead, prepare him to oversee your interests. You could prepare Esau to accept Jacob's rule."

"Esau is the older."

"The older will serve the younger."

"So you say!" His words made her draw back, and he saw that he had wounded her, as her words had hurt him.

"So *God* has said." Her words were hushed. "You do not believe me." Her expression grew suddenly closed, shadowed.

"I did not say that." Yet he could not deny it.

"You said enough." She pulled her hand from his and wrapped both arms around her in a self-protective pose.

The flap of the tent rustled, and Isaac turned to see Haviv stepping into the darkened interior. He approached, looking uncertain. Isaac motioned him forward, relieved to be through with this conversation.

"What is it?" He ignored the sense that Rebekah had moved farther away, glancing toward her only briefly to see her leave the tent.

"Your brother has arrived, my lord. We are ready to take the body to Machpelah."

Isaac's stomach tightened at the news. Ishmael's presence always posed a challenge and left Isaac's emotions taut as bowstrings. And now with the added grief over his father . . .

He glanced from Haviv to Abraham's still form once more, feeling bereft of father and wife—and apparently at least one son—all in one blow. Ishmael would not make the emotions lighter. But he could not avoid dealing with them.

He moved with Haviv to the door of the tent. "Take me to him. We leave at sunset."

⁂

A full moon lit the path on the trek from Hebron to the cave of Machpelah. Isaac and Ishmael, Jacob and Esau, and Ishmael's two oldest sons, Nebaioth and Kedar, carried the bier while servants walked before and behind, carrying torches to light the dark places along the way.

Rebekah clutched Deborah's arm for support as the two followed at the head of the women, Selima and Lila and the other maids making a closely woven group. The piercing cries of the mourners made Rebekah's heart twist in pain. But the pain was not for the loss of her father-in-law nearly as much as it was for what she had done to her husband.

She looked at him, his back straight and strong, his muscles flexing as he gripped the rod holding the bier. She knew the weight of his father's body rested most heavily on his shoulders—if not physically, then surely emotionally. Isaac stood as the leader of the clan now, with no other to look to for guidance. And she had added to his burden in the tent of mourning, bringing up a subject that could have waited.

Would she never learn to curb her tongue?

She released her hold on Deborah and wrapped both arms about herself. Guilt gnawed her middle as the group at last came to a stop near the large oaks of Mamre. The outline of the cave came into view. Isaac had brought her here once to see where his mother rested, but from then on he had stayed away.

Had he stayed away? Who knew where he went on those many treks he made to wilderness areas and beyond?

"Will you go with them into the cave?" Deborah's voice barely registered.

How well did she know her husband? What did he really do when he left her in the camp and went off alone or with Haviv or Esau?

A touch on her arm made her jump.

"Are you listening? Your husband is speaking."

Deborah's hissed whisper brought her thoughts into focus. She turned and met the woman's gaze with a silent nod.

"My father was a great man," Isaac was saying, his voice carrying beyond her, its clear tones marred by the hint of sorrow.

She studied him in the torchlight, feeling the pain in his eyes, and suddenly wished she could rush into his arms and hold him close, beg him to forgive her for making him feel worse than he already did.

"Adonai once promised him that he would become the

father of many nations. Three wives have given him eight sons and grandsons too numerous to count. Adonai has fulfilled His promise and rewarded our father's faith." He looked at Ishmael, and Rebekah sensed something pass between the brothers that had not been there before. Was that a flicker of respect in Ishmael's brooding eyes?

At Ishmael's slight nod, acknowledging Isaac's words, she shifted to look at her sons. Esau stood close to his uncle, and she did not miss the furtive glances he cast Ishmael's way, the admiration sparking in his expression. Had Isaac's favorite son ever looked at him with such respect, such longing? The thought troubled her further, and she pressed a hand to her middle to quell the unease.

"He was a man of intense passion in life, and one obedient to Adonai Elohim even unto death," Isaac said, drawing her eyes to him once more.

His face carried an expression of awe as he spoke the Name, making her look heavenward. Even the stars seemed brighter somehow, as if the night approved of Isaac's words.

She felt herself nod in agreement as her gaze shifted to Jacob, finding the same awe in his eyes, and when this son looked at his father, she saw respect, even longing. Why could Isaac not see how this was the son who was worthy to inherit the promise, the blessing, and his affection over the other?

Isaac stepped aside and allowed Ishmael the chance to speak, but the man waved his right to do so away. She glanced behind her at the waiting throng, forcing her irritation in check. Ishmael had brought only his sons with him to the burial, so the crowd surrounding them now belonged mostly to Isaac. His refusal to speak was fitting, perhaps, though clearly not a good reflection on how he felt about his father.

A sigh escaped her. Why were relationships between a father and his sons so difficult?

The sound of movement and the sway of the torches made

her turn to watch Isaac again as he took his place once more at the side of the bier. The men lifted Abraham's body and took the steps to the cave below. She followed and glanced back at Deborah, motioning her to come as well. She did not want to go there, to look on the linen-wrapped bodies, but she could not bear to allow her husband and sons to do so without her.

They stopped again at the cave's entrance, set the bier on the smooth stones, and the four younger men gripped the large rock guarding the entrance and shoved it aside. The scraping of stone on stone grated on her ears, and she gritted her teeth against the sound. She looked at Abraham's body and wished again that she had known him sooner, known him when Isaac was a boy. If she had understood the father, she might better understand her husband and her sons now.

She strained to hear the hushed voices of the men, but she only half heard the giving of directions and the grunts as they bore the bier in strong, masculine arms and disappeared into the cave. Moments later the men emerged, the stone was shoved back into its slot, and the men moved back up the stairs.

Rebekah waited with Deborah, unsure what to do. Esau never glanced her way, but Jacob stopped at her side and slipped his arm through hers. She smiled into his eyes.

Isaac came up behind both sons but barely paused in his climb back up the steps, as though he could not be free of the place fast enough. His jaw was set in a grim line, and he did not look at her, causing the guilt and regret to mix anew within her.

She felt Jacob's grip and tug as he silently led her to follow the men. Looking at him once more, seeing the affection for her in his gaze, she felt a small measure of relief to know she was loved.

But as she lay alone in her tent that night, it was Isaac

whose arms she missed, Isaac whose heart she longed for. And she knew from experience that his return to her would be a long time in coming.

***

The period of mourning for Abraham lasted seven days, with talk and feasting and celebration of the great man's life. Ishmael set his tents just outside the circle of Isaac's camp but spent each evening at the door of Isaac's tent, breaking bread and talking as they had never done before.

Rebekah stayed near the shadows, listening and watching with increasing distress as her son Esau asked his uncle Ishmael question after question, until the two fairly dominated the discussion. Only when Ishmael discounted the goodness of Adonai did Isaac finally speak.

"I do not see how you can call Him good, Brother, after what He put you through," Ishmael said. "Or perhaps it is our father you blame for nearly taking your life on the mountain?"

Isaac stroked his bearded chin, his look thoughtful. "I do not blame our father, nor do I blame Adonai's command to him. Look around you at the many blessings Adonai has given. You have twelve sons and are the wealthy prince of a mighty clan. Our flocks and herds are flourishing, the land has yielded grain when we need it, the rains fall mostly when they should. Has our father's God not blessed us both? Does this alone not make Him good?" Isaac leaned forward on his cushion and rested both elbows on his knees, his expression challenging.

Ishmael ran a finger along the edge of a golden goblet of spiced wine, but his gaze never left Isaac's. "You are to be commended, Brother. You make a good point." He glanced at Esau and smiled, then faced Isaac again. "I will admit, God has blessed us both with sons and flocks and the fruit of the land, but if our father's God is truly good, why put His people to the test? Why allow my mother to be sent away? Why command you be killed? Our father's God was not kind to our mothers in either case. So I will ask again—how can you say that He is good?"

Rebekah stilled, stunned by the depth of the question and the bitter tone that accompanied it. Did Ishmael still carry the scars of his youth, as her husband once did?

But of course he did.

"You ask a hard question, my brother." Isaac's words held assurance and calm, and Rebekah felt a small measure of peace as she looked once more in his direction.

"I did not expect you to have an answer." Ishmael's tone moved from bitterness to the familiar mocking, but his eyes held a hint of yearning, as though he wished Isaac would prove him wrong.

Silence followed the comment, and one glance at Isaac told Rebekah he was carefully crafting his response. But what could he possibly say to such a thing?

A shiver worked through her, and she suddenly wished Ishmael had never voiced such thoughts. What good would it do for her impressionable sons to question their God before they had even lived long enough to know Him? And yet surely they were old enough to hear, to ponder, to question, as Isaac had done. Still, worry niggled her thoughts as she glanced from one son to the other, reading doubt in the eyes of one and curiosity in the eyes of the other.

"God is good because He is," Isaac said at last, drawing her attention back again. "He does not need a reason to do what He does, and He is not answerable to us when He chooses to test our faith. But we can see His goodness in the things He has made, in the very creation that surrounds us." He pointed through the tent's opening to the shadowed trees and the sounds of night animals surrounding them.

"If God is good, why do evil men live?" Ishmael pulled a

small dagger from the leather pouch at his side and held it between them like a shield. "I could kill you in your sleep, and who would stop me?"

"I would stop you." Esau jumped up to stand between his father and uncle.

Ishmael laughed. "And so you would, young nephew." He put away his weapon, and Rebekah released a breath.

Ishmael rose up and leaned forward until he was nose to nose with Esau. "But if you were not home, or if your father were off by himself in the hills with no one to watch out for him . . ." He let the thought linger until even the air in the tent grew hot, uncomfortable.

Ishmael removed his dagger and set it away from him, then leaned back against the cushions, his hands behind him. "And now"—he looked directly at Esau—"in my defenseless position, your father could lift his sword and plunge it into my chest, and who would stop him?"

"I would cut his throat before he could reach you, Abba." Kedar's voice carried a thinly veiled threat.

Ishmael laughed again, but Isaac sat silent, waiting.

"If our father's God were to sit by and allow such a thing from either of us, then He cannot be good. He would destroy evil if He were." Ishmael leaned forward again, his look so intense Rebekah could feel the heat of it from where she waited in the shadows. "But how do we know it isn't Elohei Abraham who created evil in the first place? How do we know He isn't glad to use it against us?" Ishmael leaned back once more, took a long drink from the goblet, wiped his mouth with the back of his sleeve, then returned his dagger to his side.

"You see, my brother," he said, his look confident, strong, "you cannot really know this God our father worshiped. I do not see Him as so very different from the gods of my mother's people or the gods of our father's family. He just disguises his intentions better than most." A smug smile, as from one who is certain he has won a debate, creased his lean, angular face.

Questions swirled in Rebekah's mind, and fear twisted in her middle as she witnessed the admiration growing in Esau's eyes. He was fully enamored with his uncle, and she felt him slipping away with each word of the conversation.

Isaac shifted in his seat and folded his hands in his lap, his eyes focused on them as though they were clay tablets with words that could answer his brother with eloquence. His silence begged to be filled by more than the sipping of wine, the chewing of sweet cakes, and the whispers of Ishmael's sons.

At last, when Rebekah thought she could not bear his contemplation a moment longer, he lifted his head and looked deeply into Ishmael's dark eyes. "I am not in the place of God to give an answer to all of your questions, my brother, but this one thing I know."

At his pause, Rebekah held her breath and glanced around the tent. Every eye focused on her husband—Jacob's with the most interest.

"Adonai Elohei Abraham is not a God who delights in evil. If He did, He would not have destroyed the world with the flood. Noah would not have felt the need to preach repentance, and our father Abraham would not have been called out from a city of foreign gods to follow after Him.

"Do I understand why you were sent away or why I was bound and laid on an altar like a lamb to be slaughtered? No, I do not. But I have heard God's voice on that mountain, and I know He delights far more in obedience, which our father fully understood, than in the circumstances that allow evil to prevail."

Ishmael drew a hand over his beard, studying Isaac for the space of several heartbeats, but at last he looked away, signaling an end to the debate. "I cannot say I agree with your conclusions. I do not see His motives as more benevolent than any other of the gods I serve."

"Can the gods you serve, the gods of wood and stone, speak? Can they lift even one finger to do what is just and right?" Isaac's gaze was unflinching, and Rebekah wanted to cheer her husband's response.

But Ishmael's expression was closed, his hooded eyes shifting slightly from Isaac to his sons. At his nod, they stood as one.

"I will allow that neither one of us can know for sure what our father's God is like," he said, his tone brooking no further argument.

Isaac stood, and Jacob and Esau rose with him.

Isaac embraced Ishmael and kissed each cheek. "You leave tomorrow?"

After seven days, Ishmael would want to return to his clan, and Rebekah would be happy to see him go.

Ishmael nodded, at last showing the soft hint of a smile. "Ready to see me off, are you, Brother?" He returned Isaac's kiss of departure and clapped him on the back.

"Of course you know you are welcome to stay as long as you like." Isaac walked with his brother through the tent's opening, their conversation drifting out of earshot, Ishmael's sons following.

Rebekah moved from her place in the shadows and set about clearing the goblets and scraps of food left on the golden trays, her ears attuned to the night sounds and the voices of Jacob and Esau as they moved from the tent.

"I want to go with him."

Esau's words stilled her hands, her heart suddenly thumping hard against her ribs. She walked closer to the tent's opening.

"Go with who?" Jacob's tone held surprise. "Uncle Ishmael?"

"Who else? Did you not hear his stories of the hunts he has

carried out, of the mighty game he has killed? He could teach me better use of the bow. He is more skillful than Father."

Esau's excited voice held persuasion, and she knew in an instant that if he turned those pleading eyes on Isaac, he would promptly get his way. She must not let him.

"All I heard was his disdain for our grandfather's God. Does this not concern you?"

Rebekah breathed a sigh that Jacob had been listening with discernment, that he cared about the weightier matters.

"Of course. But have you not thought these very same things? Uncle only voiced the questions we have all raised at one time or another. And how can we know anything for certain? Have you heard God's voice?"

"Abba has."

"So he says."

Esau's words came out harsh, despite his attempt to lower his voice, and Rebekah did not miss the signs of anger bubbling within her firstborn son. Did Isaac realize how Esau felt? The boy was too easily persuaded, too quickly influenced.

Images of Haviv and Nadab flashed in her mind's eye. Haviv, who had married Selima and remained a faithful servant, loyal to their God. Nadab, who had stormed off and married a Canaanite and abandoned his family, Isaac's camp, and their faith. She could not let Esau end up like Nadab.

She stopped, looked across the camp where Isaac bade Ishmael farewell. The men would rise before dawn and be on their way, leaving her little time to convince Isaac to keep Esau here. The boy would make a strong case. But she could be just as convincing.

26

Holding a clay lamp in one hand, Isaac slipped through the entrance of his tent and lowered the flap, closing himself in semi-darkness. A deep sigh lifted his chest, but the burden would not dislodge, the turmoil of the evening resting heavily on his shoulders.

Ishmael's questions had not troubled him for his own sake. He had wrestled with the questions of God's power and goodness since his youth. He had not understood the test of faith that led his father to obey a seemingly outrageous command, one that the gods Ishmael served might easily demand, but one his father's God would not. Adonai had called his father out from among such beliefs and practices. To ask it of him was so foreign to all that his father had come to know of Him that he would not have obeyed at all if not for the fact that he knew Elohim's voice. There had been no mistake. Isaac understood that now.

But his children did not, nor would they until they had lived their own hardships. If only he could instill this understanding deep within them so they might be spared their own tests of faith. Would Esau's faith be tested and grow in the company of Ishmael? Should he allow the boy to go with his brother as Esau had pleaded with him to do?

He rubbed the back of his neck, certain the pounding of his head would not be eased until he closed his eyes in sleep. Weariness swept through him, but as he moved from his sitting quarters to his sleeping chamber, he stopped abruptly. Rebekah sat among his bed cushions, her hair undone, her expression earnest.

"What are you doing here?"

The hurt in her dark eyes made him wish the words back the moment he had spoken them.

"That is, I did not expect you."

She merely nodded and dropped her gaze as her hands twisted the fabric of her robe. She still wore the garments of the day, as though she knew he might send her back to her own tent. The thought stirred him to gentle his response, and he set the lamp on the low table and came to kneel beside her.

"I am sorry, Rebekah. I am tired and worn out with the many voices of argument and reason. I do not wish to speak any more this night . . . but I can see you are distressed or you would not be here. So please, tell me quickly that we may both get some rest." He reached for her hand, hoping to still her fidgeting and coax her to hurry and speak.

She lifted her head, and his heart melted at her pleading look. "You must not allow Esau to go with your brother." She kept her voice low, though the tone implored him. "I watched him tonight, and I heard him tell Jacob that he wanted to return with his uncle. But Esau is too eager to please his uncle, and I fear he will fall into Ishmael's ways if we allow it." Her words ended in a rush, and she pulled his hand to her chest, where he could feel the rapid beating of her heart. "Please, my lord. I know he will ask you." She paused, and he knew she could read the look in his eyes. "He already did?"

Isaac nodded. "He could speak of little else the moment Ishmael returned to his tents."

"What did you say to him?"

Isaac lifted his free hand, which suddenly felt weighted with age, and pulled the turban from his head. "I told him I would think on it. I will tell him in the morning before dawn."

Crickets picked up where his last words left off.

"You must tell him no."

Her tone and the insistent way she spoke sparked irritation within him.

He pulled his hand from hers. "I will take your opinion into consideration." He put his back to her and removed his robe and tunic. He lifted his night tunic in one hand, then thought better of it and turned to face her.

She lifted wide eyes to his, then lowered them, the heightened color of her cheeks barely visible in the lamp's flickering glow.

He settled himself among the cushions and studied her. "Put aside your robe and come."

She looked at him and opened her mouth as if she would say more, then closed it and did as he had asked. His heart stirred as she nestled in the crook of his arm, the feel of her soft skin and the scent of her hair filling him with desires he had ignored for too long. He kissed her, letting his lips linger, and looked deeply into her eyes.

"I share your worries, Rebekah. But I also know that a boy too restricted is a boy who may one day rebel far worse than he might have. Remember Nadab."

"I do! This is why I do not want Esau near his uncle. He is too vulnerable, too easily swayed—"

He held a finger to her lips, then slowly moved it aside and kissed her again, more deeply this time, until her rigid form relaxed in his arms.

"I'm sorry, my lord, I just—"

"Shh . . ." He sifted his fingers through her undone hair and pulled her closer. "No more tonight."

She released a sigh that he sensed signaled her own irritation, and he knew her well enough to know she would bring it up again in the morning. But for tonight he allowed himself to forget his cares, forget the days of mourning his father and the struggles of brother and sons, and enjoy the pleasures of the one he loved.

The next morning dawned too early, and Rebekah's tension rose with her. She had been right to come here, to be with her beloved as they had not been in many months. How was it that they had allowed their sons to fill their days and nights, to keep them from each other?

And yet she knew the neglect was due in part to the conflict they faced about the promise she had received from the Lord—the promise that he struggled to accept. She had avoided his bed when he angered her, when he favored Esau over Jacob, and he had gone off on his desert treks over the same slight.

The thought shamed her. Had their love truly come to this—this vying for power and place between two sons? Would they really allow the future to pit them against each other?

She dressed quickly in the chill air, grateful for the sputtering wick that had not yet gone out. She refilled the oil in the lamp and moved through the spacious tent to the closed flap.

Isaac had somehow risen and left before she'd awakened. The thought made her heart skip and dance with sudden fear. Had Ishmael already left? Had he taken Esau with him? She should never have been so demanding the night before. Isaac's pride could make him decide against her just to prove that he could. It was his decision, after all. And she could tell he did not agree with her.

She lifted the flap and blew out the lamp's flame, then set the lamp on a low post near the entrance. Pink shades of coming sunlight bathed the eastern ridge, casting a rosy glow over the camp. Her feet felt the dew's cool dampness as she walked hastily across the compound toward Ishmael's tents. She found the tents disassembled and packed on camels already mounted by Ishmael's sons. Isaac embraced his brother as they gave each other their final farewell.

She scanned the crowd, her heart pounding, searching. But there was no sign of Esau. Was he up ahead with the caravan or still in his tent? But surely he would be up and ready if Isaac planned to allow him to accompany these men.

Ishmael turned his back to Isaac and climbed atop his beast, commanding it to rise. And then they were off, traveling the merchant road to the south, headed back to Ishmael's hills.

Isaac watched them go until they became small in the distance. At last he turned and saw her. He approached, smiling.

"I hope I did not wake you." He traced a finger along the outside of her face, his expression warming her.

She shook her head. "No. I wanted, needed, to be up." She glanced beyond him to the road. "So you told Esau no?" She longed to look at him, to read the emotions in his eyes, but could not bring herself to do so.

"What do you think?" His fingers beneath her chin coaxed her to face him, and she could not pull away.

"I think you did the right thing." She was right, wasn't she? "That is, I didn't see Esau among the men."

Isaac's brows drew together, and a shadow passed through his eyes. He turned them both back toward the camp and placed one arm around her shoulders. "I have promised to let Esau visit soon. When he is a little older."

She stopped walking, forcing him to halt with her. She must choose her words carefully. Did he not just give her what she wished? Who knew what time would bring to them? Esau might decide a visit unnecessary, or Isaac might be convinced to change his mind. The thoughts calmed her anxiety, and she gave him what she hoped was a grateful smile.

"Thank you, my lord. Perhaps when he is older, he will be strong enough to withstand your brother's influences." She slipped her arm through his. "In the meantime, we must teach him more of Adonai and to be kinder to his brother, to be more like his father, to prepare them both for the future."

She made a move to continue on, but Isaac did not join her. She turned back, realizing once again that she had said the wrong thing. If she could only make him see . . .

"Is something wrong, my lord?" She shivered, knowing the cool morning air was not the only cause, burdened by the look in his eyes.

"I know you are the mother of my sons, beloved. And I know you had a hard time when you carried them. Whether God spoke to you about them . . . I am not in the place of God to know such a thing. I did not hear the words, and I am not certain I accept them."

Her heart sank in the space of a breath. "You don't believe me."

"I am not sure I want to."

"But why? Is it because Jacob is not what you expected in a ruling son? Are you so ashamed of your younger son that you would pick the older, the one who questions your faith, ahead of him?"

The shiver grew until her hands shook. She wrapped her arms about her, begging her limbs to be still.

His heavy sigh filled the space between them. He dragged a hand over his beard, as though the action might force the words from his mouth. "I am not ashamed of Jacob, beloved. I just see more qualities of leadership in Esau. In time, if his faith grows and he learns greater trust in Adonai, he will make a fine prince to carry on my father's name. As the firstborn, that is his right."

"Ishmael was your father's firstborn, but God chose you."

The words hung between them, slowly burned away by the heat of the rising sun.

Isaac looked westward, his face shadowed by the trees above them. "My father was promised a son by my mother. Ishmael would not have been born if my parents had trusted in that promise. As for our sons"—he turned to face her—"God has given me no such word or promise regarding either of them. While I do not deny that He could have spoken to you, I do not know." He touched her cheek. "You were so overwrought, beloved. Could you not have heard what you wanted to hear to ease your burden?"

His words, his doubt, rocked her, until the shaking grew to shocked stillness.

"You think I am lying to you? You think the vision was all the working of an overwrought mind?" Her voice dropped in pitch with each word—words too unbelievable to utter, yet still they came. "If you do not trust me, your wife, who do you trust, Isaac? If our God speaks only to men, then how do you account for his visit to Hagar or his words to your own mother? If God did not speak to me, then who did? I did not make the words up in my mind. Adonai told me, 'The older will serve the younger.' If you do not believe this, there is nothing more I can say to you." She looked long and hard into his eyes, her heart dying within her at the uncertainty she saw in his.

She turned away from him, tears clouding her vision, and ran all the way back to her tent.

* * *

Isaac slung a goatskin of water and another that held a mixture of dates, raisins, and almonds over the side of a donkey, then fastened his pallet to the back. He left his tent standing, the rest of his provisions tucked inside. He would sleep under the stars or in the shelter of a cave this night, and perhaps many more nights to come.

Anger, vivid and deep, spurred him to hurry, to retreat from the battle he knew would be quick to ensue if he stayed. He loved Rebekah with an ache so fierce he feared it would consume him, and yet her insistence, her claims to knowledge he did not share, only fed his feelings of inadequacy. She questioned his leadership, did not respect his decisions—in fact, had not respected them since the twins were born, ever since he had merely humored her vision, never truly embracing it as his own.

Had Adonai truly spoken to her?

The question prodded him, its fervor relentless. He could not act on her word alone. How could he? Even his father had not been faced with such a plight, had he? He searched his mind for memories of the things either parent had told him, but emotion blinded him with every step.

He cinched the last of the provisions beneath the donkey's blanket, gripped the reins, and started forward. Distant wails coming from Rebekah's tent should have touched him somehow, made him turn back to her, to apologize for not believing her. But how could he? He was not ready to face her again. Not yet.

He plodded forward, grateful Haviv had been in the camp to accept his quick instructions. He moved past the circle of tents toward the road that followed the path Ishmael had taken that morning. Afternoon light was dappled where the clouds moved to hide the sun from view and then disappeared moments later to give the sun the space it demanded. Much as he needed such distance now from the clouded views of his wife and sons.

How had everything changed so quickly in the short week since his father's death?

Emotion clogged his throat with the memories, but at the sound of running feet coming up the path, he tamped it down, quickening his stride. He would not let her persuade him to stay. He needed time alone.

But the sound was not that of a woman running. The footfalls were too heavy, too fierce. He turned to see Esau rushing toward him, his tunic girded about his waist, a sack flung over one shoulder and a bow and quiver over the other.

"Father! Let me come with you." He pulled up beside Isaac and stopped, panting for breath. "I won't be any trouble." He lowered his sack to the earth. "See? I have brought all that I need."

Isaac glanced from the sack to the bow and arrows, then looked into his son's earnest gaze. His chest lifted in a sigh. How could he refuse him? But how could he allow this if he was ever to get any relief, any understanding of Rebekah's claims?

"Please, Father. I could hunt for us. You know you prefer wild game to fruit and nuts." His broad grin lit his dark eyes, coaxing a smile to Isaac's lips.

"You would not enjoy my company, my son." He stifled the urge to sigh once more, instead turning to continue on his way.

Esau hurried to join him, keeping pace at his side. "I do not care if we talk. I just want to be with you."

His young legs slowed to match the donkey's stride while Isaac's mind churned with reasons to make him turn back the way he had come. But a part of him wanted him here, needed the reassurance that Esau was not what Rebekah claimed. That he was right in his assessment of the boy.

He glanced at his son. Red hair poked beneath a striped turban—Rebekah's handiwork—and his chin was beginning to show the same curly red hairs that covered his body and would fill his cheeks with the beard of a man. How different this son had been from his twin, even from birth. Esau, the hairy one, while Jacob's skin was smooth and light brown like his mother's.

He looked at him a moment longer, then allowed a slight nod and was rewarded with Esau's exuberant whoop. He chuckled and felt some of the anger dissipate. "Very well. You may come. But do as you said and keep your silence. I am weary of words."

How often had he thought the same and said so to Rebekah? Why was it so hard to talk to each other as they had in the early years of their marriage? The twins had changed her, changed them.

They walked in silence, Esau keeping good to his claim to hold his tongue, until they had reached the field where the barley had grown to nearly full height. The harvest would be upon them soon if the latter rains fell as they should. But the season's heat had been harsher than most, and the threat of drought worried him. He glanced at the sky, too bright in its nearness, then looked toward his son.

"We will make camp up ahead in the cave at the side of the hill."

He motioned with his hand and looked at Esau, suddenly grateful for his company. As much as he enjoyed time alone, he did not realize how discouraged it made him feel, how often his thoughts circled back to the same things he had thought before, and how difficult it became to get past his frustrations. Had he done Rebekah a disservice by going off and leaving her alone with the servants so often over the years? And yet, some of his trips could not be helped. There were flocks to oversee and fields to attend.

"I am glad you came," he said.

He smiled at Esau, pushing past the excuses that he continually raised against the boy's mother. How could he treat the woman he loved with such distance? This was exactly how his mother had treated his father after his binding, and he had hated the separation of his family. Why could he not break the cycle?

Esau's wide smile warmed him. "I thought you might need someone . . . I heard Ima weeping." He shrugged as though a woman's tears were a daily occurrence. In truth, Rebekah rarely wept, and never so bitterly as he had heard this day.

"I should have gone to her."

Dare he admit such a thing to a child? Well, not actually a child, but still young enough to not understand such things.

Esau reached the cave two steps ahead of Isaac and dropped his things onto the dry earth. He turned and took the donkey's reins from Isaac's hand. "She was not ready to listen to you, Abba. You were not ready to speak with her." He tied the donkey to the branches of an overhanging tree. "You will settle things between you when we return."

His confidence soothed some of the rough places in Isaac's heart, but at the same time he knew it was not as simple as that. As long as he and Rebekah held to different goals for their sons, as long as she believed something he did not, there would be a divide between them—as wide a chasm as the Jezreel Valley between its opposing mountains.

The thought pained him, but he could not share it with Esau. Maybe it would be best not to think on such thoughts at all.

He unloaded the donkey's packs and brushed its rough coat. He was weary of trying to understand Rebekah or what had caused her to cling to a vision he did not share.

Did You speak to her, Adonai?

But the question went unanswered, doing nothing to ease the frustration he had with her. Very well then, he would do as he had never done before. He would stop trying to make sense of his wife. He would instead enjoy this time with his son, and when he returned, he would put their disagreement and Rebekah's vision behind him, behind them both.

27

Rebekah turned over on her pallet in the darkening tent, her body drenched in sweat that mingled with her tears. Her throat ached and her eyes felt puffy. She shivered in spite of the heat of the late afternoon and wrapped both arms about her, certain her world had tilted so completely that it could never be put right again.

How was it possible? Had she misunderstood Isaac from the start? Had he ever trusted or believed her? If he did not believe that Adonai had visited her during her pregnancy with the twins, he must not have believed her when she told him of the angel who had visited her just before Eliezer came to meet her. She had trusted Isaac with that revelation.

A sob broke through, but she stuffed a fist to her mouth, not willing to cry out again. She must get hold of herself.

The entrance flap of her tent parted, letting light filter into the deepening darkness. She lifted her pounding head from the mat to see who dared interrupt her, then fell back among the soft pillows when she recognized Deborah.

"Why have you come?" Her voice, raspy from the strain of weeping, sounded like it came from another source, not her. She draped an arm over her eyes, wishing she could sink even further into the darkness and never speak to another soul again.

"I came to help you." Deborah moved about the room, and Rebekah peered from beneath her arm to watch. Deborah carried a clay pot in one hand, steam rising from it as she poured a stream of liquid into a clay cup. She turned and handed it to Rebekah. "Drink."

Rebekah looked away, not wanting to be told what she should do. She was a child no longer, and she did not need such coaxing.

Deborah touched her arm, her grip gentle. "You will feel better if you drink this." Her tone was firm but kind, and Rebekah gave up her resolve and faced her friend.

She sat up and accepted the cup, inhaling a mixture of mint and tarragon. She sipped, then straightened while Deborah sorted pillows and plumped them around her, making her more comfortable. A deep sigh released the tension from her chest.

"Do you want to tell me what has brought this on and why Isaac has left the camp?"

Deborah's words nearly made her spill the tea.

"He left the camp? Why would he . . ." She let the words die on her tongue. It was his habit to go off alone when he was troubled. What else did she expect? Except in every other case he had said goodbye, reassured her of his love, and told her how long he would be gone.

"What happened between you two?" Deborah touched her arm, and her eyes held such compassion that Rebekah could not hold her gaze.

She looked beyond her, shame heating her face. "Isaac does not believe me. Has never believed me." She shifted to face Deborah. "He thinks I am lying to him, or worse, that I am a woman crazed! He denies the fact that Adonai spoke to me about the boys before their birth. He thinks that in order for it to be true, Adonai should speak to him as well." The words came out shrill even to her own ears. "He doesn't believe me, Deborah." Her voice was a whisper now. "What am I going to do?"

Deborah's dark eyes, still lovely though lined with age, met hers with a searching look. At last she took the cup from Rebekah's hands and pulled her close, as a mother would a young child. No words passed between them as Deborah held her, but Rebekah sensed the woman was praying as she rocked back and forth, drawing Rebekah with her. Moments passed in silence until Deborah finally leaned away and cupped Rebekah's cheek in her palm.

"Dear one, is it possible that you misunderstood his intent? What did you say to him to cause such a reaction? What did he say to you?" She brushed damp tendrils of hair away from Rebekah's cheeks and tucked them behind her ear, soothing her with the action.

She thought back on the morning—had it been only a few hours ago? "I said nothing that hasn't been said before. I only told him that I did not want Esau to go with his uncle, to spend so much time with him." She paused, searching her mind for what she had said. "I told him we must teach Esau more of Adonai and to be kinder to his brother, to be more like his father, to prepare them both for the future." She looked at Deborah, imploring her to agree with her. "He suddenly seemed upset with me and told me he did not agree that Jacob would rule over Esau. He does not think God spoke to me. He thinks Esau should keep the right of the firstborn."

She choked on the last words and fisted her hands in her lap, forcing her body to stop its trembling. "Why can't he see and accept the truth? Why can't he help me to train Esau to accept this, like Bethuel accepted Laban's rule? It is not so unusual. Even Isaac is head over his father's household instead of Ishmael. Why can he not see this?" The questions drained her, and she sank back onto the pillows, spent. "I have lost him, Deborah. If he will not accept the truth of my vision, the truth God spoke to me, then we will never agree on anything regarding our sons again." She grew suddenly still at the thought, her whole being saturated with the awful truth.

"You have not lost him, dear one. Isaac loves you more than his very life. Anyone can see his affection for you." Deborah refilled the cup, urging her to rise again and drink. "But is it possible that you have pushed him to accept something that God has not yet revealed to him? Perhaps the vision was for you alone until such time as the boys are ready to rule in Isaac's place."

Rebekah took another sip of the tea, calmness growing within her. "Do you think he will eventually accept this then? Is it only that I have pushed him too soon?"

Was it possible? And yet, she was not sure she could forgive the tone or the meaning behind his words. How could she look on him again with respect if she did not have his trust?

"A man's pride is a fragile thing, Rebekah. You must be patient and let Isaac see the difference between his sons, how the one favors his faith and the other does not. Let Jacob arise to be the leader Isaac wants. Then he will believe your words. Right now, Esau is more outspoken and charming and has more in common with his father."

"But that is not true! Isaac and Jacob are far more alike in spirit. Both of them think and feel deeply, and both are gentle and loving and kind." She looked away, struck by the character of the man she had loved for so long, the man who had walked away from her without a word. This was so not like him. Had she pushed him too far?

"Esau can be gentle and loving. He is more temperate with his father than he is with you, I daresay. I think both of your sons can feel the tension between you and Isaac, dear one. It concerns them. If you continue to favor Jacob over Esau, if Isaac continues to favor Esau over Jacob, and if you both do not resolve your differences, it will be the boys who suffer for it." Deborah's sigh filled the space between them. "Both of them will suffer."

Rebekah stared into the contents of the cup for a long moment, her heart aching with the pain, the truth, of Deborah's words.

Oh, Isaac, why can't you see?

But perhaps Deborah's point made sense. She could not blame Isaac entirely. And the twins were only fifteen. They had many years ahead before they would be given the blessing. Isaac had many more years to live, God willing.

But she need not sit idly by, waiting for things to change or hoping Isaac would see things her way. She must groom Jacob, training him to be all that the vision, the word of the Lord, had in store for him. If Isaac would not listen, Jacob surely would.

Resolve tightened her muscles, and she stood, retrieved a cool cloth and dried her tears. Deborah rose with her and placed a hand on her shoulder.

"So you are well now?" She looked at Rebekah, uncertain.

Rebekah forced a smile that she prayed Deborah would find genuine. "I am well. Somehow we will work things out. When Isaac returns, I will welcome him."

She would not do to him what his mother had done to his father, no matter their differences. Somehow she would find a way to convince him, with or without words.

Isaac spent a restless night tossing on his pallet at the mouth of the cave, finally giving up the notion of sleep, and rose at the first hint of dawn. He kindled the fire that had long since died during the night, listening to Esau's soft snores. He studied his son in the pale pink light, his heart yearning with affection. The boy stirred, rolled over, and flung an arm over his head, his movements as violent as the passion with which he lived. Longing, even envy, touched the edges of Isaac's thoughts. How he wished he could be like his son, so self-assured, so quick to make decisions. Surely Esau possessed the marks of a good leader. If he had the right guidance and training, the men and women of the camp would do exactly as he wished.

But will he do as I wish?

The thought came from a place deep within, and he could not tell if the desire was for obedience to him as Esau's father or to Adonai. Esau showed interest in the questions of life, but only on the surface. He did not explore them to their depths as Ishmael had done, as Isaac himself did on his visits to the desert, to the fields, and among the sheep. Esau would not have taken time to sit long enough to give the words of Adonai that much thought. Would he?

The first twittering birdsong met him as he left the fire to draw water from a nearby stream. As he bent low at the water's edge, he looked to the opposite bank, where the water line dropped too low for this time of year. He filled the skin, glancing toward the eastern ridge. Waves of heat that should have dissipated with the night still hovered over the cloudless sky, threatening drought.

He stood but did not return to the fire. Instead, he trudged up the incline to look down over his fields in the plain below. The sky brightened further, and he picked his way down the low hill until he came to the first heads of barley. He fingered the stalks, frowning. Already the signs of too little water and too much heat were evident in the thirsty green stems. There was not enough water in the stream to divert to the fields even if he brought a hundred men to carry it.

He turned back, releasing a sigh, the weight of the goatskin too light in his hands. This was not good. They would lose the crop, and the herds would have little place to forage for food if they stayed in this place.

Concern rippled through him as he walked back to the fire. Esau sat before it, a camp stove set over the flames and a handful of wheat berries already toasting above it.

"Where did you go?" Esau met Isaac's gaze, then glanced toward the skin in his hands. "I could have gotten that for you. You should have awakened me."

Isaac smiled despite his anxiety. "I dare not come near a man who thrashes about so in his sleep."

Esau gave a sheepish grin. "Jacob used to holler at me when we were small and shared a tent. I whacked him in the night, waking him." His grin turned wicked. "He only thinks I was asleep the whole time."

Isaac lifted a brow. "You mean to tell me those bruises were intentional?"

He could not stop the amusement from lifting the corners of his mouth. The boy had caused Rebekah many a lost night of rest. Just as he had surely caused her with his unexplained absence even now. He should have told her he was leaving. Should have reassured her of his love, despite their differences.

Guilt pierced him, but Esau seemed not to notice.

"Can't let my little brother think he's stronger than me, now can I? A few smacks when he isn't expecting it don't hurt anything." His gaze glanced off Isaac's, and sudden color heightened his already ruddy hue.

Perhaps neither of them was immune to feeling guilt over the hurt they had inflicted. But he let the matter pass.

"We will turn back to camp today," he said, kneeling beside the fire to heat the water and herbs he carried.

"So soon? But we just left yesterday, and I had hoped . . ." He looked in the distance to the south, away from the camp.

"Had hoped what?" Isaac narrowed his gaze, trying to

read his son's intentions. That his son might want to spend time with him was tempting . . .

"I had thought . . . that is . . ." Esau stirred the wheat berries with a tree branch to keep them from burning.

Isaac waited, but it appeared Esau had changed his mind. "There is a famine on the horizon, and we must prepare for it."

Esau's brows drew together in a frown, and he looked as though he wanted to speak. Again Isaac waited, as Esau wrapped the thick part of his robe around his hand and pulled the camp oven from the fire to cool.

"We could stay with my uncle," he said, at last meeting Isaac's gaze. "There was no talk of famine in the hills where he lives."

Isaac studied his son, noting the eager light behind his eyes at the mention of Ishmael, and with the knowledge he felt the slightest hint of sadness. Was the boy too taken by his uncle? Ishmael did not carry the promise passed down from Abraham. Perhaps Rebekah had been right. But he could not trust that thought.

"We will send men to seek greener pastures and move where the water still resides," he said, mixing the mint leaves into the heated water to steep. "We will not be joining Ishmael." He glanced up to read Esau's expression. The boy's disappointment lasted but a moment.

"To Egypt then?"

Esau's eagerness did not diminish with the change of location. Isaac released a sigh. Perhaps it was only adventure he sought.

"I do not know where Adonai will lead us, my son."

"But Egypt has water, Father. The Nile flows continually, and they say that famine never visits the black land." He reached in his sack for a handful of dates and cheese and popped some in his mouth, then handed the rest to Isaac.

Isaac took a handful of both, fingering the dates' smooth, sticky surface. He glanced at the cloudless sky, already feeling the heat rising with the sun, which threatened to bake the earth before it had fully risen. Sweat broke out on the back of his neck, and he rubbed the spot as he popped the dates into his mouth. He broke off a hunk of the soft cheese and tucked the rest into his pouch.

"We will return to camp and discuss our options with Haviv and Eliezer." He met Esau's gaze. "We will go where God leads."

He waited, assessing Esau's reaction, but he seemed suddenly interested only in the food and the fire. Isaac poured the tea into clay mugs and handed one to his son, content with the silence and the interruption of twittering birds greeting the dawn.

When the meal finished, Esau cleaned up the utensils and packed the donkey's sacks while Isaac put out the fire. But as they turned west to head back to camp, Esau approached Isaac's side once more.

"Abba?"

"Yes, my son?" Isaac gripped the head of his staff, holding tight to the donkey's reins as he braced for what he sensed was coming next.

"What if I waited out the famine with my uncle? I would be one less stomach to fill, one less person to worry over. He did invite me to stay with him. And if you are going to move us regardless, then wouldn't now be a good time for me to make that visit?" He rested a hand on the donkey's mane and met Isaac's gaze across the animal's back.

Isaac looked at his son, Rebekah's warnings rising in his thoughts. And yet, as he saw the earnestness, felt the pleading in his tone, he could not help wondering anew whether her fears were unfounded. The twins were no longer children. Each one had to decide what he would believe, whether or not he would follow in the faith of their grandfather Abraham. It was not a decision Isaac could make for them. Perhaps time with his uncle would help Esau see the difference in the two households and long for his father's faith.

He looked beyond his son's head to the distant hills where Ishmael lived. It would take a few extra days to make the trip, but perhaps the boy was right. If Isaac took him there now, he could return and have that time alone and consider how best to make Rebekah see his view of things.

He paused but a moment, the decision made. "Very well, my son. I will take you to Ishmael. Perhaps if we hurry, we can catch up to his small caravan before they reach the hills. I will send for you when we are settled in our new location."

Never mind that they could use Esau's help in packing and moving to wherever they were going. His loss would mean less conflict between the twins, and perhaps less conflict between himself and Rebekah.

He did not stop to ponder that he was only fooling himself.

28

Rebekah stirred the lentil stew with the whittled branch Jacob had fashioned into a scraping utensil, her heart anxious, aching. Would the turmoil never cease? How was it she had lost both husband and one son in the space of a few weeks? But Abraham's death had changed Isaac, and Ishmael's visit had made Esau bolder until she feared she did not know either one anymore.

Their argument and Isaac's absence had lasted nearly a week, and when he returned, Esau was not with him. Isaac had given in and taken him to Ishmael only days after he agreed it was too soon, that the boy was too impressionable. The threat of famine should not have changed anything. Esau should go with them to wherever they were going.

Her stomach knotted at the sound of voices entering the camp and coming closer to the central fire. She peered through the sides of the open tent, where she stood over one of many cooking fires, to see Isaac and Haviv in deep discussion.

The ache intensified. Isaac had confided little in her since his return, saying only that they would be packing up the camp and moving west toward the sea. He had not shared her bed or stayed to talk after the evening meal since Ishmael had left nine days earlier.

The knot turned sour as she pondered the thought, and she felt the threat of tears. He stood so close, yet so far. How she missed him! Missed what they had once shared. But how could she get it back when neither one of them was willing to compromise? Bile rose in the back of her throat, and she struggled to swallow it.

A touch on her arm made her jump, making acid stick in her throat. She whirled about, nearly dropping the stick into the stew pot. "Jacob! You know better than to scare me like that." Had she been so absorbed by her thoughts that she had not heard his footfalls?

"I'm sorry, Ima." He placed a comforting hand on her shoulder. "But Father is asking for you."

She met his sober gaze and stiffened. "If he wants me, let him come to me." She lifted her chin and looked away, her anger bubbling.

"Ima." Jacob's gentle tone brought tears to her eyes. How could she treat him so? At least this son cared for her feelings, even if his father and brother did not.

She turned to look at him, and her grip tightened on the stick as she stirred and scraped, feeling the broth thickening. "He should come to me." But she dropped the pitch of her voice, knowing she did not mean it as fiercely as it sounded.

"How would it look to his men if he humbled himself to seek you out? Please, Ima, do not force him to step beneath his pride like that. Do not make him lose the respect of the men in the camp. If you do not heed his voice, who will?"

Jacob rested both hands on her shoulders and kneaded the tenseness until her muscles grew less rigid, her anger slowly dissipating. Of course he was right. Her bitterness would not accomplish her goals for Jacob. She must find better ways to appease and convince.

"You will come with me," she said. She glanced around the tent and spotted Selima at the other end. She called to her to take over stirring the stew, then straightened her head scarf and followed Jacob to the central fire.

"Here she is, Father."

Jacob's announcement brought Isaac's attention from Haviv to her. He smiled, but there was no laughter in his eyes or joy in the action.

"Rebekah, Haviv tells me that Abimelech, king of the Philistines in Gerar, has not felt the effects of the famine. He has accepted our request to settle in Gerar, and we will leave at first light. Please have your maids pack the belongings and be ready to go." He held her gaze, obviously awaiting her nod of acceptance, but she could not bring herself to acknowledge the wisdom in leaving with such speed.

Silence settled between them, and she felt the eyes of Haviv and Jacob on her.

"Is there a problem?" Isaac asked when she did not move or speak.

Warmth heated her face. She should not make him coax a response from her. That he even cared that she answer dissolved some of the ire from her heart.

"We shall do our best to be ready, my lord," she said at last, offering him a tentative nod. "We have accumulated many things, and a day or two longer might cause less burden on the men and women in their packing." She looked at him, searching, unable to keep the longing for him from invading her thoughts.

Isaac's look turned thoughtful, and he glanced briefly at the distant sky. She followed his gaze, uncertain what it was that he studied in the bright, cloudless heavens. His eyes swept the camp, then he glanced at Haviv before coming to look at her once more.

"I will send every available man to help you. But the sky

does not bode favorable for us to stay here. I sense a storm brewing, and it will not hold rain."

"One with sand and wind?"

He nodded. "The conditions are right, and while the trees here might shelter us, the sooner we can get to the coast, the better for the flocks and herds—for everyone."

His urgency suddenly made sense, becoming her own.

"I will do as you say." She turned, then thought better of it. "Shall I get started now?"

He smiled fully this time, and she felt a measure of relief in knowing her attempt at peacemaking had had its desired effect. "Yes, thank you. I will be along soon to help you."

She turned to leave, glancing back over her shoulder. "The food is ready. If you would eat now, we can pack the cooking utensils and eat flatbread and dried fruit in the morning."

He nodded his agreement, and she lifted her skirts and hurried across the short distance to the cooking tent. There was much to do, and the packing would be an almost overwhelming burden. But Isaac's gentle tone and genuine smile had given her new hope. She would make things right with Isaac whether she agreed with him or not. She would not move to Gerar with a heart of bitterness.

The trip to the outskirts of Gerar took three days for the members of the camp, longer for the herds, before they had passed the last of the burned-out grasses and dry wadis. Isaac walked the length of their makeshift encampment, listening to the sounds of nightfall and the soft voices of men huddled around enclosed fires. Women and children lay on pallets in a few of the larger tents that had been set up for protection against the night. They would unpack the rest of their goods when they arrived in Gerar tomorrow.

The thought both comforted and worried him as he paused

at the tent that housed Rebekah and her maids. Would the change in location give them a new start, allow them to set their differences aside? Surely they had lived through worse disagreements down through the years of Rebekah's barrenness and troubling pregnancy.

But as he looked at the tent, longing to call her out to him, to hold her close, he glanced down at the entrance and spotted Jacob stretched out near the tent's door, a guard against the night. His stomach tightened at the sight, a mix of pride and jealousy rivaling for space within him. How could he be jealous of his own son? And yet, had not Rebekah turned more often to Jacob than to him of late?

He searched his mind for a time, an event that had caused her to turn away, to favor Jacob over Esau, over him. Had it been since the twins' birth, with the vision she claimed? The vision that had divided them from the start?

No, even if the vision were true, she had been a caring mother, loving both boys, devoting herself to their care. No one in the camp could call her neglectful, and at times he had feared she would smother them as his mother had done him. There had to have been a time—something that caused the change.

But despite the longing to understand, he could not place the cause. She had favored Jacob long before Abraham's death.

The memory made him move on, but he was surprised at the grief he still felt. Since his father's death, he needed Rebekah more, not less. Needed her laughter and her love. But he had spoken little with her during the journey, and she had fallen exhausted on her pallet soon after dusk each night.

His feet crunched stones and dry twigs as he walked toward the tree line circling the camp, and the black sky overhead winked down on him with stars too many to count. A throat cleared, and he looked toward the sound, seeing Haviv striding toward him.

"Is everything settled?" He fell into step with Haviv and continued toward the seclusion of some overhanging oaks.

"All is well." Haviv ran a hand along the bumpy bark. "But there is news you should know."

Isaac waited, crossed his arms over his chest. "Tell me." Though by the look in Haviv's eyes, he sensed he would prefer not knowing.

"The traders we met at the pass had news of Gerar, of the men of the place." Haviv stepped back from the tree and rubbed a hand along the back of his neck, clearly troubled. "They do not fear Adonai as we do. They do not respect a man's property, particularly the women in his household . . . not even his wife. If our women go to market alone or mingle with the women of the city, they will be at risk. And I fear . . ." His pause was too long.

"You fear what?" A lump formed in Isaac's throat.

"I fear that the more beautiful women in our group will be at the greatest risk. Selima. Rebekah." Haviv let the words hang on the breeze, his look saying more than words.

"My father faced this in both Egypt and Gerar before I was born. Surely the new king of Gerar is not as debased as his father, for even his father repented of taking my mother without thought, and Adonai protected her even then."

But fear still found its way into Isaac's heart, and he wondered if his father had lost faith for lying to the men, saying his wife was his sister, or if he'd been wise in the way he approached both kings.

"Is the situation dire? Should we turn back or go south to Egypt?"

Haviv shook his head. "I do not know what is best. My father lost his first wife in just such a manner, by an unworthy king." He shifted from foot to foot and glanced over his shoulder, as though he feared the men of Gerar were already close enough to hear them.

"What will you do with Selima?" He could not have every man in the camp claiming to have no wives, to make every woman a sister. The lie would be too obvious.

"I do not know. I will accompany her to market or keep her only in the camp. She has our youngest to attend. A babe on her hip should be a strong deterrent."

Selima had given Haviv five strong sons and four daughters in their nearly thirty-five years of marriage, their youngest still not having weaned. But Rebekah had borne only Esau and Jacob with many years since their birth. She carried the body of a younger, still beautiful woman, not worn down with childbirth as Selima had been.

"Perhaps if we moved farther south," Haviv was saying, "toward Egypt, we would find the land still fertile, less arid."

"There is desert between here and Egypt. We face danger either way." Isaac looked once more to the starlit heavens. "I will think on it and pray." He met Haviv's gaze. "I will give you my decision before we break camp in the morning."

Isaac picked up a handful of stones, sorted through them for several smooth, round ones, tucked them into the pouch at the left side of his belt, and readied the sling in his right palm. He moved away from the camp, letting the moon guide him along the path at the side of the hill, aware of every sound, every flap of wings, every cricket's mating cry. The hoot of an owl drew him to look up at the sky, and he caught its form silhouetted in the moon's bright glow.

The familiar awe filled him at the sights and sounds of night, and he continued uphill, attuned to his surroundings, until he came to a secluded rock enclosure near the cliff's edge. The camp lay below him among the trees, partially hidden from his view, and he felt a measure of comfort in its nearness.

But he also felt a sense of respect for Adonai as he stepped into the wild of night. He walked farther into the rock recesses, his eyes adjusting to the darkness. The place appeared to be deserted, and after inspecting the area for animals he did not wish to disturb, he settled onto a large rock, resting his back against the rock wall.

Starlight danced above him, and he stared at their formations, identifying the Bear and Orion and some constellations that his ancestors would have worshiped and deemed deities. How could a man think the stars held power or answers over the world, over his life? The voice of God he had heard long ago—*that* held power over a man.

He closed his eyes against the sight above him.

Oh, to hear Your voice again, Adonai. To know for certain You are guiding me where I should go. Are You with me as You had been with my father? Should I turn back to the dried-out plains and thirsty fields? Should I return to Hebron? Or go south to Egypt? Where, O Lord, would You send Your servant?

He sat listening to the night sounds until the crickets' voices died away and the howl of distant jackals faded from his hearing. His eyes felt weighted, as if heavy stones rested upon them, and though he struggled to open them, to look once more to the heavens, he could not lift his lids. His breath drew in and out in a normal rhythm, his chest lifting and falling. He sensed sleep would soon overtake him but felt as though he already dreamed.

Warmth settled over him, and he relaxed, cocooned in an ethereal vision between night and day, light and darkness. The bleating of a ram, like the one caught in the thicket the day of his binding, met his ear, and he turned his head, expecting to see it once more ready to take his place. Instead, he looked into the face of a man he did not know, who stood in the glow of the light.

"Do not go down to Egypt."

The man spoke, and the voice thundered as it had that day in Isaac's ears, familiar and fearful, yet he was not afraid.

"Live in the land where I tell you to live. Stay in this land for a while, and I will be with you and will bless you. For to you and your descendants I will give all these lands and will confirm the oath I swore to your father Abraham. I will make your descendants as numerous as the stars in the sky and will give them all these lands, and through your offspring all nations on earth will be blessed, because Abraham obeyed Me and kept My requirements, My commands, My decrees, and My laws."

"I will do as you say, Lord." As the words left his lips, the light vanished, and the weights lifted from his eyes. He looked up and blinked against the blinding light of stars too numerous to count.

I will make your descendants as numerous as the stars in the sky.

A little thrill rushed through him. Jacob and Esau would bear sons, and their sons would bear sons, and his children's children would possess all the lands that now lay dry and fallow. Someday they would flourish again.

He slowly stood. In the unspoken request of obedience came the knowledge that he would be blessed because his father had believed and obeyed, even to the point of great loss. As he must be willing to lose as well, to sacrifice all to the obedience of Adonai.

To what end? Could he do as his father had done?

The thought brought with it a rush of memories. Strength failed him as he saw himself in the place of his father. His sons were almost the age he had been at his binding. If Adonai asked it of him, could he so fully obey?

He shuddered and sank to his knees beside the rock, wrestling with the question long into the night.

29

Rebekah led a heavy-laden donkey through the gates of Gerar the next day, just one of the throng of men, women, and children in their camp. Isaac moved at the head of the group, and she could see him walking tall and determined many paces ahead of her, Jacob at his side.

A twinge of pride lifted her chin. If Esau had been with them, Jacob would not be standing as Isaac's right-hand man. Esau surely would have taken his brother's place. Perhaps Isaac had been right in letting the boy go off with his uncle after all. It would be Jacob whom Isaac introduced to the king as his son. Jacob who would carry the appearance of Isaac's heir.

Please, Adonai, let it be so.

Buildings of hardened clay rose on either side of a paved stone street as she clutched the donkey's reins harder, leaving behind the tent-enclosed merchant stalls and the calls of men to come and peruse and purchase their wares. Heat filled her face at some of the ribald comments cast toward the veiled women. She felt the clasp of her head scarf to make sure it held secure over her face.

"What do you make of this place?" Selima sidled up alongside her, holding tight to her young daughter's hand. She leaned closer, but her gaze did not hold Rebekah's, flitting first right, then left, taking in the town whose grandeur grew the farther they progressed.

"I don't know." Rebekah glanced over her shoulder toward the merchants' stalls and spotted a lone man ambling beside their caravan, attempting to get closer to the women huddled at the center of the group. She looked quickly away, her heart suddenly pounding. King Abimelech's palace grew closer, but the thought did not comfort. "Do you think we are safe here?"

Selima shrugged but pulled her daughter closer, lifting her into her arms. "You do not need to hurry so. What did you see back there?"

Rebekah looked straight ahead, realizing she had picked up her pace and was nearly on top of the donkeys in front of her. "A man is following us." She swallowed, holding back her fear.

Selima met her gaze, her own showing a hint of alarm. "What can one man do among so many? The men surround us. Surely we are safe." But she tightened her grip on her daughter just the same.

Rebekah stepped nearer to Selima, tugging the donkey to her until they nearly melded as one. A man's whistle and crude remarks drifted closer, and she knew his intent was not honorable.

"We must tell our husbands," she whispered into Selima's ear. "Take the donkey's reins. I must tell Isaac. Where is your mother?"

"She is behind us, walking with my girls." Selima's older daughters were young, though one was near marriageable age.

"Send someone to get her. I want her to come with me." Rebekah cinched her robe closer. Her breath hitched as she continued to walk forward while Selima worked her way to the women and girls straggling in the rear. *Please hurry!*

She glanced behind her once more, aware that several others had joined the lone man until a small crowd of them now followed their company. Her heart quickened its pace, and she darted a look in Isaac's direction, but still he did not turn her way.

Her hand wrapped tighter around the donkey's reins, and she had to take care not to stumble as she glanced behind her once more. Relief filled her at the sight of Deborah rushing to her side.

"Shall I take the donkey while you find Isaac?" Deborah's expression told her that she shared Rebekah's fears.

"One of the servants can lead the beast. I want you to come with me." She handed the reins to one of the maids, then motioned for Deborah to follow.

She wove between the sweating women and beasts until she at last reached Jacob's side. Deborah waited one step behind her as she touched his arm, got his attention, and moved in to stand next to Isaac. He turned to look at her, surprise lifting his brows.

"My lord, there is trouble." Her breath felt tight within her chest. "There are several men trying to get close to the women, and these men . . ." She tilted her head in the direction of the merchants. "They are very crude and offensive, my lord."

Isaac looked into her eyes but a moment, then glanced beyond her to where the commotion stirred. "We should not have come." He breathed the comment, but the look in his eyes told her she had not misunderstood him.

"Then let us turn around at once and go to some other place." She would have grabbed his arm and tugged him with her if she had thought for a moment that it would urge him to act quickly. But as the king's courtyard stretched before them, Haviv's deep voice cut off Isaac's response and turned their attention to where he stood several paces away, standing on a short section of the palace wall.

"What is the meaning of this affront to our women and children? We seek peace among you and have the permission of the king to enter."

As he spoke, Isaac left her with Jacob and Deborah and moved to Haviv's side.

One of the men shouted from the back of the crowd, "Any woman entering our gates gets our attention, stranger. Any real man ought to know that."

Guffaws and back slaps followed the remark, raising the hair on Rebekah's arms. She watched Isaac speak quietly to Haviv, then turn back to them to whisper something in Jacob's ear. Within moments the men of Isaac's camp had woven their way in among the women, a shield against the citizens.

But what was their small group against an entire town?

A trumpet's blast jerked her around, and she felt Jacob move in front of her as guards and flag bearers emerged from the palace and hurried through the courtyard to the stone gates. Isaac turned away from the uncouth men while Haviv jumped down from the wall, and the two strode to the head of their group. Jacob fell into step behind them, and she felt herself and Deborah swept into the palace by the king's flanking guards.

They moved through ornate oak doors along intricate inlaid tiles set in patterns of birds and beasts and gods similar to those she had known in Harran. They stopped in a chamber larger than her tent, where the guards left them. Isaac and Haviv stood near the door, speaking too softly for her to hear, but Jacob touched her elbow and bent low.

"Abba told me to protect you," he whispered. "He said for us to keep quiet. He will speak to the king and see what is to be done."

She smiled into his eyes and nodded, longing to touch the soft growth now covering his chin. How tall he had become! She suddenly realized with a certain sense of loss that he was no longer the child she had once carried in her arms.

"I do not like it here," Jacob said, his low tones meant for her ears but his gaze directed at his father's back.

"Nor do I."

A servant approached only moments later, gave them strict instructions on royal protocol, and led them to the king's receiving chamber. They knelt at a thick line of deep blue tiles, a barrier for all who would approach the steps that led upward to the king's throne.

"Rise and speak."

The commanding voice came from the right of the king.

Rebekah rose slowly and glanced in front of her, following Isaac's silent lead.

"You have come from a distance," the king said, his voice welcoming but his expression flinty, causing her an instant sense of distrust.

"From Hebron, my lord king." Isaac gave a slight bow.

"To what purpose have you come?" The king curled one hand around a scepter of polished, ornamented gold.

"To seek refuge from the famine. To settle on lands near your city, to cultivate and to care for our little ones and our herds." Isaac's voice held a calm Rebekah wished in that moment was hers. But the unsettled feeling in her middle would not leave.

"We are most happy to have you. Our merchants will be pleased to have your business, and you may in turn settle on the land south of town. There are fields beyond there where you can plant and plenty of land for your animals to graze."

Rebekah kept her head lowered but attempted a glance at the king, surprised at his gracious gift.

"I will be happy to pay you for the use of the land," Isaac said. "Please name your price for its use."

The king waved the request away with his free hand, but he did not smile. "We will discuss those details later. I am sure you are weary from your journey. Go and settle your families, then return tomorrow and we will talk."

Isaac bowed low and then rose. "Thank you, my lord king. It will be as you say."

Rebekah felt a sudden urge to rush from the room but forced her anxious feet to still, awaiting the king's dismissal.

"Who are these men and women you have brought with you?"

The king's voice and tone stopped Rebekah's blood, and for a brief moment she thought she might faint. She lifted her head to glance at Isaac, but his back was to her, and she could not draw on the strength she needed from him. She heard Jacob's quick intake of breath and silently thanked God that Deborah stood beside her.

"The young man is my son, my lord king." He gestured toward Haviv. "And this man is my chief steward." Isaac turned slightly to one side and beckoned Jacob closer to stand at his right side. At any other time the action would have pleased her, but a fear she could not name suddenly slithered up her back, and she felt exposed and alone.

"The women are your wife and sister?"

Rebekah longed to meet the king's gaze, to understand his question, but the meaning at once became clear.

"The older woman is your wife, of course. But the younger one is too old to be a daughter. A sister? A cousin, perhaps? She is quite beautiful." The king's words held the challenge of one who is not to be crossed, one whose word is right and just and obeyed without question.

Fear took wing inside her, and in one glance she recognized that same desire she had seen in countless men throughout Harran years before, desire she had not faced in that possessive, controlling way since she'd married Isaac.

Silence followed the remark, and Rebekah's heart squeezed until she felt an almost physical pain.

Tell the man the truth so we can leave.

But when she glanced up to find the king's gaze fixed solely on her, she knew in a heartbeat that he did not want to hear the truth. The truth would be dangerous to them all—to her, to Isaac, perhaps even to Jacob. For what use did a king have for a husband and a son of a woman he desired?

"She is my sister."

The words did not register past the sudden throbbing in her head. She closed her eyes, keeping her head discreetly lowered, begging the room not to sway.

"Your sister, you say?" The king sounded clearly pleased, a lion crouching, observing its prey.

"Yes, my lord." Isaac's voice sounded far steadier than it should have. Did this lie not trouble him? Yet surely he would still find a way to protect her.

"Very good. We will keep that fact in mind." He tapped the end of his scepter to the floor. "You may go."

Rebekah did not breathe again until they were safely out of the king's chamber, and if not for Jacob's steadying arm, she would have melted into the paved stones beneath their feet. But she could not weaken or show her fear. Not here.

She felt Isaac's presence at her side, his breath against her ear. "Come quickly and do not look back."

She gathered her skirts and hurried beside him.

Isaac led the company of men, women, and children to the outskirts of Gerar to land within the jurisdiction of the Philistine king and under his protection. Weariness followed him, the kind caused not by lack of sleep or too much exertion but by the realization that life had taken a turn, and the change would not bring peace.

"At least he accepted us." Haviv kept pace with him as Isaac pushed himself to mark out the area before the sun sank another notch toward the west. He would feel more at ease once he could see the women safely settled and could speak alone with Rebekah.

What had possessed him to give in to such a lie? How could he stop men from trying to claim her?

"I would have done the same thing in your position," Haviv said as Isaac finally stopped at the copse of trees lining the field Abimelech had commissioned for him. "What other choice did you have?"

"I would have told him the truth if the townsmen had made me more at ease. I do not think the men of Philistia accept strangers because they are friendly." Isaac lifted an arm to sweep the space before them. "This is where we will settle."

"Do you think our lives are in danger because of our women?"

Haviv's question only churned the fear already growing in Isaac's gut.

"Yes." He hated the cowardice the king had evoked in him. He had faced death before, had seen the power of God to protect him. Had not God told him to settle here rather than Egypt? The thoughts battered within, leaving his soul bruised and beaten.

He tied the donkey he was leading to the branch of a tree and set about unloading his tent from its back, then looked up at the sound of Rebekah's voice. An ache so deep he could not reach it filled him as he studied her. She lifted her head to look at him. He had failed her. He could read it in her assessing censure, in the hurt that caused the light in her eyes to flicker.

"Let us get these tents raised and be quick about it."

The barked command sounded like it came from someone other than him. But her tent was the best place to speak to Rebekah alone, to reassure her away from listening ears and gossiping tongues.

Rebekah stood at the threshold of Isaac's tent as the sun gave up its fight to stay suspended in the west and sank with an array of potent reds and golds into the night. Her heart beat as a new bride's as she waited, holding back a mixture of emotions she could not gather into one place or keep still within her. What could he possibly say to her that would ease the pain of this new betrayal, this cowardice?

And yet, how could she blame him? She had seen the king's look, and she knew what men in power could do to those beneath them if they so chose.

She drew in a slow breath as he appeared in the door of his tent and extended a hand to her.

"Come." His voice was low, husky, and she obeyed without a word. "Sit. Please."

She settled herself among the cushions in his visiting area, beyond the partition that separated it from the chamber where he slept. Would he treat her as the sister he claimed her to be? How far would the lie take them? Would he take Deborah to wife to give truth to the king's suspicions?

But she did not voice the questions.

"I hope you know that I had little choice in the presence of Abimelech." His look held hers for a lengthy moment, as though willing her to agree, but she could not give the nod of affirmation she longed to. "I was a coward . . . and afraid."

"You were doing what you had to do to protect your family. No one can fault you for that." Her eyes searched his. Love for him suddenly filled her, and she knew in a heartbeat that she meant every word. "I saw the way he looked at me, the way the men of Harran used to look. It is not love that guides their words. It is desire, pure and simple."

"Desire misdirected and greedy, nonetheless, and a danger to us all." He sighed, but the action seemed strained. "I will tell him the truth when I meet with him tomorrow. If I die, I die."

"No!" She hurled herself toward him and wrapped both arms around him. "Let him think what he will for now." She nestled herself against his heart, could feel the steady pounding in his chest. "In time, after we better know the place and the people, then you can tell him. Why take such a risk?"

"God protected me from my own father. Surely He can do the same from a heathen king."

"But what if He doesn't? Your father was commanded to do what he did. This king does not listen to Adonai or care to do what He says." She scooted closer still until she heard his breath hitch at her nearness. "Please, my lord."

His arms came around her, and he kissed the top of her head. How long had it been since he had held her thus? Not since the week of Abraham's death, before their fight about the twins and the angry words that had been flung between them. He rubbed circles along her back, and she felt the tension and fear slip away.

"How can I treat you as a sister? I cannot bear to be apart from you."

His whispered words thrilled her. Never mind the arguments or the things that remained unsettled. She needed him, and in that moment she knew that she could not lose him, even if it meant giving up the things that had been keeping them apart. Surely they could settle their differences.

"We will have to practice discretion." She reached up to kiss his cheek, her breath soft against his face. "I can act the part of a sister, if only you do not keep apart from me at night." She smiled as she met his gaze, a gaze ignited with warmth and acceptance, something she had not felt from him in far too long.

He kissed her, a reminder of all she had missed in his absence. He gently rubbed both of her cheeks with his thumbs and traced a line along her jaw. "I am not sure we are truly safe here." She heard the uncertainty in his voice.

"As long as you are with me, I am safe." She spoke to reassure herself as much as him.

30

Isaac raised a hand to his eyes, a shield against the glare, and looked with satisfaction on the plowed field. The abundance of the last harvest had surprised him, yielding more than double what he would have expected. How good God was! How small his own faith!

He released a sigh and smiled at the even rows where young men and women of the camp scattered seed from pouches hung at their sides. Pockets of laughter filtered to him from the young men while the girls gossiped between the rows. There would be joy in the camp tonight, a pleasing sound he had grown to anticipate in the years they had lived in peace near Gerar.

He turned to one of three sets of yoked oxen, undid the latches, and lifted the wooden beam from the oxen's necks, then inspected the wood for any signs of roughness or splintering. Deep male voices grew closer, the familiar sound of his overseer and oldest son. He looked up at Haviv's and Esau's approach and set the yoke aside, a sense of apprehension rising at the sight of their matching frowns.

"What is it?" He glanced beyond them to see more men drawing close, his chief shepherd and several servants coming up behind.

"The Philistines have stopped up the wells, even the wells Abraham dug when he lived in these hills. We had to go in search of streams to water the flocks and herds," the chief shepherd said. "This is not a good time while the females are with young. We need those wells."

Isaac glanced at the field where the seeding continued unhindered. The rains were not yet upon them. The wadis would be dry until they came, the wells of even greater import. "We will have to unstop them or dig new ones."

"Which would you have us do?" Haviv asked.

"Unstop the wells my father dug." Isaac looked to one of the approaching servants. "See to the yoke and oxen. I will have a talk with Abimelech in the morning. Haviv, you will come with me."

"Can I come too, Father?" Esau's long legs brought him quickly to his side. "I have not yet met the king, and I would like to."

Isaac stopped and looked at his son, his memory flashing with sudden fear. "Now is not the time, my son." He had not yet told King Abimelech the truth about Rebekah. He did not need to complicate matters with another son. "I need you to oversee the servants with the wells."

Esau scowled at the response, but he did not argue. How much the boy had changed during his time with Ishmael! He was stronger, bolder, and the growth of a man's beard had fully formed now along his neck and jaw.

Isaac watched Esau turn and stalk off after the servants and breathed a relieved sigh.

"The women might like a chance to visit the markets while we visit the king," Haviv said as they entered the camp. "It has been months, and Selima pesters me about needing new pots since a few of ours have cracked with daily use."

"What is wrong with the pots we make here in camp?"

"Apparently, the Philistines use different dyes in the designs or etchings along the top. I don't know. She claims they make sturdier tools than we do too."

Isaac stopped near the line of tents, his thoughts churning with indecision, with what to say to the king. "I don't think this is a good time."

Haviv nodded his acceptance, but the following morning Isaac changed his mind when Haviv arrived with Selima and several maids in tow.

"They asked if you might reconsider. If the group is large enough, they should be safe."

Rebekah looked to him, pleading, and Isaac shook his head in defeat.

"I thought you did not like Gerar." He glanced at Rebekah as he bid Jacob and Deborah and several male servants to join them to increase their company.

"I don't. The men are uncivilized and crass."

He released a frustrated breath. "Then why do you come?" Could the men in his employ, could his son, protect her?

"Because there are goods there we cannot make ourselves." Her smile made all his arguments turn to dust. "Besides, after living so long untroubled, surely we are safe."

He did not agree but did not argue.

"Outings are always enjoyable when my men surround me." She took his arm and sidled close. She did not mention Esau's absence, and he did not ask her why. Graver issues stretched before them now. Issues of water rights and grazing lands.

The markets teemed with life, and the reason became clear the moment they set foot in the main square. Heavy-laden camels and donkeys blocked the intersection that led to the Way of the King, and Isaac immediately regretted his timing. But there was no turning back now.

They made their way past the stalls, weaving in and out of a large Syrian caravan, swarming market stalls, and vagabond children darting around the legs of the buyers and sellers, trying to snatch whatever they could to feed their too-thin bellies. He must do something soon to see that the children were fed, to make sure his kindness actually reached them and not their greedy guardians. The thought troubled him, as so many vices of Gerar often did, and he knew he would not rest until he sought a solution.

The sweaty smell of too many bodies mingled with that of spices and camel dung, familiar and pungent, assaulting his senses. He grasped Rebekah's hand and pulled her close, a protective feeling washing over him. He motioned the group to follow as he maneuvered his way, finally breaking through the crowd to start the trek along the main thoroughfare. The streets of paved stone burned with the heat of the late morning sun, and the number of people thinned out the closer they drew to the palace gates.

"I should have known better," he said, bending close to Rebekah's ear. "The crowds are not safe. I cannot leave you women with only one young man and a few servants to guard. You will stay with me." He squeezed her hand and released it.

She nodded and offered him a smile that warmed him. "When you finish with the king, you can take me to the stalls. A woman does not come all this way only to have the delights of Damascus denied her."

He laughed at the way her mouth curved just slightly into a pout. He touched her cheek, letting his fingers trail a line along her jaw, his gaze lingering. "How can I argue with such a request? Of course, you will have your fill of merchants and goods from Damascus once I convince the king to give back the wells his men have stolen."

The thought grew heavier with the reminder of why they had come, and now he had the added worry of having brought the women and Jacob when they had no safe place to wait. But the palace gates rose before them now, and Haviv stepped closer.

"The women and Jacob can wait in the portico beneath the shaded columns. I will speak to one of the guards to make sure they are not disturbed."

Isaac examined the ornate columns, where all manner of carved beings stood guard over the heavy oak doors, and limestone benches with clawed feet lined the walls beneath the overarching roof. "It appears we have no other choice."

His heart beat faster as they approached the seated guard to state their business. The man seemed to regard Jacob, assessing his height and strength, then assessed the two male servants, and finally glanced at the women, pausing too long to study Rebekah. He lifted a brow and looked at them with curiosity, but he said nothing as he motioned to the bench near the doors, where they would wait.

"Follow this man." The guard pointed to another armed sentry, and within moments Isaac and Haviv were escorted inside, announced without fanfare, and presented to the king.

"Why did you deceive me?" The king's question brought the blood rushing to Isaac's head.

"Deceive you, my lord king?" He waited, searching for a reason for the hostile glare piercing through the king's adornments.

"She is really your wife! Why did you say, 'She is my sister'?"

Isaac swallowed hard. How did he discover the truth? But he did not voice the question. Whether it was right or not, the time had come.

"Because I thought I might lose my life on account of her." Who could cross the king and live?

The fire in Abimelech's eyes did not lessen. "What is this you have done to us? One of the men might well have slept with your wife, and you would have brought guilt upon us."

Isaac lowered his gaze to the tiles but did not offer a word of defense, as there was none to give. Silence settled in the room, broken only by the scratching of the scribe's tools on clay and parchment. A sharp clap of the king's hands seemed sudden, though only a moment had passed as Abimelech called on a servant standing nearby.

"Yes, my lord king," the servant said loud enough that it caused Isaac to look up. But the anger he expected to see in the king's face had smoothed into an unmistakable mask of disdain.

"Spread the word to every man living anywhere near Gerar, saying this: 'Anyone who molests this man or his wife shall surely be put to death.'" The king once more held Isaac's gaze. "Go in peace."

Isaac bowed low. "Thank you, my lord king. May you live forever."

Relief spread through him in a rush the moment they rejoined Rebekah, Deborah, Selima, and Jacob in the portico. At last the truth was made known.

He took hold of Rebekah's arm, all thoughts of water rights forgotten.

***

"What do you plan to do about the wells? We dig them out only to find them filled in again. And the quarreling has almost come to blows."

Haviv stood at Isaac's side as two servants hefted the heavy stone from the mouth of a well that Abraham's servants had dug when Isaac was a boy. Back when water rights and living among the peoples of the land had seemed far less complicated to his innocent eyes.

He stepped closer once the stone was removed, half hoping to see the steps that led to the spring below. But unsettled earth filled the cavity to the rim.

"We have enemies among the king's herdsmen." He rubbed a hand along his jaw and leaned more heavily into the staff he had stuck into the earth. In the months since his last visit to the king, the protection he'd enjoyed had not appeared to extend to his servants or shepherds.

"The men are jealous of your successes. God has blessed you mightily. You can't deny it." Haviv's tone held a hint of pride, as a man might feel for the success of his friend.

"I don't deny it."

God had promised blessing because of his father's faithfulness. Was he merely the recipient of another's merit? Was the faith of his father earned or given in grace?

"So what do you propose we do?"

The bleating of sheep sounded in the distance, and Isaac looked toward the hills, where he spotted his chief shepherd leading the flocks away from the stopped-up well in search of existing water. The thirsty animals could not wait until water was found beneath their feet.

"We will do as the shepherds are already doing. We will move to another area and try again." Isaac turned away from the earth-filled well and headed back toward the camp. "In the meantime, I will talk to Abimelech again and see what can be done."

But the following day, as he waited once more in the receiving chamber of the Philistine king, the answer did not please him.

"Move away from us. You have become too powerful for us," Abimelech said.

Isaac bowed low, then rose, suddenly aware that in a different set of circumstances this king should be bowing to him. But the thought did not cheer him. What he possessed was a gift; whatever blessing he carried, something another had earned.

"I am sorry to have worried you. My men are no threat

to yours." He dipped his head, acknowledging the authority of the man. "But to put your mind at ease, we will pack up and leave within the week."

He left the king's presence, sensing the man's relief, albeit relief mixed with an animosity that he could not hide beneath the shadow of the crown he wore.

Isaac met Haviv, who waited just inside the doors to the receiving chamber. The two walked in silence along Gerar's thoroughfare, past merchant stalls now quiet with the midday sun, and through the Philistine gates to the valley beyond.

"That was unexpected," Haviv said when they were a safe distance from the guards and walking through the fields toward their camp. "I thought he was going to toss us into the streets with that glare he does so well."

Isaac smiled at Haviv's attempt at humor, but he could not shake the sobering feeling that always accompanied change. "I think he was angry and afraid of us. Though I fail to see how two lone men posed any threat to him."

"He was probably thinking about that small army of men you have trained that could attack his town at your word."

Haviv's sarcasm elicited a chuckle from Isaac, lessening his unease. "We will move from the valley back toward Beersheba, where my father once lived. There are wells along the way that we will dig again, but we will take our time getting there."

They neared the copse of trees that provided a protective barrier to the tents on the other side along the valley floor.

"If I may ask," Haviv said, "why not move directly there, away from the king's territory?"

Isaac rested his staff in the dirt and looked beyond Haviv toward the west and the town they had just left. God had blessed him here, had told him to stay and not move to Egypt. "I must seek Adonai's will before we move too far. Who knows but it might yet be His plan for us to stay in the area where my father's wells were dug? We will move in that direction, and I will seek His face."

Haviv nodded, his expression one of acceptance. "It will be as you say."

They returned to the camp to break the news to Rebekah.

Rebekah bent over the loom, her fingers deftly working the threads. The pattern of four stripes repeated itself, with the yellows and whites like streaks among the thicker reds and blacks. Esau would be pleased with the design, as it was an exact copy of one worn by a passing wealthy merchant on his way north, though he would not appreciate the care and skill she put into making it just so. He never noticed the things she did for him, not the way Jacob did. He was too busy running after foreign women and taking his weapons into the hills to hunt.

She released a tightly clenched jaw and leaned back, examining the robe taking shape beneath her hand. The work was good. The garments would be Esau's best, and she would keep them with her when he did not need them. He would surely ruin or misplace them if they were left with him.

She looked up at the sound of birdsong, her heart lifting as it always did when she expected Isaac's mimicked tunes. But disappointment quickly replaced her hope of seeing him. It was just a bird after all.

Why did she still cling to a memory? He rarely whistled such tunes for her now, though he surely still did so when he went out to the fields or spent time with the sheep. Wistful longing accompanied that thought. She had not been to the fields or followed him into the hills since the day they had set foot in Gerar so long ago. The fear of being found out as husband and wife had caused a loss of much-needed privacy and too little time alone. Even now that the truth was known, he did not come to her as he once did. If only he were not so stubborn . . .

She fingered the threads, mentally counting the rows. The robe was nearly half done, and when it was completed, she would present it to Isaac to give to Esau. Perhaps then he would believe that she loved Esau too.

A sigh formed within her, and she slowly let it out and looked through the open sides of the tent toward the hills, toward Gerar, where Isaac and Haviv had gone early that morning. The mist of dawn had long since lifted, and the women of the camp had settled into their normal daily routines, though Deborah had yet to join her at the loom. Selima needed her mother to help with her children more than Rebekah needed her help with the weaving. But she did not enjoy the loneliness such times afforded.

She straightened, rubbing the small of her back, then chose another color to weave into the warp. Male voices made her look up again, and this time she spotted Isaac coming toward her. She jumped up from the low stool where she had been sitting and hurried into the sunlight.

"You are back so soon! Did the king accept you? Are the water rights secure?"

She had overheard the discussions, the arguments Isaac and Haviv had raised during many an evening meal. Even Jacob had given an opinion she thought fair, but Isaac seemed only interested in hearing Haviv's comments. Esau had been off doing as he pleased.

Isaac took hold of her elbow and gently guided her back into the weaving tent, out of the sun's glare and out of earshot of the servants in the camp. "Order the servants to pack our things and be ready to leave in three days. We are moving away from here."

How familiar this conversation. She lifted a brow in question. "But what of the wells? I thought now that we have grown to such a large company, the king enjoyed our protection."

He studied her a brief moment. "The king is the one sending us away. He feels we are no longer protection but a threat."

"A threat?" Her gentle husband a threat? Ridiculous!

"Yes." He glanced beyond her, as though searching for something to convince her.

"If the king says to go, we will go. There are better places to live, in any case."

He gave her a quizzical look, and she struggled to understand the thoughts behind his dark eyes. "Is there something more, my lord?"

He shook his head. "Have you seen Esau?"

A bitter twinge pierced her that he should desire to leave her so quickly to go off in search of his favorite son. "Jacob is in the camp, but I have not seen Esau." Let him be reminded that he had one son he could count on to be nearby, to do his bidding.

Isaac glanced beyond her, but she did not miss the firm set to his jaw. "Tell Jacob to meet me near the donkeys. And send a servant to find Esau."

"He is probably off in search of a wife."

The boy cared not a whit what she thought of his exploits. Perhaps this move would be good for him, get him away from the foreign women of Gerar.

Isaac looked thoughtful, but there was a sternness in his gaze she did not like, one he had turned her way only when they had argued about the twins.

"Perhaps it is time we seek a wife for him then."

"He is barely twenty!"

"The age does not matter if the man is ready."

"Esau is not responsible enough for such a thing."

"And I will not expect his mother to coddle him and keep him from the life God intends if he is ready to bring a bride into the camp." His words were firm, and she did not miss the challenge in his gaze.

"I do not coddle him!" she hissed, glancing beyond him, fearful the servants would overhear.

"No, you reserve that for Jacob."

The stinging words felt like a slap to her cheek. She flushed hot, and his dark eyes pierced hers. When had he grown so angry with her? Is that what he really thought? She would admit to enjoying Jacob's desire to live near the tents, to come and go with the sheep rather than spend days away in the hills hunting in the wild. His malleable spirit had allowed her to train him, to teach him all he must know to be ruler of the camp one day. But of course Isaac resented this.

"I do not coddle Jacob either." She finally spoke, but the words were barely above a whisper now.

Isaac stared at her, then shook his head as though the whole discussion were a frustration to him. "I thought we were past this. I did not come here to argue again. Just send for Esau and start packing. Be ready to leave in three days."

He turned and walked away from her without a backward glance, leaving her feeling like a child who had been severely chastised. She put a hand to her burning cheek, grateful to be alone in the tent, to recover from the shock of all of Isaac's words.

31

Rebekah tucked a stray strand of hair beneath her head covering, but it was useless against the wind that seemed determined to whip both her hair and the scarf from their proper place. She gave up on the third try and faced the cool breeze coming down from the hills, not caring what she looked like or who might see. Strange how time had changed her. There had been a day in her youth when her beauty had been her prized possession, the envy of many a woman, the desire of many a man. When had she stopped caring?

She trudged forward, at last setting her jar in the stone impression at the well of Shibah, the last and final well Isaac's servants had dug near Beersheba, where they had settled and made peace with the Philistines. How long ago it seemed to her now.

She lifted the rope that held the pitch-lined wooden bucket and lowered it to the spring gurgling in the depths below. The younger servant girls could handle this task, but today she needed the distraction and the time to clear her head.

She strained against the rope, heavy now with the full water bucket, and startled at the sound of male voices behind her. She gripped the rope tighter and hurried to pull it up, her pulse jumping within her. But one glance behind her put her heart at ease.

"Ima, let me get that for you."

Jacob's welcome voice warmed her, and she could not help but smile at the man he had become. How strong and good he was!

"Do you think your mother so weak that she cannot draw water?" She hefted the water over the lip of the well and grasped it in her hands, carried it to the stone jar, and carefully poured it to the rim. "Would you like some?" She offered him what was left in the bottom, then noted the men, Haviv's oldest sons, who were with him. "There is enough for you and your friends, my son."

He took it from her and drank, then handed it to one of the men. "Thank you, Ima." He sat on the side of the well and looked at her, his smile mischievous.

"I know that look, Jacob. You are too pleased with yourself."

"I have good reason to be." He laughed, and she thought the sound almost musical. He glanced at his two friends whose smiles stretched wide over tan, bearded faces.

"Tell me quickly, lest I die of curiosity."

She leaned against the well beside him, struck again by the way the passing years had matured him. She ought to seek a wife for him soon, and not from the neighboring tribes as Esau had done. One wife, as she had been to Isaac, not like those two bickering heathens Esau had married without his parents' permission. She held back a powerful urge to sigh, to give in to the weighted feeling she carried too often of late, the one that made her feel ancient and useless. If not for Jacob, what good would her life be? She and Isaac had grown so distant . . .

"It all started with lentils," Jacob said, pulling her thoughts back to the present and causing laughter among the three men.

She was far too distracted and distraught these days, and she blamed it on Judith and Basemath, the daughters-in-law she did not want.

"Lentils?" She pulled the scarf closer and turned her back to the wind, facing Jacob. "What are you talking about?"

"Lentils and your son's famous red stew," Haviv's firstborn son said.

"Well, famous now," said the other. "And it will be a long time before Esau asks to taste it again, if I were to bet on it."

She frowned and crossed her arms over her chest, leveling her most stern look at her son, but she could not keep the pride from filling her at the way he smiled when he returned her look with an amused one of his own.

"Do not look so distressed, Ima. This news will please you. I promise." He placed a hand on her shoulder and leaned back against the well, stretching both legs out and crossing them at the ankles. "I took some of the lentils from the last harvest and added some vegetables and the spices you favor. The pot hung over the fire, and I checked on it now and then. I intended to surprise you with it during the evening meal, but Esau came into camp famished from being out in the fields, not to mention that his trek into the wilderness yielded nothing."

"Your father will be disappointed."

Isaac had grown even fonder of the wild game Esau hunted as he aged, since his own arm had weakened against trying to hold the bow.

"Not as disappointed as he will be when he hears what Esau agreed to do." The comment brought a sober look to his dark eyes, and for a fleeting moment Rebekah wondered if Jacob also regretted whatever had taken place between himself and his brother.

"What did Esau agree to?"

She felt the slightest wave of apprehension fill her. Esau's wives already caused both her and Isaac enough grief. They did not need trouble beyond the normal silent animosity between their sons as well. Animosity driven by the rift that had grown between herself and Isaac, a chasm she could not seem to breach despite her best efforts.

"He sold me his birthright for a pot of my stew."

The words rocked her, and she stared at her son, mouth agape, until she realized how awkward she must look to him, to his friends. She closed her mouth and searched his gaze. "Tell me you are serious and not making sport of me."

"I would not do such a thing." Though he had teased her many times in the past.

"Why would your brother despise his birthright so much that he would toss it away to fill his belly?" The idea was ludicrous—it made no sense.

"Apparently, he did not care, Ima."

She held his gaze, saw the slightest waver, as though he were trying not to squirm under her scrutiny, much as he had done as a small boy when she had caught him in a lie. "You coaxed him into it."

He inclined his head in a half nod, and that mischievous smile courted the edges of his beard. "You could say so."

"Tell me."

He shrugged. "He came in from the fields, saw the stew, and demanded I give him some. I said he could have a bowl if he sold me his birthright first. He agreed. I made him swear it, and he did."

She looked at him long and hard, glanced beyond him to his two friends whose smiling faces affirmed Jacob's words. Was this Adonai's way of fulfilling the promise He had made to her all those years ago?

Satisfaction filled her. Isaac would have to believe her now! And she would make sure he knew the full tale, would force Esau to admit it if she must. Then when Isaac was ready to give the final blessing of the birthright, she would remind him that it belonged to Jacob now.

She smiled into Jacob's eyes and patted his knee. "You did very well, my son. God will surely bless your efforts." She chose not to dwell on the niggling thought that perhaps God's plan might have come about in a different, less deceptive way.

Isaac stood at the edge of the field that housed the well of Shibah, watching the exchange between Rebekah and Jacob. He shaded his eyes with a hand, the glare of the sun more troublesome than it had been in his younger days. A cloudy film made things in the distance harder to discern, but he knew his wife's laughter in a crowd and the sound of her favorite son's voice.

The favoritism saddened him, as it always did when he thought on his sons. When had they taken sides, choosing one against the other? Except for the two women he had married, Esau had grown to make his father proud. Why could Rebekah not see it? It was Jacob who owned her heart, even taking Isaac's rightful place. Had their disagreement come to this?

He shook his head, his thoughts turning wistful. He loved Jacob. And Jacob did seem to possess a greater perception of Adonai's ways, but he had no desire to get out in the fields with the servants, to lead by example, and he was much too content to stay near the tents with his mother. If God had chosen this one over the other, Isaac simply could not see it.

He gripped his staff and walked toward the well. When had walking the uneven ground become so difficult? When had one hundred summers stopped feeling like forty?

A sigh forced its way through his lips, and he turned toward the laughter coming from the group at the well. If only he and Rebekah could share such laughter once more. Surely there was a way to mend their differences. And yet, he wasn't sure he was willing to sacrifice Esau on the altar of Rebekah's choices.

Jacob greeted him with a smile. "Abba! How good of you to join us."

His welcoming voice eased some of the tension around Isaac's heart, and he accepted his son's kiss with a smile.

"I could not help but be drawn by your laughter." He looked at Rebekah, searching her face for the comfort he longed for, that she used to offer him.

"Jacob was relaying a story, my lord. You know how well he tells them." Rebekah moved to his side and touched his arm, her expression serious. "You must listen to all that he says."

Something flickered in her eyes that made his knees suddenly weak as a newborn calf's, and he quickly lowered his body to sit beside the well, listening as Jacob told the tale of Esau selling to him his birthright. Anguish filled him, and he could not move or speak.

"Is this true?" He looked at Haviv's two sons, who nodded affirmation, then held Jacob's unflinching gaze.

"All of it, Father." He knelt at Isaac's side and rested his head on Isaac's knee. "I am sorry if this displeases you."

Isaac drew in a breath, willing his limbs to obey his commands, and at last rested a hand on Jacob's head. "Your brother's despising of his birthright displeases me." Did the right of the firstborn mean so little to him? Isaac could not fathom a hunger that could not be assuaged some other way than by making such a rash choice. "The birthright is yours," he said, though he still could not make his heart believe it.

"The birthright and the blessing."

Rebekah's voice broke through his mind's fog, and he looked at her. This was what she had wanted all along. So be it.

"The birthright and the blessing," he said, patting Jacob's head.

Jacob rose up from his knees and kissed him.

The summer's heat bore down on the camp even though the sun hit at an angle that suggested day was ending. The shade of the tent could not lift the oppression, and the intermittent breeze did little to rustle the leaves or cool Isaac's skin. He opened his eyes to watch the women grinding grain and stirring some sort of stew or syrup, gossiping all the while, their voices like chattering birds. If only he could clearly see their faces as their shadows passed before his tent or recognize Esau's children as they played somewhere nearby. But time had robbed him of most of his sight and left him with little pleasure.

He rubbed a hand over his beard and sighed, recognizing Rebekah's voice calling to Selima and, moments later, Jacob's deeper one coming closer.

"Abba, Haviv and I have come."

The cushions rustled beside him, and he felt Jacob kneel and kiss his cheek. His son smelled of a mixture of sheep and spice, as though he had just come from the cooking pots or the sheep pens. Perhaps both.

"Good, good. Come and sit and visit for a while."

The sounds of the men settling near him told him they

had complied with his wishes. When had life become more about spending time with loved ones and less about working the fields, gathering and setting aside for winter's store?

"My lord, there is news of Ishmael." Haviv's quiet voice held the hint of concern Isaac had come to expect from him. Concern matured by the heartache of losing his brother Nadab to his own choices, and by the deaths of his parents Eliezer and Lila several years before. Few were left of Abraham's generation.

"Tell me." Though he already sensed the truth.

"Word has come through a messenger sent from Kedar, Ishmael's son, that Ishmael now rests with his fathers. They buried him several weeks past."

"And they are just now sending word?" He would have traveled to bid his farewell if he could have done so with ease. But at one hundred and twenty-four years, he did not move about as he once did. Blind men did not go anywhere of their own accord.

"It would seem that they sent word as soon as they could, my lord. The distance is not a close one." Haviv always managed to make the truth realistic.

"I am sorry for Uncle Ishmael's loss, Abba." Jacob touched his shoulder, and Isaac lifted his face in the direction of his voice.

"Has your brother Esau been told?"

Esau was the one who would miss Ishmael the most. Esau still visited his uncle from time to time, staying away longer with each visit, giving Isaac and Rebekah even less respite from the two Canaanite wives he left behind. At least when Esau was home in the camp, he managed to keep peace between the women.

As Jacob's sigh reached his ears, he regretted asking after his brother. "Esau left the moment he spoke to Ishmael's messenger. I do not expect he will return for several weeks now," Haviv said, speaking for Jacob.

"He left without a word to me?" The boy could have at least said farewell. The thought pained him, but he did not voice it. "He is impulsive. He will miss his uncle."

"Yes." Haviv cleared his throat. "He did not take the women or children with him, so perhaps he will return more quickly."

Isaac grunted. "Would that he had." He lowered his voice. "Is there not enough strife in the camp since he brought them here?" He and Rebekah had grieved long and often over Esau's two Canaanite wives.

"Is there anything I can do for you, Father, in Esau's absence?"

Jacob's voice held a thin thread of hope, and Isaac wondered not for the first time what he had done wrong that this son should think he did not accept him. He only favored Esau to make up for Rebekah's lack.

"Father?"

The question brought his thoughts up short. Had his mind wandered again? "Yes, my son?"

"Can I bring you anything? Is there anything you need?" The voice had shifted slightly away from him, as though Jacob desired to leave.

"No, no. I am fine. You may go and complete whatever tasks your mother has for you." He offered a feeble wave to send him off and listened as his son's steps retreated.

"He is not a child that you should send him to his mother." Haviv's tone was gentle, though the words held reprimand.

Isaac rubbed a hand along his beard and blinked, wishing for one moment that when he opened his eyes they would see as they once did. "I forget sometimes." How faulty his thoughts were of late! Though the moments of his childhood seemed sharper in their focus, the early years with Rebekah were a bittersweet memory.

"I know you do. But you would do well to remember that

your sons are men now. Men fully capable of leading the men of the tribe in your place."

"You think me old." But of course it was true.

"I do not think you old. Your father lived to one hundred and seventy-five winters. You have many years ahead of you." Haviv leaned in close so that his breath touched Isaac's ear. "I think you must prepare your sons to lead after you, however. Bless them and give them control as your father gave you."

Isaac settled back among the cushions and caught a whiff of stew carried to him on the breeze, drawing nearer with each breath.

"Are you ready to eat, my lord?" Rebekah's tone held a smile, and he sat straighter, grateful for the interruption.

"Yes, if you will stay with me and share the meal." He turned toward the sound of her voice. "I will let you join your family," he said, sending his words in Haviv's direction. He did not need the man telling him what to do. Not now. Not while he had yet to grieve his brother's death.

"I will speak with you again later, my lord."

Isaac heard the man walk away but did not respond.

***

Days passed with unending sameness, and though Isaac conferred often with Haviv and Jacob over issues arising in the fields with the shepherds and herdsmen, and listened to the normal laughter and bickering among the men and women of the camp, he could not shake the desire to hear Esau's voice once more. How long would he stay away? Still, he knew the trek to Ishmael's camp was not one a man traveled quickly.

Afternoon shadows blocked the heat of the sun several weeks after Ishmael's death, bringing with them a welcome respite. Isaac settled among the cushions in the receiving area of his tent, the sides drawn up to let in the breeze. He briefly dozed, then jerked awake, his thoughts troubled and weary.

Was Haviv right in his assumption that Isaac had many more years ahead of him? Would he live long in this state of blindness? The thought pained him, making him suddenly long for Sheol. He had lived a long, good life already, so what need was there to continue in it? He was old and useless, and it was time he passed on the blessing of leadership to the son who would inherit that blessing. The blessing Jacob should now receive.

But Jacob had stolen Esau's birthright. Did he really deserve Adonai's blessing as well?

He shifted, silently cursing his inability to see the colors of the cushions Rebekah had made to brighten his surroundings. Cushions he had taken for granted in his sighted years. He tilted his head at the sound of male voices coming near, tuning his ears to listen more closely. But a moment later the voices quieted and someone stepped into the room, his presence obvious by his heavy breathing and the scent of the fields clinging to him.

"Father, I am home." Esau knelt at Isaac's side. "How good it is to see you."

Isaac warmed to his son's presence and lifted his arms toward the sound of his voice. "Come closer, my son. Let me feel your kiss on my cheeks."

Esau leaned in and did as Isaac requested. Isaac responded in kind, then pulled Esau into a fierce hug. "You are back. Why did you not tell me you were leaving?"

"There was no time, Abba. A caravan had just passed along the route toward Havilah, and I wanted to join them. It is safer to travel in numbers." Esau touched Isaac's knee. "But I regretted my impulsiveness and wished I had told you. I would have taken you with me if I could. Ishmael's sons were pleased that I came. I gave them your condolences."

Isaac felt his pride lift at Esau's words, his commanding tone, the practical reasons for his choices. "Thank you, my son. You have done well, have carried yourself like a man and a fine representative of our household."

It was true. Jacob would never have been able to broach the territory where Ishmael lived without returning with some kind of ill will between the groups. Jacob could please his mother and the men and women of the camp, but he did not carry the understanding to appease other tribes.

The thought beckoned him, and he turned toward his son with new vision. Vision that did not need physical sight.

"My son," he said, renewed resolve filling him. He had always known that Esau would make a great leader one day, and it was time he followed through on that belief.

"Here I am." Esau leaned close again, the scent of the fields filling Isaac with a deep sense of rightness, of peace.

"I am now an old man and don't know the day of my death." He reached out a hand, fumbling until he touched Esau's bearded face. "Now then, get your weapons—your quiver and bow—and go out to the open country to hunt some wild game for me. Prepare me the kind of tasty food I like and bring it to me to eat, so that I may give you my blessing before I die."

Esau did not respond quickly, and Isaac feared he would refuse the blessing on account of the birthright he had so easily despised. But surely it was his impulsive nature that had made him act so rashly. Surely he did not truly despise his heritage and all that his father believed.

"It will be as you say, Father. I will go at once." He bent to kiss Isaac once more in farewell and quickly stood. "Pray that your God heeds my success."

As Esau's footsteps retreated, Isaac did just that.

❧❧❧

Rebekah took a step back from the entryway of Isaac's tent, her blood pumping hard and fast, her mind working to understand what she had just heard. Isaac had promised the blessing to Jacob. Could he truly have just changed his mind and gone back on his word? Or had his word been given under compulsion, something he had never intended to keep?

She held her breath, willing her racing heart to calm, as Esau emerged and turned left toward the tents that sat across the compound, the tents that housed his two wives and sons. He had to be weary from his recent journey, but he would waste no time leaving again to do Isaac's bidding.

How could Isaac do such a thing?

She smoothed her hands along the sides of her robe, trying to still their sudden trembling. She could not let this happen. Isaac was simply too old and his memory too weak to realize what he was doing. She would help him see. Should she go in and talk to him, to convince him to bless Jacob before Esau returned?

Indecision made her palms slick with sweat, and her heart picked up its pace once more. She moved away from Isaac's tent and crossed the compound toward Esau's with an attempt at casual indifference, her mind churning. Should she confront Esau?

But no. While this son might have once despised his birthright, he surely desired the blessing now. A blessing he did not deserve. A blessing Isaac should not have offered.

She came to the entrance of Esau's tent and paused. How could she explain her presence here? She avoided contact with his wives at every turn and could not afford to confront them now. Gliding past in the pretense of moving toward the well—never mind her lack of jar to carry the water—she stopped at the back of the tent, darted quick looks in every direction, and pressed her ear toward the tent's back wall.

"Are you going so soon, my love? You just now returned!" Basemath's whiny voice rose above the din of his sons' clamoring and Judith's loud, mournful sigh.

"I promise you, I will soon return, and when I do, it will be for blessing far greater than we have yet seen. Soon we will send my brother to the hills, and all that my father owns will be mine."

The women squealed at Esau's boast, and with it came a sudden surge of anger rushing through Rebekah's body like hot coals. She stepped away from the tent and moved along the tree line until she was half hidden by a row of servants' smaller quarters. She watched, waiting for Esau to leave, her anger growing, her thoughts roiling, until resolve wound her decision tightly around her heart.

Esau emerged from his tent, bow and sling hung over his shoulder, his stride arrogant and sure. She waited until she could no longer see him as he disappeared over a rise toward the open country, then lifted her skirts and hurried to find Jacob.

She found him in his tent, resting in the early afternoon heat. "Jacob, my son." She bent low and shook him, rousing him from sleep.

"What is it, Ima?" He shook his head and rubbed a hand over his face, though he still carried the look of one held in a dream.

"Wake up and listen to me." He blinked at her sharp tone and sat up straighter.

She knelt at his side. "Look, I overheard your father say to your brother Esau, 'Bring me some game and prepare me some tasty food to eat, so that I may give you my blessing in the presence of the Lord before I die.' Now, my son, listen carefully and do what I tell you."

She waited but a moment, assured of his full attention. They were alone, but she kept her voice low nonetheless. "Go out to the flock and bring me two choice young goats so I can prepare some tasty food for your father, just the way he likes it. Then take it to your father to eat, so that he may give you his blessing before he dies."

Jacob stared at her as though she had completely lost her senses, raising her ire. "But my brother Esau is a hairy man, and I'm a man with smooth skin. What if my father touches me? I would appear to be tricking him and would bring down a curse on myself rather than a blessing."

She batted the thought away with a wave of her hand. "Let the curse fall on me. Just do what I say, my son. Go now and get them for me."

Jacob waited but a moment, then rose, grabbed his blade from the floor at his side, and hurried from the tent.

Rebekah walked with calculated slowness to her tent, thoughts turning over in her mind as she entered the darkened interior. Normally, the sides would be lifted to let light and air into her quarters, but she thanked the Unseen One that she had left them down this morning, affording her the privacy she needed. The garments she had woven that long-ago day for Esau—the ones she knew he would not fully appreciate but had worn with pride because Isaac had given them to him—sat tucked away in a corner of her tent, in a basket of clothing she had refused to send off with his wives. The decision would prove useful now.

She lifted the basket's lid, pulled the colorful robe from its place near the top, and held it to her face. She sniffed and sighed. The robe still carried Esau's scent. He had worn it to the fields on more than one occasion, against her wishes. Another providential gift that the smell of the land still lingered within the threads.

Setting the robe aside, she retrieved her store of spices from where they hung along the rod that held the tent's roof aloft, snipped several strands of rosemary and dill, and dug into her stone jars of cumin and caraway seeds. She carried them to the cooking tent, glad that it was too early for the women to be about the preparations for the evening meal, and set to baking the spiced flatbread Isaac loved.

Jacob soon returned with the kids, and they set to work skinning them and cutting up the meat into small chunks. While Jacob began the stew, adding the spices at her direction, she scraped the skins free of any last bits of flesh, rubbed them with water, and then smoothed the insides with oil to soften them. She quickly found her bone needle and thread and attached the skins to Jacob's hands, where the robe would not cover, and the smooth part of his neck that remained exposed above the collar.

Hours passed, and Rebekah gave an anxious glance toward the hills in the direction Esau had taken, fearing that God would indeed bless his efforts and he would return too soon.

"What if Esau returns before my father finishes his meal?"

"If he returns, I will distract him."

Jacob allowed her to dress him in Esau's robe, the bowl of steaming stew and tray of flatbread sitting on a low table nearby.

"But what if my father recognizes my voice? I will be cursed before I can enter the tent."

"You will tell him you are Esau. He cannot see you. He will believe you once he smells your brother's clothes and touches your skin."

Silence settled as they looked at one another.

"You must do this, my son. Your future depends on it. Adonai chose you to inherit the blessing, and I will not let your father give it to your brother in your place."

"You ask a hard thing of me, Ima." He looked into her eyes, unflinching, but she held her ground, knowing what he did not. They had no other choice.

"I only ask you to fulfill the promise as God intends." She crossed her arms, challenging him with her sternest look, until he glanced beyond her, his sigh defeated.

"I will do as you ask." He bent to retrieve the tray, glancing back at her once as he left the tent. "Stand guard and mimic a dove's call if my brother draws near."

"I cannot mimic such a thing. Only your father possesses such a skill."

He shrugged. "Then whistle a tune I will recognize." He brushed through the entrance, striding away from her.

She hurried to keep up, to listen near the tent's walls. But she would be no use to him whistling. She could not make her lips do such a thing.

She would pray God's blessing on her plans instead.

Jacob hesitated at the threshold of Isaac's tent, but he did not look to see if Rebekah had followed. The sides of Isaac's tent were raised, and Rebekah knew he could not see her, but just the same, she stood in a hidden place near a corner out of sight.

"My father," Jacob said, his voice a slight warble.

"Yes, my son," he answered. "Who is it?"

"I am Esau, your firstborn. I have done as you told me. Please sit up and eat some of my game so that you may give me your blessing."

Silence followed Jacob's comment, and Rebekah held her breath, waiting, irritated. How many years had she endured Isaac's exasperating patience?

"How did you find it so quickly, my son?" he said at last.

"Adonai your God gave me success."

Good. The exact thing Isaac had prayed for Esau. She felt a measure of pride at Jacob's shrewdness.

"Come near so I can touch you, my son, to know whether you really are my son Esau or not."

Rebekah stilled, her heartbeat slowing as though suddenly frozen in her chest. Did he know? But he would have recognized Jacob's voice.

Please, Adonai, let him believe Jacob's words. The prayer seemed ludicrous, but her need to pray it remained.

She longed to peer into the tent to see what Jacob would do. Did he set the dish near his father so that the scent of the stew would distract him? Did he have the courage to continue the ruse to the end?

"The voice is the voice of Jacob, but the hands are the hands of Esau."

The goatskins had convinced him. She held back a breath, her heart now beating faster within her.

"Are you really my son Esau?"

Blood pounded in her ears as she strained to hear.

"I am." Jacob's voice sounded stronger, more convincing this time.

"Bring me some of your game to eat then, my son, so that I may give you my blessing."

Rebekah heard movement and could barely catch the sound of the bread dipping into the bowl. She glanced about the camp, but the women still worked in the tents, away from the heat of the sun. Childish voices drifted here and there, but they played far from Isaac's tent. No sign yet of Esau. She leaned closer, silently begging him to finish eating and be done with the task.

"Come here, my son, and kiss me."

Her heart skipped a beat at the words before taking off at a wild gallop within her. Shallow breaths escaped her, and she feared he would hear. She took a careful step away from the tent but stilled at the sound of Isaac's voice.

"Ah, the smell of my son is like the smell of a field that Adonai has blessed. May God give you of heaven's dew and of earth's richness—an abundance of grain and new wine. May nations serve you and peoples bow down to you. Be lord over your brothers, and may the sons of your mother bow down to you. May those who curse you be cursed and those who bless you be blessed."

So it was done. Murmurs too quiet to hear followed the

blessing, but at last Jacob emerged from the tent and met her at the farthest edge, where the peg held taut the goatskin roof. A wide smile creased his face, but the joy was short-lived. A commotion came from across the compound, and Rebekah grabbed Jacob's arm and hurried him toward her tent.

Esau had returned from the hunt.

Isaac leaned against the cushions, relieved. It was done. The blessing had been given, and Esau would indeed be blessed. Rebekah's vision had been wrong. Hadn't he known it all along? If Adonai had truly spoken to her, if Jacob had truly deserved the birthright, he would not have needed to resort to deception to receive it. Rebekah had simply been overwrought, her pregnancy too troubling. Surely she had imagined meeting the angel of Adonai. Many a woman had experienced similar imaginings, if some of the men in his camp were to be believed.

He reached toward the low table at his side and felt for the cup of wine Esau had left for him, lifted it to his lips, and drank deeply. But the satisfaction of being right did not settle in the deep places of his heart as he had expected it would. Had he done the right thing? Rebekah had been so certain, so convinced of Adonai's will for the twins throughout their years. It had been the cause of many an argument, yet she was unwilling to give in despite his pleas that she do so. He had considered her unwillingness a lack of respect, had determined to somehow prove her wrong in the end, despite his promise to Jacob after Esau sold him the birthright.

Was he wrong?

Uneasiness settled within him, and he checked himself, frustrated with the rambling thoughts of a foolish old man. What did it matter? Esau was the firstborn. He deserved the blessing, and Isaac had given it. Somehow Rebekah would come to accept it, and all would be made right between them again.

But a moment later, as footsteps sounded outside his tent once more, a sense of foreboding filled him, making each movement languid.

"Father?"

A dim shadow further darkened the room, and a man moved closer. "My father, sit up and eat some of my game so that you may give me your blessing."

The foreboding grew, and his heart thumped hard within him. "Who are you?" The question came out raspy, as though spoken through dry reeds.

"I am your son, your firstborn, Esau."

Swift and violent trembling shook him, and he could not get his hands to hold steady. He dropped the goblet, felt the wine spill over his robe.

"Who . . . who was it, then, that hunted game and brought it to me?" He swallowed and told himself to breathe. "I ate it just before you came, and I blessed him—and indeed he will be blessed!"

Silence lasted the space of several heartbeats as Esau seemed to come to grips with the truth. Isaac startled as a moment later Esau's voice rose in a loud and bitter cry.

"Bless me—me too, my father!"

"Your brother came deceitfully and took your blessing."

Which meant Rebekah had also deceived him, making him the greatest of fools. Had God truly spoken to her then? Had He allowed this to come about because of Isaac's own stubbornness, his refusal to believe her? But Elohei Abraham did not need to deceive to accomplish His will.

"Isn't he rightly named Jacob? He has deceived me these two times. He took my birthright, and now he's taken my blessing!" Esau's voice cracked, and he leaned closer, grasping Isaac's hand. "Haven't you reserved any blessing for me?"

Sorrow rose within him, and suddenly the meal Jacob had deceitfully fed to him churned to bile in his gut. How foolish he had been to bless him so thoroughly, reserving nothing for his brother.

"I have made him lord over you and have made all his relatives his servants, and I have sustained him with grain and new wine. So what can I possibly do for you, my son?"

"Do you have only one blessing, my father? Bless me too, my father!" Tears mingled with Esau's words, and the pain of it wrenched Isaac's heart.

When at last Esau quieted, Isaac gripped his hand and pulled him close to kiss him. "Your dwelling will be away from the earth's richness, away from the dew of heaven above. You will live by the sword, and you will serve your brother." He paused, searching his heart, silently praying for something he could offer this favorite of sons. He turned unseeing eyes toward Esau and gently held his face in his aged hands. "But when you grow restless, my son, you will throw his yoke from your neck."

Isaac kissed each of Esau's cheeks and allowed him to take his leave. At least he would not remain a servant to Jacob forever. In the end, he would rule his own tribe in his own land. In that, Isaac rested his hope.

34

Rebekah lifted the jar to her shoulder, the effort strained, and walked toward the well of Shibah, her legs moving slowly as though weighted with sand. The hour was early, dawn's crest barely visible above the eastern ridge of earth, but Rebekah could not wait for the other women of the camp to awaken. She had spent a restless night on her mat and found little comfort in its proffered rest.

Sluggish and anxious, she moved along the tree line, past Esau's tents, until she had climbed the low incline and descended to the well in the low-lying valley below. Dew tickled her feet where the grasses rose over her sandals, and she shivered. The morning chill would be gone soon enough. But she found no comfort in the thought.

She took her time going and coming, the anguish of the night invading her every breath and Esau's bitter cries mingling with her misery. What had she done? Could there have been a better way to secure blessing for Jacob? Must she have resorted to hurting Esau so deeply?

He would never forgive her. And now, if the rumors were true . . .

She looked up toward the camp and saw the shadow of a woman silhouetted on the low hill, facing her. Rebekah lifted the full jar again and began the trek home. The figure moved to meet her. She drew in a relieved breath at the sight of Deborah.

"I feared Judith or Basemath had risen early to come here." She looked at Deborah for the briefest moment, unable to hold her steady gaze. "I cannot bear to face them."

"Perhaps it is Esau you should fear, mistress." Deborah rarely referred to her as mistress anymore, a sure sign of her disapproval, and it added to Rebekah's guilt.

"Do you not think that I already fear his reprisals? My son is impulsive and hot-tempered. But what else could I have done? Isaac would have thwarted Adonai's plan! I could not allow him to do such a thing. He may not believe that God spoke to me, Deborah, but I know what I heard, what I saw." Rebekah's words came out rushed, and still she felt the urge to talk until no words would come. She drew a calming breath and forced herself to release it.

"God's plans can never be thwarted, dear one. He chose Jacob from before his birth. He would have found a way without your help." Deborah's pointed look made her squirm as though she were still a child. "I fear the damage is only beginning."

Fear spiked like bursting flames within her. "What do you mean? What have you heard?"

Deborah sighed and looked into the distance, as though seeing something only she could see. "Esau is making threats against his brother. He is consoling himself that once his father dies, he will kill Jacob."

Alarm jolted her, and she stopped, gripped the jar with both hands, and lowered it to the earth, nearly tripping as she strove to steady it. She lifted her head to search Deborah's face, to discern some misconception, to be sure she had heard correctly.

"Jacob must not stay here."

Deborah nodded her agreement. "No, he must not."

"But where can I send him?" A sudden sense of loss filled her, followed by waves of deep grief. "He must go home to Harran, to my brother Laban." The thought did not comfort, though at least with Laban, Jacob would be safe.

"It is said that your brother has daughters." Deborah's smile was weary and sad.

"Yes, this is a good plan. Isaac will allow Jacob to flee if he goes in search of a wife in Paddan-Aram." Rebekah held Deborah's gaze, noticing the lines along her temples and the drawn pull to her mouth. When had her servant aged so much? But Deborah was the one person she could trust to see that Laban welcomed Jacob, to see that he was protected and cared for and found a wife to guide and please him. To love him, though no one could ever love her son as she did.

"You must go with him." She crossed her arms, trying to look convincing, though in truth she needed some place to put them to still the shaking. "Laban knows you, Deborah, and Jacob will need someone to comfort him, since I cannot go with him."

Deborah did not immediately answer, and Rebekah knew that what she was asking was perhaps more than the woman was willing to give, since Selima and her children would remain with them. The thought made her pause, but in the next moment, she shored up her resolve and held Deborah's unflinching gaze.

"You would ask me to leave my daughter, my grandchildren?"

Rebekah slowly nodded, her resolve weakening. How could she send her nurse, her confidante, away? "It would be only for a time. I couldn't bear to live without you both for long. Just long enough for Esau's anger to subside and for Jacob to choose a wife. A month, maybe longer. Nothing more." She would send for them the moment Esau's wrath abated.

Deborah looked at her for another lengthy moment, then shook her head. "I cannot go with him, Rebekah. This is a journey Jacob must make alone."

Rebekah took a step back and nearly lost her balance, so rocked was she by her nurse's words. "But he needs me. And if I cannot go with him, which I cannot, then you need to go in my place."

But her argument had lost its earlier strength. Isaac's long-ago accusation returned in full force. *I will not expect his mother to coddle him and keep him from the life God intends.*

I do not coddle him, she had said, referring to Esau.

No, you reserve that for Jacob, he'd said.

The memory of his comment made her limp, weak. She sank to the earth and wrapped both arms about her knees.

I do not coddle him. But she did. And as she felt Deborah kneel at her side, saw the firm set to her jaw and the compassion in her gaze, she knew. Deborah was right, as Isaac had been.

Weariness came in waves, and she looked into Deborah's tender yet unflinching gaze. "I don't know how I will live without him."

Deborah lifted a veined hand and cupped Rebekah's shoulder. "It is time you both learned how to do so."

Rebekah could not meet her gaze. "I cannot let him go." But she had no other choice. She closed her eyes and forced her exhausted limbs to rise. Lifting the jar once more to her shoulder, she pushed one weighted leg in front of the other. "I will appeal to Isaac on Jacob's behalf to send him to my brother. Why should I be bereaved of both sons in one day?" For as she walked, a new thought struck her. If Esau killed Jacob, Haviv, on behalf of Isaac, would be forced to kill Esau to avenge Jacob's blood. She could not abide such a thing. She would die of guilt and grief.

"If Adonai is willing, we will all live to see another sunrise," Deborah said.

Rebekah could not bring herself to think of that as good.

Isaac rolled over on his pallet, forcing his weary body into a sitting position. But the effort had lost all meaning and desire in the past month. Everything had changed with Rebekah's deceit and Jacob's departure to Paddan-Aram.

He rubbed a hand along his beard and licked his lips, tasting the salt of leftover tears. He had wept in silence in his tent, while Rebekah's tears had carried long and loud throughout the camp for days and days after Jacob kissed her goodbye. In the early years, he would have gone to comfort her. But now . . . now her betrayal and deceit could not break through the barrier of his grief, a grief of lost faith, of lost love.

He could not bear it.

But the death he expected would come to him soon seemed to linger far out of his reach. What if he did indeed live as long as his father had lived? If Haviv was right, he had many years left ahead of him. Sighted or not, he could not sit and wait for Sheol to open its jaws and beckon him like jackals in the night.

But he also could not stay here. He needed to get away from the voices, the whimpering nagging of Esau's women—now three instead of two—from Esau's sulking and grumbling, from Rebekah's aloofness and formality and distance. It was her guilt that kept her from approaching him. Nothing else could explain her actions since that final day when she goaded him into sending Jacob to her brother. And though he knew deep down he still loved her, he could not live with her in peace.

He was becoming just like his father, their marriage like his parents'.

His body clenched with the knowledge, and he forced his shaky limbs to stand, reached for the staff he once carried with ease, and hobbled from the tent until the sun hit his face, the warmth of its rays kissing his cheeks.

"My lord, you are up."

Haviv's voice warmed him, a steady rock in his now uncertain world.

"Yes, and I want you to do something for me." He would act even if it went against all better judgment.

"Anything, my lord. You know that."

He nodded. Seeing the barest shadow of Haviv's form, he touched his shoulder. "I do know that. You are a faithful servant . . . and friend." He smiled, though he could not see Haviv's reaction. "I want you to take me to the Negev, to the places I used to go."

Haviv paused but a moment. "How soon do you wish to leave?"

Isaac sniffed the scents of bread baking and the distinct smell of oaks and mulberry trees filling the air around and above him. He sighed with a depth that brought an ache to his heart. "Today. As soon as you can ready the animals."

"I will give instructions to my sons and be ready to leave with you after we break our fast."

Isaac nodded, then let Haviv guide him to his seat near the fire. Voices of the women came toward him, and he picked Rebekah's out among the closest.

"I have brought you some dates and cheese. The bread is almost ready." She touched his hand as she placed the tray within it, the shock of her touch surprising him.

"Your hands are cold." Was she trembling?

"Are they?" Her voice sounded lifeless.

He fingered a date but did not eat. "I am leaving for the Negev today. I do not know when I will return."

When she did not respond, he looked up, trying to see if her shadow still stood above him. It did. How he wished he could read her expression! He looked down instead, cursing his blindness. Had he always been blinded to her ways? How many years had she deceived him? Had she ever loved him?

"I will miss you," she said at last, startling him. Was she speaking truth?

"I should not be gone long."

Perhaps Jacob would return before he did, and she could have her love returned to her. She was only sad because she missed her favorite son. Nothing more.

"Is there anything else you need?" Her voice remained toneless, devoid of feeling.

"No."

She would see to bringing the bread and make sure he was well fed whether she spoke to him again or not. He could not bear to say more when there was nothing left between them.

Rebekah stood on the hill at the crossroads leading north and south, the hill where she had lost both husband and son. Isaac's back had long since disappeared from view, two donkeys and two men heading south toward the Negev where the wild things grew, where Isaac could be at peace in the surroundings he had loved since childhood.

Numbness worked through her, the kind that comes with shock too great to comprehend, with loss too great to bear. What had her life come to?

She turned to face the breeze coming down from the north, whipping the scarf about her and her robe behind her, cooling the tears that came in a steady stream over her cheeks. *Jacob!* His name hurt to speak aloud, and the memory of his last hug was fading with every sunrise. Would she see him again? Had he arrived safely in Paddan-Aram? Surely Laban would eventually send word. But no caravan had come from Mesopotamia thus far, and no message had been received.

She closed her eyes, seeing him once more, his expression solemn as he took his staff and a donkey laden with few goods to make his travel light. He had looked at her with a mixture of faith and fear, and when he held her, she had clung to him, never wanting to let go.

A guttural cry burst from within her at the memory, and she sank to her knees, the weight of her loss pressing in on her with a force too great to hold her upright.

Oh, Adonai, what have I done?

If only He had spoken to her again in the years following the twins' birth. If only He had spoken to Isaac to confirm His words. Things would have been so much different.

Dry sobs rose to choke her, but the wind caught them and snatched them from her. Would a sandstorm arise too, destroying all she had left? She crawled on hands and knees and turned to face south once more, squinting against the faintly swirling dust of the earth, knowing she could no longer see Isaac's bent form riding away from all they had once held dear.

What had happened to their love? He had loved her once. More than she could have ever thought a man capable. But the memories of their better days lived now on the fringes of her thoughts, and though she tried to grasp them, they were like the wisps of dust, floating just out of reach.

Oh, Adonai, Elohei Abraham, Elohei Isaac, hear me!

The cry broke loose something deep within her, and in that moment she knew with new clarity how much she had lost. Jacob's love for her had meant too much, his future too consuming. And she had thrown away the only man who loved her as herself, as his only, favored wife.

She lowered her face to the earth, tasting the grasses and dirt mingling with fresh tears. Both hands were clenched, fists pounding the ground beneath her, until at last, spent and exhausted, she released her hold and opened her palms facing upward.

She must go after Isaac and beg his forgiveness.

35

Isaac lifted his face toward the west, feeling the last glow of the setting sun on his weathered face. The scent of the fire Haviv had built wafted nearby, and birds spoke in their many languages among the desert trees. The oasis at Beer-lahai-roi was quiet this time of year, and the hint of winter rains hovered in the air around him. They would find warmth enough in their tents for a time but eventually would need to take shelter in the caves. One tent standing alone in the wilderness did not offer the protection from the elements that an entire camp did. Would Haviv be willing to stay with him so long away from Selima and their children?

A weight settled in the place where his heart used to be, a perpetual ache that made him feel defeated and old. Was this how his mother had felt at his father's imagined betrayal? Instead of understanding and forgiveness, she had placed a wall around her heart and set her love on her son, in the place where love for his father should have been. And she had carried the loss she felt with her to the grave.

Would he end up living her fate?

He moved into the tent, feeling his way along the wall, suddenly no longer hungry for the food Haviv was preparing. The darkness that followed his every step deepened in the shadows of the tent. His foot touched his mat, and he sank down, his bones aged and creaking with every breath.

How he missed Rebekah! But not the woman she had been of late. He missed the bride of his youth, the woman who had shared life with him before God answered his prayer and granted them twins. The twins who had come between them.

But no. It was the vision that had brought the division and this final betrayal. The vision he had refused to accept and believe.

If You meant for the older to serve the younger, why did You not tell me too?

He had been denied the knowledge, the call of God, that had sent his father off to sacrifice the only son he loved on the altar of binding, of betrayal, and then he had been denied the vision given to his wife that would have him sacrifice the son he loved on the altar of parental blessing.

Why?

Where was God's goodness now?

Ishmael's question of old haunted him as he turned onto his back and stared into the dark. Tears trickled down his face into the mat below him. Why did God keep such things from him? Surely he had been obedient, trusting. He had surrendered his whole life into God's keeping.

Not all.

No. Not this. He had clung to his disbelief in Rebekah's vision because he could not see Jacob taking Esau's place in leading the camp, in handling foreign tribesmen, in being the man Isaac wanted him to be. A hunter. A man of the wild. A man after his father's heart. Not his mother's. Not like he had been.

Truth dawned on him at the thought. When had his love for his mother turned to anger, to this running from all that she'd been, from the way she had protected him, doted on him, held him too tightly in her bonds? And he'd been running from her influence, from the fear of repeating her errors with his sons, ever since.

But at what cost?

He rose up on his elbows and closed his eyes, longing for sight. Had he rejected Rebekah's vision because his own past would not allow it? And had he lost her love in the process?

Sadness filled him as he rose to sit upright once more, his sight finally cleared to see the truth that had lain in his heart all along. He loved Rebekah. Despite everything, despite her failings and his, he loved her with a force that shook him to his inner being. He would return to her and seek her forgiveness.

And tell her that at last he believed her.

Rebekah arrived at Beer-lahai-roi two days later with Haviv's younger son guiding her, protecting her. She spoke quietly to Haviv, grateful that Isaac remained seated in the shade of one of the larger date palms, unaware of her presence. She worked quickly to put the lentils and barley to boil, season them with garlic and cumin, and stir it all together with a willow branch. Isaac's favorite stew, like the kind his mother used to make for him and his father when life was good and joy filled their house with laughter.

Oh, Adonai, Elohei Abraham, restore our joy.

When the stew and seasoned flatbread Isaac favored were ready, she carried them to his side and set the food before him. Isaac opened his eyes, though they did not see her, and sniffed the air.

"I did not expect spiced stew. You will be accused of being a woman if you continue to cook so well, my friend." Isaac laughed, obviously expecting Haviv to respond.

"I have been accused of worse." She watched his expression startle at the sound of her voice.

"Rebekah."

"Yes, my lord."

"You are here."

"Yes."

He sat very still, but his unseeing eyes moistened, and he blinked away the threat of tears. She knelt beside him, her heart as skittish as a new bride, and was suddenly cold with fear. What if he rejected her now? But she had nothing left to lose.

He reached for her hand and held it gently in his, saying nothing, then lifted it, kissed her palm, and intertwined their fingers as they had once intertwined their bodies. He pulled her close until her head rested against his chest. Tears she thought long spent rose up, filling her eyes, as he tenderly drew circles along her back.

Moments passed in silence until he slowly, deliberately, held her at arm's length. When she looked into his face, she did not see a man spent with age but a young husband, her lover, the man she had pledged her whole life to love and serve. Her heart skipped a beat as he leaned closer, and his lips lingered over hers, their tears mingling.

"I have not been the man you wanted."

"No, I have not accepted the man you are. It is I who did not appreciate what you offered me."

"I should have been stronger." His voice held strength she had not heard from him in years.

"I should have been kinder." And she knew it was true. There were so many times when she had been the one blinded. "I tried to make you like my father." Who had given her everything she wanted but not all that she needed in a man she could rely on.

"I let you fill my mother's place."

"There was no harm in that."

He shrugged one shoulder, and his eyes misted again.

"I did not see you, who you really are," she said, feeling his arms come around her again. "I only saw what I wanted to see."

"I loved you in spite of it all." He kissed the top of her head.

"But I did not treat you as I should have. If I had, I would not have favored Jacob over you." She felt his heart beating steadily beneath the tunic she had made him. One she had made more out of duty than love. She saw that too clearly now.

"I knew you loved me." His voice held such kindness, making her want to weep again.

"I did love you. I do love you. I just didn't see how much until now." She pulled back from him, holding her breath, waiting. She searched his face.

He looked at her, and for a moment she thought he could see her. Perhaps he did, for a smile began that gently grew, encompassing her, drawing her in.

"I won't let you go." He pulled her close again, and she rested in his embrace. How good it felt, knowing she was loved.

They held each other in silence once more, their hearts beating as one.

"You were right about Jacob," he said, surprising her. "God chose him to receive the blessing from the start."

She stilled, the revelation settling over her. He believed her—that God had spoken to her. If only he had accepted this sooner . . . But she would not allow herself to finish the thought.

"I should have believed you from the beginning, beloved."

"I should have trusted Adonai to show you in His good time."

Silence moved between them once more, broken only by the sound of the birds and the whisper of God's breath in the wind.

"We cannot live with regrets, beloved. What is past is gone.

Let us learn from our forefathers' mistakes and not continue to repeat them." He kissed her softly, and she knew he still tasted her tears. "We have the rest of our lives to make new ones."

She laughed through her tears but quickly sobered at the guilt that still lingered within her. "But I have lost Esau in the process. He will never forgive me."

"He will come around in time. He loves you more than he knows."

She nodded though he could not see, comfortable in the silence, silence borne of a lifetime together, of knowing they were always meant to share their love.

"In the meantime, we have each other," he said.

"Yes, we do." She kissed his cheek.

And for now, that was enough.

Note from the Author

It is said that writing is hard work. A truer word could not have been spoken for me when it came to writing *Rebekah*. I stressed and prayed over every scene, certain I would never pull the story together.

At last that day came where the final scene trickled from my fingers to the page. I typed "The End" and breathed a sigh of relief. I had lived through this!

But through the relief, another thought quickly followed. I sensed God's Spirit saying, "If I gave you the contract, I can give you the story."

The words were humbling. I had been stressing rather than trusting.

Even in faith we can doubt. But I pray that I will not stress and doubt that way again. I do not claim my words are His, but He gives the grace to complete the work. I am in awe of a heavenly Father who used a difficult story to teach me much about Himself, about His character. May I never stop trusting Him.

❧

I hope you have enjoyed reading Rebekah's story. Please know that I have done my best to stay close to the story as laid out in Scripture. Sometimes, where things like chronology were unclear and scholars more learned than I disagreed, I followed the path that made the most sense to me. One case in point is the placing of Keturah in Abraham's life. The Bible does not tell us when he married her; it only says that he took her as a concubine and together they had six sons.

Some commentators suggest that Abraham married Keturah after Sarah's death, which is possible. But it is equally possible that Abraham took her earlier. In Genesis 22, immediately after the binding of Isaac, the Bible says that Abraham stayed in Beersheba, but Sarah apparently lived in Hebron because Abraham went there to mourn for her when she died. So did they spend some years apart?

Some scholars suggest that Sarah died shortly after Isaac's binding because of the shock of what Abraham nearly did to her son. How would she have felt upon hearing the news that her husband had offered her son on an altar? Appalled? Furious? Afraid? Shocked? It's easy to imagine if we put ourselves in her place.

As for Rebekah and Isaac, this was a tale that was very hard to tell. The Bible gives us little to work with when compared to the great detail given to Abraham and Jacob. The story needed to have a relational rather than an action-oriented focus. In the end, I discovered a greater hero in Isaac than I expected. And in Rebekah, I saw the dangers of an overbearing mother/son relationship.

As always, any errors, as well as the fictional parts of this story where Scripture is silent or confusing, are my own. I hope you will turn to Genesis and read the story of the patriarchs in context. The truths hidden there are fascinating!

In His Grace,
Jill Eileen Smith

Acknowledgments

To the team at Revell—I am so grateful for each one of you! Special thanks there go to:

Lonnie Hull DuPont—I love working and laughing with you! I am honored to call you editor and friend.

Jessica English—I can't imagine a better person to edit my work. You have a way of wording things that takes all the pain out of making changes!

Michele Misiak—I love your can-do attitude and laughing with you on the phone. Thanks for such great marketing advice.

Cheryl Van Andel—you wow me with your cover designs! Thank you for giving me a sneak peek at some of the behind-the-scenes choices! I LOVE this cover!

To my agent, Wendy Lawton—I am so blessed to know you and to work with you! Thank you for all you do!

To some special family and friends: Mom, Elaine, Jill Marie, Karen, Kathy K., Kathy K., Kathy R., Kathy F., Maureen, Robin, Joyce, Judy, Sue—thank you for being real and for our shared faith and friendship.

To my family: Randy, Jeff, Chris, and Ryan—life holds such joy and meaning because you're in it. I could not have understood Rebekah's story without knowing and loving you.

To the many family, friends, and influencers that for lack of space I did not name—please know you are thought of with gratitude and love.

Most of all, to *Yeshua HaMashiach*, Jesus, Messiah, my Deliverer, my Savior, the only true sacrifice for sin—thank You for doing what Isaac could not.

Thank You for loving me that much.

Jill Eileen Smith is the author of *Sarai*, book 1 in the Wives of the Patriarchs series, and the bestselling Wives of King David series. When she isn't writing, she enjoys spending time with her family—in person, over the webcam, or by hopping a plane to fly across the country. She can often be found reading, testing new recipes, grabbing lunch with friends, or snuggling one or both of her adorable cats. She lives with her family in southeast Michigan.

To learn more about Jill or for more information about her books, visit her website at www.jilleileensmith.com. You can also contact Jill at jill@jilleileensmith.com. She loves hearing from her readers.

Meet

JILL EILEEN SMITH

at **www.JillEileenSmith.com** to learn interesting facts and read her blog!

Connect with her on

Jill Eileen Smith

JillEileenSmith